M.J. FORD

THE
HIKER

av**on**.

KT-377-280

Published by AVON
An imprint of HarperCollins*Publishers*
1 London Bridge Street
London SE1 9GF

www.harpercollins.co.uk

HarperCollins*Publishers*
1st Floor, Watermarque Building, Ringsend Road
Dublin 4, Ireland

A Paperback Original 2022

First published in Great Britain by HarperCollins*Publishers* 2022

ISBN: 978-0-00-845335-0

1

Typeset in Sabon by Palimpsest Book Production Ltd,
Falkirk, Stirlingshire

Printed and bound in the UK using 100% renewable electricity
at CPI Group (UK) Ltd

For Matthew Tute, my fellow fellsman

Prologue

Castor tossed his head, batting her in the shoulder, nostrils flaring.

'I know, but it has to be done.'

She rubbed the cream into the scratches on his flank. It was still a mystery how he'd come by them a couple of days before. Her mother thought it must have been barbed wire, though Alice didn't see how it could have made such markings, not unless he'd somehow collided against it in a really strange way. There were five diagonal gouges, side by side. Not deep, thankfully, but it would prevent her from riding in the short time they had left together.

Castor stamped and snorted.

'What's *up* with you?' said Alice. 'It can't hurt that much!'

She had a clue, of course, and she suspected his mood didn't have a great deal to do with the injury. Castor had always been able to read her, better than any human being, and certainly better than anyone in her house. In many ways, he was her closest friend on the estate, his stable a refuge, away from the dark, joyless rooms and watchful staff.

He lowered his nose again, resting it in the crook of her neck, as if to say sorry for the outburst.

'I'm going to miss you,' she said.

His breath warmed her neck.

The new term at St Hilary's started in two days – nine weeks away from home and the stables. They had horses at school too, dreary and stubborn things, not like Castor in any way. Riding them was joyless, for all concerned.

The creak of the stable door made her half turn.

'Will you be hacking out, miss?' asked a familiar, gruff voice. 'I could saddle Pollux.'

'No, Bill. Not today. I thought I might go for a walk.'

'I'll let your mother know,' he said.

She bit her lip. *Why can't they leave me be for ten minutes?* 'You don't have to do that. I'm not going far.'

'Clag's coming in,' said Bill. 'Could be heavy.'

'I'll take my coat. I know the way.'

When she was sure he'd retreated, she ran a hand along the underside of Castor's jaw. The stallion's pulse was strong and fast.

'It's okay,' she said, to comfort herself as much as him. 'I'll be back later.'

He snorted a soft breath. They'd been inseparable, from the moment he took his first wobbling steps in the stables. The mare who'd birthed him, Ariadne, had bled out the same night, and Alice had been the one who had cleaned him up, then sat beside him with the bottle, every three hours, a ten-year-old keeping the newborn foal alive. Neither Mr Farrah nor her parents had had great hope, but she'd

2

proved them all wrong. She was the first and only person to ride him – he'd thrown her cousin Fiona, who fancied herself the better rider; Alice had tried not to laugh. Over time, as they began to jump, their bond had only grown.

Last year, when her parents had revealed their scheme to send her off to board, Alice had spent a whole night in the stable, wet face buried in Castor's neck, his scent the only thing keeping her anchored in the world. Their relationship had changed. Not a surrogate mother and child any more; something more like siblings. With no brother or sister, it was Castor who she'd poured out her secrets to – her hatred of her parents, her friends and enemies at school, the boy she was in love with. Even if he didn't understand the words, she knew from his kind and patient gaze that he understood something.

Alice left the stable, casting a brief look towards the house, scanning for silhouettes of figures lurking in the many windows. Pollux – her mother's horse and Ariadne's first foal – wouldn't do for the place she was going. She took the south-western path, alongside the old dyke, one of the many earthworks that had survived the estate's long history. It followed the camber of the slope, before striking gently uphill to higher moorland, where the bridleway, a public footpath, would take her towards the village. The sky above was bruised, promising rain, maybe even a storm, but she could feel the wind at her back, moving it away.

She prayed Daniel had been able to get away too, because if he hadn't, she didn't know what she'd do. They hadn't been together for three days, since a few snatched moments behind the barbecue stand at the village summer fête, and those seventy-two hours had been dreadful, cooped up in the house, trying and failing to complete her French assignments, thinking only of the next time she'd be able to see him.

Checking her watch, she saw it was quarter to two. She was running late, so she decided to come off the bridleway, skirting through the old quarry. Not only was it a shortcut to their meeting spot on the outskirts of Hartsbridge, the contours of the landscape were such that she couldn't be seen, or potentially followed, from the manor. She was sure that one or two of the regular staff knew about her relationship, and she wouldn't put it past her parents to have a spy. Not that they'd see it that way.

She gazed back towards the house as she reached the crest above the quarry, or to where the house had been, and she saw she needn't have worried – Bill was right about the clag. A thick white mist had taken it completely. The moorland vanished into the sky and it looked like the edge of the world. For a moment, Alice let herself fantasise that she could go back and find it truly disappeared, an empty space where the looming walls once stood, all traces of the buildings and its inhabitants gone. What she would do then, she didn't know. The taste of imagined freedom was strange and intoxicating.

Her boots disturbed loose slate chips as she descended through the old workings. The slag heaps and crumbling chimney of the smelting house were all that remained of the former ironworks – the river that once flowed through had long ago been redirected to the new reservoir further down the valley. Her friends from school, some of them wealthy themselves, always found Brocklehurst Hall and the surrounding estate fascinating, set among the sweeping Pennine moorland. They were mostly from the city. She tried to explain it was actually very boring and lonely.

A skitter of rocks somewhere at her back made her stop and turn, heart spiking. It was a sound that made no sense, because out here she was alone, moving through the landscape. She saw no one else on the path though.

The first spots of rain began to fall, spattering on her Barbour coat. She scanned left and right. Down below, by the trickle of the brook, were the ruins of several stone huts, their walls and roofs collapsed. Looking at them, she had the first, curious sensation that she was not alone. Beneath the stillness, something else lurked.

'Hello?' she said. Maybe one of the staff had followed, after all. Mr Farrah had been watching her saddle up. He was always watching her.

Further down the slope, she heard the *snick* of stone on stone.

'Danny?' she said. There was no answer. 'Danny, if that's you, this isn't funny.'

The desperation in her own voice appalled her. There was no reason at all for Danny to be out here. He couldn't even have known she'd come this way.

Her eyes locked on the dilapidated buildings. No more than old workshops, or tool sheds, unused for two hundred years or more. There were shafts running under the ground, Dad said, but they were sealed up.

Under the gap in a slate roof, something moved quickly. A black form, right there, now standing completely still. Her breath caught, trying to make sense of it. Her mind thought 'sheep', knowing full well there were no flocks this high. It moved again, disappearing into the hidden recesses of the old shelter.

For some reason, she couldn't budge. Sheep didn't move

like that. Curiosity, or fear, pinned her to the spot. Her eyes were fixed on the roof, daring herself, and the world, to show the thing again.

It did. This time, it hesitated there. Just blackness, crouched in the ruins. She was more sure than ever that she was looking at an animal. At fur. And much bigger than a sheep. Not a farm creature at all. It was too furtive. Something deep in her being – the instinct of prey in the presence of a predator - told her it had been watching her for some time. It told her to run.

She began to climb the slope, as quickly as she could. She heard the shifting of stones behind her, and realised it had emerged. But when she looked back again, she couldn't see anything.

'Dan!' she shouted. Hoping he might miraculously appear.

The slope was steep, and her hands gripped at anything they could to haul her higher – rock or heather. The mist had thickened as she came out of the gully. She couldn't see ten metres and now that blank canvas filled her with despair. Which way was the house?

'Help!' she screamed. Her voice came out in a thin cry, like her throat was being squeezed. Still, she tried again, calling into the mist.

She looked back, but there was nothing. No, not nothing. She heard more steps, irregular and quick. Breathing too – grunting, heavy breaths of something massive, chasing her down.

She turned and was about to scream again, when fire raked down her back, ripping through her jacket. A weight forced her to her knees, her hands shooting out to break the fall, but the pressure was too much. The scream became a wail as her face buried in the heather. The grunting, growling, filled her ears, and when she tried to roll over, its bulk pressed her into the ground. She managed to turn her head a fraction, before something pushed it down, so hard she feared her skull would crack. She felt its breath on her face.

'Please . . .' she said. 'Please don't.'

And then, first in her peripheral vision, she saw its teeth and all the fight left her body as the stories of the schoolyard came flooding back. The nightmares she'd had as a child, buried, she thought, forever.

Something from the past, that didn't belong here.

Chapter 1

SARAH

'The police are here to see you.'

And with those words, a normal day in the office is anything but. My first instinct is a client. Some enraged, slighted husband, backed into a corner, has taken things too far. It happens rarely, but there was an horrific incident, when I was just starting, involving acid . . .

'Ms Kline?' says the receptionist. 'Shall I send them up?'

'Did they say what it's about?'

A pause, then, 'Apparently it's a personal matter.'

My hand tightens on the phone and a series of horrendous images flick through my head, like the slides in some hellish PowerPoint presentation. Doug lying on a roadside somewhere, surrounding by broken glass. Bystanders, one or two already pulling out their phones in macabre fascination. A panicked driver saying how he wasn't going fast, how the man came out of nowhere, how he didn't see him until it was too—

'Thanks, Nia. I'll meet them at the elevators.'

The line goes dead, and I'm left with tingling fingers, my lips suddenly cold. Shock. The blood responding to my panic, taking evasive action from my extremities to the vital organs.

A personal matter. It has to be Doug. The scenario seems inevitable – a logical progression from dread to doom. The slide show flashes up a police officer crouched at Doug's side, reaching into his jacket pocket. Then the organ donor card he carried in his wallet. I'm listed as his next of kin. That's why they're here. He must have been out for a lunchtime run – part of the latest marathon-training cycle – pounding the city streets on his way to one of the big parks, veering off onto the road to avoid the flow of pedestrians. The roads are all busy round his office. Motorcyclists tearing between cars in a blind rush, impatient taxi drivers pulling daring manoeuvres, tourists in hire vehicles trying to get to grips with London traffic. Those bus drivers, looking for a yard's advantage and trusting any Londoner to have their wits about them. And Doug – *my* Doug – probably thinking about keeping his heart rate stable, or his running form, or listening to his earphones, his mind on other matters entirely. He might not even have known what hit him. Just a screech of brakes . . . then nothing. The sort of thing you read about all the time on the news, and thank God it's not you or yours.

I split into two people. One's detached, almost indifferent. A protective measure to find space, to keep calm, to take a step back. This cool and collected version of me drifts towards the window and watches the other, pale and waxy as a corpse herself, plucking her coat from the back of her chair and rushing from the room. It wonders how that woman will cope if a week before her wedding some terrible accident has befallen her fiancé. She'll be this tragic stereotype – the woman who buried her husband on the day intended for her nuptials, dress never worn, gifts returned, future cruelly snatched away.

A few seconds pass, and I follow the other me down the hall.

Katriona comes out of the loo, and we almost collide.

'Sarah!'

'Shit. Sorry.'

'Are you okay?'

The shadow me thinks Katriona's looking radiant as always, and wonders the name of the perfume she's wearing and where she got those blue teardrop earrings (are they *genuine* sapphires?), but the real me – the flesh and blood, trapped in the moment, the one with the heart thumping like a drum – doesn't have time to take that sort of thing in at all.

'Er . . . yes.' I don't want to explain. I can't really, until I know what's going on.

I sense Kat's eyes following as I keep going, and the dread in my gut is like a rock, making it hard to walk. My visitors – *the police* – will have to have passes issued, then there'll be a wait at the bank of elevators. I picture two of them. Their grim, apologetic faces, like undertakers. Men with black hair and black eyes and black clothes. Crows seated on a branch, surveying carrion.

From the elevator lobby on the fifteenth floor, a huge window gives a view across the city. Soaring glass and metal sprouting like exotic plants among a bed of regular Georgian

11

grandeur. It's normally a comforting view – the potent, thrusting city in which I dwell – but my nerves are fizzing with anticipation and it looks fragile today. Vulnerable. If Doug's been hurt, none of it matters. I think of a mushroom cloud bursting silently in the distance over the rooftops and await the shock wave roar that will sweep me, and everything else, away in glass and fire and dust.

The numbers over the elevator doors provide an illuminated countdown. At 14, a light chimes, and the doors open.

Their faces are not quite as lugubrious or commiserating as I expected. A man and a woman; he in his forties, she a decade or so younger. He's tall, pale and thin, with a wet-shaved head and a neatly trimmed beard. She's Asian, short, hair in a tight plait, and carries a document case, which looks curiously old-fashioned. Both are wearing the same sort of plain and discreet office clothes as everyone on my floor. Almost, anyway. Even if I didn't know they were police officers, there's something not *quite* right about them. His tie knot droops a half-inch, revealing his top collar button, and his cuffs are buttoned too. Neither would be acceptable among my colleagues: they teach you how to dress in law school and if you don't fit in on that score, you'll find someone has a quiet word. Cufflinks are a must and top buttons should only make an appearance two drinks into a work night out. She's smarter, but the jacket isn't tailored properly – too short at the wrists. Her shoes are flat, so though we're probably the same size, I feel like a giant in my heels. Ungainly too – at a distinct disadvantage in this encounter.

'Ms Kline?' says the man.

I nod and hold out my hand. 'Is it Doug?'

The officers share a confused glance with one another.

'Doug?' says the man.

'He's my fiancé. Is he okay?'

He shakes his head. 'Ah, no,' he replies, before adding, 'I mean, this isn't about your fiancé.'

My hand goes to my chest, in a way that shadow-me briefly considers theatrical. 'Oh, thank God. I thought . . .' My mind hits reboot. 'What is it, then?'

The woman smiles reassuringly. 'This is just a routine enquiry.' She lifts the document case a fraction, in a gesture that seems involuntary. 'Is there somewhere private we could talk?'

I'm forgetting myself. The elevator lobby is no place for this sort of conversation. 'Of course. Follow me.'

I take them back to my office. Through the partition, a couple of the associates on my floor look up with idle curiosity. The police officers probably look like auditors of some sort. They have that slightly worn and weary look of those who sit in cramped, poorly lit offices drinking lukewarm coffee and spilling sandwich crumbs onto their paperwork.

I close the door and gesture to the two seats opposite mine. There's a picture of Doug and me on the desk, half-reclining on a gondola beneath St Mark's. It was the night he proposed. I'm laughing wildly, because I was tipsy and because the gondolier had pretended he was about to fall in with my phone in his hand. I normally move it when clients visit, as a matter of course. Divorce lawyer rubbing in her happy relationship gives the wrong impression.

'I'm Sergeant Sadler,' says the man, taking a chair. His accent is pure south London, but his pronunciation is clipped, like he's putting on airs. 'And this is Constable Sanjit. We wondered if we could ask you a few questions. It's about your sister, Gemma.'

'Gemma?'

The name comes out of my mouth like it's a foreign word I'm learning for the first and the officers look at each other quickly, before returning their gazes to me.

'You do have a sister called Gemma Kline?' says Sadler.

'I did . . . I mean, I do,' I say. 'Look, sorry. I haven't seen her for a long time. We're not really close. Is she all right?'

My brain is still playing catch-up with this sudden, unexpected change of direction. Of course this is about Gemma. It would hardly be the first time she's got herself in trouble with the law. I remember picking her up from the station when she was fifteen on a Friday night, when Mum was in no fit state to drive. A fight. Someone had been bottled, if I recall correctly. Gemma hadn't been directly involved but proved difficult enough with the attending officers for them to place her in custody.

Constable Sanjit has placed the document case on her lap, and taken out a notebook and pen from her inside jacket pocket. 'When you say, "a long time"?'

I note they haven't answered my question. In fact, they seem a little impatient. Blunt, even. Like *I* might be the problem here. I choose not to rise to it.

'Over five years,' I say. I look at the electronic calendar on my desk. It's the ninth of September. Mum's funeral was in February – a blustery, wet, miserable day that I'd obviously rather forget. We'd sheltered under bucking umbrellas and the wreath blew off the coffin as they carried it into the crematorium. I was crying and Doug rushed forward to pick it up. 'Five and a half.'

'You haven't spoken at all since then?'

'Not once.'

If they'd seen the argument we had afterwards, they'd understand.

'Look, what's this about? Has something happened to her?'

Sanjit closes the notebook and looks to the sergeant. He gives a discreet nod. Then she breathes a long sigh through her nose, before her sad brown eyes rest on me. 'We're assisting Durham Constabulary in their enquiries into the movements of a man called Mark Lake. We believe he was in a relationship with Gemma.'

The name rings a bell. 'She had a boyfriend called Mark. The last thing I heard, Gemma lived down on the South coast though. Not up north. Nowhere near Durham.'

'That's right,' says the constable. 'We traced Mark's current address in Brighton. Gemma lived there with him, but we haven't been able to locate her.'

'So she's missing?'

'No one has reported it,' says Sadler. 'However, there's evidence to suggest Mark, and maybe Gemma, were in some sort of trouble.'

They're playing their cards close to their chest, and I'm not inclined to give them much in return. Not least, because I can't. I'm struggling to work out how they've even found me. 'Trouble as in danger?'

The two officers share a conspiratorial glance. 'Durham found Mark's car,' says Sadler. 'It had been set on fire, we think deliberately.'

I remember the one time I met Mark. Part of me is impressed that they're still together. Let's just say he didn't

15

seem like a keeper. The thought he might be involved in petty criminality is hardly inconceivable.

'Maybe it was just stolen?' I suggest.

'There was a man's body in the driver's seat,' says Sadler, not missing a beat.

'Oh, God. You mean he's . . .'

'Deceased, yes. A post-mortem on his body has proved inconclusive, but Durham have no reason to believe it isn't Mark. He's not been seen for several days either.'

A silence falls over the office, before Sanjit adds, 'Sorry to be the bearer of bad news.'

She's misread me, I think. I didn't know Mark well enough for his death to have much of an emotional impact. 'Do you think Gemma's okay?'

Sadler stiffens, a flicker of challenge in his posture. 'We don't know what to think, which is why we need to find her.'

'I'm sorry – I don't think I can help. When did this happen – the fire, I mean?'

'A little over a week ago,' says Sadler, without checking any notes. 'Do you have a number for Gemma?'

I fish out my phone. 'I did. I wouldn't be surprised if it's changed.' I find it under 'Sis' and read it to them.

With her book open, Sanjit says, 'It's the one we've got from the flatmates, boss.' She looks up at me. 'We've tried the number. It's disconnected.'

I can sense the meeting winding up already. Sadler puts his hands on his knees to stand. 'Thank you for your time, Ms Kline.' He fishes out a card from his pocket and places it on the table. 'If she does get in touch, do give us a call.'

'I will.' I briefly inspect the card. 'Actually, how did you find me? I mean, I've really had no contact with Gemma for years.'

Sanjit, standing also, now opens the document case, a little clumsily. 'We found this among her possessions in Brighton.'

She pulls out a white card that glitters slightly. It's the wedding invite I sent to her with a letter, after much deliberation, about two months ago. With the likelihood of her address being out of date, I never expected it even to reach her, let alone for her to reply, and we haven't left a space for her in the seating plan. I'm not sure why I bothered. Conscience, maybe – some last vestige of sisterly affection. Or perhaps it was spite. A note to say 'I'm doing fine, thanks'. Hard to tell sometimes, when it comes to Gemma, how I really feel. It's always been like that.

'Out of interest, why is it you didn't keep in touch with your sister?' asks Sanjit.

'It's complicated,' I say.

The constable smiles. 'I get it. I've got a sister too. Three actually.'

As I'm showing them back to the elevators, her boss casts a glance around the office. 'What is it you do for a living?' he asks.

It's not a question I relish answering, but I've learnt the best thing to do is be vague. 'We're a family law firm,' I say, 'specialising in divorce.'

I see a cloud of confusion on Sadler's face. You don't get an office in this building doing run-of-the-mill separations. He's not wearing a wedding ring, and I make a guess he's probably on the other side of a marriage gone sour. I press the button to summon the elevator.

'We tend to represent partners exiting high net-worth relationships.'

That seems to satisfy him. His mouth twists in distaste. Lawyers generally sit somewhere high on polls of most hated professions, somewhere above conveyancing solicitors and thankfully below ambulance chasers.

'We'll be leaving you to it, then,' he says, stepping into the elevator. 'Good luck with the wedding, by the way.'

I can't tell if that's supposed to be a joke, but I raise a smile anyway as the doors close in front of them.

Walking back to my office, I think of the last time I saw my sister.

Chapter 2

SARAH – FIVE AND A HALF YEARS AGO

'Listen, I spoke to a couple of estate agents.'

I turn to Gemma. She's wearing jeans and a black hoodie and Doc Martens. 'Seriously, not now, all right.'

Her thick kohl is smeared down her cheeks. It makes her look like she's been crying, but it's more likely the weather. It's been pissing it down all day, and despite the expansive black umbrella, my shoes are soaked through. My toes are freezing, a painful near-numbness. I just want to say thanks to the other guests for coming – people I'll promise to keep in touch with but inevitably won't – and get out of here. That's the thing about funerals – it's not just a goodbye to the departed, but to the living also. Most of the guests here are bound together by tenuous family bonds, or have known each other from the hospital where Mum worked years back. Mum was the knot, and now she's gone. There'll be the odd Christmas card from these people, then over time the ties will loosen and those will cease too.

'Well, are *you* going to do it?' asks Gemma.

The wreaths are under polythene, spattered with droplets. Even so, the ink on some of the condolence cards is already smudged. The crematorium has asked if I want to take any home with me, but I don't need the flat smelling of damp and slowly rotting flowers. I even feel a bit odd taking the urn. These tokens of death feel distinctly Victorian, a way to wallow, and Mum has occupied half a lifetime's space in my mind already. She never said anything about funeral plans when alive, or scattering her ashes, and I wonder if I should just give her mortal remains to her old pals from The Artilleryman, the sorry bunch of soaks who are already sidling off to the wake. Doug is shaking hands with one of the red-nosed old duffers at the gates. They'll probably keep Mum behind the bar, toasting her every Friday night with sentiment brimming in their eyes. That's a sort of grief, I suppose, and who am I to judge?

'Gemma, can we just let it go until she's fucking cold?'

Auntie Phyll half-hears the swear word, because she looks around with a glare from the arm of her third husband.

'Sorry,' says Gemma. 'I'm going to be away for a while, and I wanted to make sure everything was in order.'

I scoff at that. Can't help it.

'What's so funny?' she snaps.

'You,' I say. 'This new interest in organising.'

'You're a real bitch, sometimes, you know?'

20

I'm not having that. Not today. 'You didn't show much interest in organising any of this,' I say, casting a glance around the crematorium. 'The funeral home, registering the death, the order of service, the invitations . . .'

'That's because you wouldn't let me. You took charge.'

'Yeah, tell yourself that.'

She looks at me with real ferocity, and I flinch, half expecting her to launch at me, tumbling us both onto the wet tarmac in an unseemly heap. The last time we fought – a proper fight – was back when we were in our teens. I'd told Mum she was seeing a boy in my year, and Mum spoke to the school, who put a quick stop to it. I told myself it was because I was concerned, that Gemma's heart wasn't really in it anyway, but the truth was closer to jealousy. My little sis with a boyfriend before me. She slapped me so hard my ear was ringing for a day after. I lost it completely and Mum found us tearing at each other's hair like wild animals on the scuffed lino of the kitchen floor.

'Lucky we've got Saint Sarah to look after everything then, isn't it?' she scoffs.

'Someone's got to. Otherwise Mum's corpse would still be on the sofa in a puddle of puke.'

Gemma looks like I've slapped *her*. Her lip trembles.

'Yeah,' I say. 'It wasn't pretty. You want to flog the sofa too once it's clean?'

I walk away, thrilled by my own fury, and manage to say a calm farewell to Phyll and whatever his name is. The thought of drinks at The Artilleryman fills me with dread. I just want to go home, get out of those shoes and have a long bath. I'll talk to Doug, convince him we only have to stay for one. He smiles at me from the gates. Doug's always much better at this sort of thing than me — small talk, bonhomie. Faking it.

★   ★   ★

Gemma can't let it rest. At the pub, I notice there's a lanky guy talking to her at the bar. He wasn't at the service, and he's not dressed for mourning, but they seem to know each other. They're having a heated conversation, heads close together, and though I don't catch it, I feel the occasional glance in my direction.

My feet are drying out a little and one drink has turned into two. It's helping.

Doug's being charming elsewhere, and it's then I realise the lanky bloke has moved right beside me. I can't see Gemma.

'Hello?' I say.

'Hi.' His voice has a slight west-country twang. He's in a leather jacket that brings with it a waft of a tobacco smell. 'Just wanted to say I'm sorry for your loss.'

'Thank you. Did you know my mother?'

He shakes his head. 'Only from what Gemma told me. Never met her.'

'You're Gemma's partner.'

'That's right. She's having a tough time. Struggling, like, bless her.'

'Struggling how?'

'You upset her, that's all.'

'I *upset* her?'

He nods innocently, like he's not read my tone at all. Like he's pleased I understand.

22

'Sorry, what's your name?' I ask.

'Lakey.' He holds out a hand. 'Mark.'

We shake briefly.

'And have you two been together long?'

'A few years.' He looks more cautious then, and I guess my face must be accurately conveying some of my feelings towards him.

'Well, thanks, Mark. I'm glad we had this talk.'

I turn away from him, but he's still hanging around. 'It's just . . .' he continues, 'about the house.'

Deep breath. '*Our* mother's house?'

'Yeah. Gemma's wondering when it might go on the market.'

Either he is grossly insensitive or plain clueless. In either case, we clearly live in different moral universes. Mark has doleful eyes. Darkish shadows under his cheekbones that looked almost like bruising. Against his pale skin, his lips are bluish and plump. His nails, I notice, are filthy.

'And why is that anything to do with you?' I ask.

'It's not,' he says, with the same guileless lack of charm. 'I'm looking out for her, y'know. She's pretty broke. A few quid'll help her get on her feet.'

'Will it? And you too?'

His eyebrows shoot up and he backs off a little, but his lip has curled. 'Nah, it's not like that, love.'

'I'm not your *love*. Glad to hear it though. Would you mind leaving me alone, please? I just cremated my mother.'

'Sorry,' he mutters, his face finally registering a fraction of self-awareness. 'Just Gem said you weren't even that close to her.'

I take a sip of my drink. The ice cubes rattle. 'Did she now?'

'Said your mum didn't look after neither of you. Cos of the drink. You didn't owe her nothing.'

Doug approaches, and I'm relieved to redirect my attention.

'Hey, sweetheart,' I say, voice clipped. 'Can we go?'

He must see the torment on my face and the man standing at my side. He looms over Mark. They're roughly the same height, but Doug has a lot more presence. 'Is everything okay?'

'Fine. I'm just done in.'

'Right,' he says, eyes still on Gemma's boyfriend. 'I'll settle up.'

As he does, I leave Mark at the bar. I don't say goodbye to anyone and make my way to the porch area of the pub to get my umbrella. Gemma is standing here, smoking, looking out onto the rainswept carpark and the junction beyond. She catches her breath as she sees me.

'Your boyfriend really is a piece of work,' I say.

'What's that supposed to mean?'

'Telling me all about Mum and how I feel.'

'Mark's a good guy.'

'He really isn't,' I reply.

'Cos he's not a lawyer?'

'Well, does he even have a job?'

'He's a mechanic, actually. You have no idea what he's like. He works bloody hard.'

'He seems very keen to flog Mum's house.'

'Must be nice not worrying about money.'

'I gave you money, remember? Last year. A grand. What happened to that?'

'And I told you I'll pay you back.'

'I don't want it back.'

'Then why did you bring it up?'

'Because . . .' I don't know what to say. I wish I *hadn't* brought it up.

She looks at me with contempt.

I can feel the skin flushing across my chest and collarbones, giving me away. I want to say any number of things to Gemma. How she doesn't *deserve* Mum's money, because she upped sticks and moved out the moment she could, leaving me to clean up the mess, to pay the bills, to deal with the cycles of rage and despair. But, in the moment, it's too much. I know I won't get the words out clearly, and she'll have won.

'You think you're better than everyone,' continues Gemma. 'You look down your nose at me, at Mark. I bet you even do it to your boyfriend. I just wish you could *see* yourself.'

'That's rich,' I say, eyeing her outfit. 'Just sort your life out.'

'Fuck you.'

★   ★   ★

As final words go, it seemed pretty conclusive. Doug and I drove away, and I was still too angry to process things. In the days after, I relived and rescripted the conversation, by turns dialling up my anger to heights of rhetorical violence, or lowering the temperature to make peace. Neither fantasy offered satisfaction. I thought many times about calling Gemma, trying to build bridges, but it had never happened. And in the end, it became easier not even to think about it. I asked an overpriced, reliable solicitor to handle the sale of the house and arrange for half the proceeds to go to

Gemma. It wasn't much in the end – a two-up two-down ex-social housing, miles from the Tube and a long way from the gentrification slowly emanating from EC1. She got all Mum's jewellery too, not that it would have been worth much. I certainly didn't want it.

And when Gemma didn't bother to say thank you, that was it.

Money well spent if it meant I never had to worry about her again.

Chapter 3

GEMMA – THREE WEEKS EARLIER

A woman's voice was calling out plaintively from along the dimly lit corridor, and Gemma was struggling to work out which room it was coming from. She'd been on her feet for thirteen hours, and the blister that had formed and burst on her left heel made her eyes water with each step along the worn carpet. She'd covered the extra two hours for Petra, who had a problem getting a sitter for her kids.

Some of the doors in the Nightingale Wing were kept open all the time, for safety reasons, but Gemma knew the residents in those couldn't be the source of the noise. The first floor was entirely made up of the more severe dementia patients – those with no prospect of discharge. Many never left their beds at all, only occasionally rising to anything that could be called consciousness. Nevertheless, Gemma cared for them just as she did everyone on the floor.

As she continued down the corridor, she realised the cries were coming from room 6 – Eileen, or Mrs Waters as she preferred to be addressed by the staff. Gemma knocked and entered. The only light in the room came from the muted television – flashing across the face of the elderly woman half-reclining in bed.

'You need the loo, sweetheart?' she said. Eileen could still walk with the help of a frame, and there'd be no need to call for stronger arms to support her.

The old woman didn't reply for a moment.

'You all right, Mrs Waters? It's late.'

'Is it today my Simon's coming?' she said. With her teeth out, the lower half of her face was collapsed and gurning.

Simon was the name of Eileen's late husband, but she'd attached it to her son-in-law, David. He visited dutifully once a month, and had only been in the week before.

'It's night-time, my love,' said Gemma. 'He might be here tomorrow. We can check in the morning if you want. Why don't you go back to sleep for now?'

Eileen didn't protest as Gemma plumped her pillow and pulled the blanket back up gently over her nightdress. She was staring at the ceiling.

Gemma switched off the TV, casting the room in shadow. 'Night night, Mrs Waters.'

She closed the door gently, as Petra came bustling down the hall, wearing a thick winter coat. 'Thank you, thank you!' she said.

'You found someone?'

'A friend's daughter. She's only fourteen, but she's a good girl.'

Petra fished in her purse, pulled out a twenty-pound note, and offered it to Gemma, who shook her head.

'It's too much,' she said. Petra took her hand, and pressed the note into it. Gemma half-heartedly mouthed, 'Ten's plenty.'

'No, it's good,' said Petra. 'Did Mrs Panerjee ask anything?'

'I don't think she's come out of the office.'

Petra nodded. 'Good.'

The home manager was strict with the roster. She didn't appreciate personnel chopping and changing hours at the last minute.

In the small staffroom, Petra took off her outer layers while Gemma donned her own coat and hat. 'Any dramas?'

'Not yet,' said Gemma with a smile.

The night shifts at Elm House tended to be uneventful and lonely, punctuated only by the odd toilet visit or bed change. Occasionally, the doctor needed to be called, but mostly it was a long drag until dawn, when the kitchen staff would come in to begin their preparations for breakfast and the morning round of checks began.

'See you tomorrow then,' said Gemma.

★　★　★

The freshness of the night air always took her by surprise after the musty central heating of the home, and she took a few deep breaths while she sent a text to Mark asking where he was. She was hungry, having eaten half a quick dinner off the kitchen counter five hours earlier. She couldn't remember what they had in the fridge at the flat.

A map pin came back, on the seafront. A message read, *With Kash x.*

Elm House was a kilometre up from the beach at Hove,

and she wandered down, trying to ignore the blister. She couldn't afford new shoes at the moment – the extra twenty would have to go towards the rent arrears.

They were far enough from the centre of Brighton that there wasn't much traffic around on a Monday night. Occasional taxis drifted past.

The sea at the bottom of the shallow hill was a dark expanse, waiting. Once Gemma reached the promenade, she turned east towards the lights of the city. Figures walked on the shingle, or huddled together. She heard Mark's voice before she way him – picking out his shape leaning against one of the exposed wooden groynes that marked off the waterfront. She climbed down a set of stone steps onto the shucking pebbles and crossed the beach towards him. She saw Kash too – lifting a glowing joint to his face. She smelled the sweet weed-smoke hanging in the air.

'Hey,' she said.

'Hi, Gem,' said Kash.

Mark held out his arms and she fell into them. He kissed the top of her head. 'How was work?'

'Long,' she said. 'Got an extra couple of hours though.'

'That's good,' he said.

His voice was flat, with something left hanging, and she extricated herself from his arms. 'What's up?'

Mark looked her in the eye. 'Frank laid me off,' he said.

'You're kidding.'

Mark shook his head. His eyes looked moist. 'He said he was sorry, but business hasn't picked up. Can't blame him.'

'You've been there over a year! What about Tom?'

'Tom's his cousin.'

'And he's a lazy bastard, you said. Always making mistakes.'

Mark shrugged. 'Still family, though.'

Gemma felt sick. Mark's job at the garage was just about all that kept them from drowning. They still owed two grand to their landlord from the year before, before Mark had found the job with Frank. Luckily for them, Des, the old-timer who owned the property, was chilled with them paying the debt off in tiny chunks each month. Now without Mark's income they'd only slip further behind.

'What are we going to do?' she asked. A familiar feeling of desperation, dormant for months, gnawed at her insides.

'They were looking for staff at Aldi last week,' said Kash.

'I'll go tomorrow,' said Mark. 'Something will turn up, babe.'

'Always does,' added Kash. He reached out the joint to Mark, who took it.

Kash worked at one of the big chain gyms as a personal trainer, as his bulging biceps could attest. He was always dressed in designer gear, and his trainers glowed white. He occasionally drove an old Merc, though she got the impression it belonged to one of his brothers. Mark said they were into 'other stuff', but Kash was the golden boy of the family and kept away from the dealing.

'This is good gear,' said Mark. He tipped his head back and blew smoke rings up over the decaying wooden groyne. The light breeze coming off the sea took the smoke inland towards the sad-looking amusement arcade. Lights flashed inside, but there were few customers that Gemma could see.

'Home-grown, mate,' said Kash.

Mark looked at the joint with a frown. 'Serious? Your folks know?'

Kash laughed. 'Nah, I mean it's English weed. Not an import.'

He extended it to Gemma, who shook her head. She didn't care much for weed at the best of times. On an empty stomach, it was likely to make her sick.

Kash was seated on the sea wall just above and pushed himself off, landing with his heels in the ricocheting pebbles. 'You didn't hear it from me, but there's this big house, somewhere up north. Hartford, or something. They grow it in the grounds.'

'Ballsy,' said Mark.

Gemma didn't know how he could be so relaxed. Her wages might just cover this month's rent, due in a week's time, but they'd be left with no money for food or bills. And after that, they were stuffed. Her mind made a token effort to search for other sources of money; each was a dead end.

She watched Mark take another drag and hand it back. He was putting on a brave face, but he wasn't stupid. He knew they were in a hole as well as she did.

And no one was going to pull them out this time.

Chapter 4

SARAH

'You don't owe her anything.'

It's the same evening after the police came to the office. Doug swirls the remains of an expensive Malbec around in his glass, watches it cling in viscous arches to the inside. The restaurant diners are thinning out around us as it gets near to eleven p.m. Those that remain are mostly the corporate crowd, and there's one table made up entirely of men in suits who've been getting increasingly loud since their last course disappeared and they've been gradually soaking up more booze. They've just ordered shots, and the poor waiter looks like he's anticipating a late night.

'I'm not sure what I can do anyway,' I reply.

Doug tips the last of the wine into his mouth, then sets down the glass.

'You want coffee?'

I shake my head. Last thing I need is caffeine keeping me awake. I've enough to think about already.

Doug scribbles an imaginary bill to the waiter. 'She's probably fine though. Like you said – the darkest Pennines don't seem the destination of choice for your sister. And it sounds like they're not even sure it *was* this Mark guy inside. The car might have been sold on, or nicked.'

He has a point. The thought of a body burned so badly it's impossible to identify turns my stomach. I assume they'll do some sort of DNA testing to confirm.

'By the way,' Doug continues, 'the venue called today. Seat coverings have arrived; they're four short.'

I groan. 'What a shocker.'

Doug grins. 'Don't worry – it'll get sorted.'

He reaches across and takes my hand on the tablecloth. The engagement ring catches the light and sparkles.

'You know what,' I say. 'When the police came today, I was worried it was about you. Thought you'd been flattened by a bus while out running.'

He chuckles. 'Not possible. Rest day today. It's almost like you don't religiously follow my training regimen.'

'I mean, it is *fascinating*,' I reply, with an eye-roll.

I pull my hand back as the waiter approaches with the bill on a small silver platter. At our backs, one of the businessman guffaws loudly at a joke I didn't hear, slapping the table and rattling crockery. The waiter looks at us apologetically.

'Miles and Susanna have had to move their flight though,' says Doug. 'They're coming straight from the airport.'

'Sue's never been late for anything,' I reply. 'She'll probably be knocking on the cockpit door, telling them she can fly the plane herself.'

We've been organising this wedding for what seems like an eternity, but it's still a mad panic as the day draws near. Flowers, stationery, hotels for family, the marquee, ever-changing dining options for kids and vegans, cake, gifts, musicians for the ceremony, the band for afterwards . . . What with the firm as well, my head's spinning. Not that Doug hasn't pulled his weight. We'd wanted to marry in the summer, but work was just too mad, so we've settled for autumn. It's all completely weatherproofed though – marquees, heaters, fifty hired umbrellas. Barring a natural disaster, in nine days' time we'll be husband and wife.

'And Olly still hasn't pawned the rings?'

'No promises, there,' says Doug. He lays his card on the platter.

Olly's his best man. Nice guy, hampered by a troublesome gambling problem far enough in the past that we're starting to joke about it, at least behind his back.

'Actually, I was going to ask . . .' says Doug, looking a bit more serious. 'He's with Liz again . . .'

'Oh yes?' The saga of Olly and Liz has been going on for years.

'He wanted to know if she could come. I said yes. We have one space.'

'I guess so.' Given today's events, Gemma making a sudden appearance seems less likely than ever.

'Not to say they won't be off again in a week's time, of course.'

The waiter comes back and takes our payment and wishes us a pleasant night.

Doug wipes the corners of his mouth with a napkin and tosses it on the table. 'Just going for a pee.'

As he heads off to the loos, I twirl the engagement ring on my finger. There was a time I never thought we'd get married. The things you see in my line of work are enough to give you more than a healthy scepticism of the institution. And the announcement caused a few raised eyebrows at the office, especially when I confided – and it was quickly spread about – that we weren't even signing pre-nups. It's no secret I'm the main breadwinner in the relationship – not that Doug's IT salary is anything to sniff at.

We're pretty much the last of our friendship group – bar Olly, naturally – to tie the knot. The weddings have all blended into one over the years. The country houses, the town halls, the garden receptions, the champagne. Okay, there was Miles and Susanna's in France – a beautiful rural church and dinner in the vineyard. That was something else. Her dad in his wheelchair, coming down the aisle at her side . . .

I'll be making that walk solo of course. I don't remember my father at all – he wasn't around much when I was young, and vanished completely when Mum was pregnant with Gemma. I've never even seen a picture of him, and it seems rude even to use the term 'father' for a man who never did anything to earn it. There was a time growing up when I used to fantasise about a strange, handsome man appearing at the front door, with a bunch of flowers and a suitcase and tears in his eyes. Eyes just the same shade of hazel as mine. When the daydream really took hold – when I let it – he was rich, too. He'd explain that he was a different person now, ready to change. We'd go to live with him, and he'd get help for Mum, and our lives would be altered completely.

Romantic, silly ruminations that I could lose myself in for a few minutes, especially when things at home weren't too bad. When they were – when Mum was drinking heavily – I'd try to enter that world of fantasy, but the spell never worked as well, like a lodged door that couldn't be opened. Later, when I could've looked for him (we've plenty of investigators on the books at work), something always stopped me. I don't need him now, and I don't want him to think I do.

I wonder if Gemma ever had the same thoughts. Somehow I doubt it – she was never much of a dreamer.

I take out my phone, and it still shows the message I've written but not sent: 'Gem, it's Sarah. Are you okay?'

The constable was right. Each time I've rung in the hours since their visit, it's the same emotionless, automated response. *The number you've dialled is not available . . .* She might have changed her number, but more likely the phone is just switched off. Would she answer anyway, if she knew it was me calling?

Doug's coming back from the toilets, and he has his jacket over his arm. 'You ready to go, Mrs Thomas?'

'Oh, God – don't call me that. Not yet. It sounds so old-fashioned.'

I send the message, and slip the phone into my bag.

He grins. 'Not long now until you're *all* mine.'

Chapter 5

GEMMA

'We could sell the car?' she suggested.

'It's worth fuck all, babe,' said Mark.

Gemma didn't doubt it. 'We might get a couple of hundred quid. Frank might take it.'

'For scrap, maybe. Sixty max, though.'

They sat either side of the small table in the kitchen on Windsor Place, both nursing mugs of tea. After a totting-up, they'd had four hundred pounds, another two-fifty coming in from Elm House in five days' time. They could pay the rent, but Mark thought Des would let them off for another month if they pleaded. He'd composed and sent a text explaining their situation a couple of hours earlier. As yet, there was no response.

The supermarket prospect had come to nothing – the two positions already filled by the time Mark got there. The manager hadn't even wanted to keep his details on record in case something else turned up. Mark admitted he'd got angry, so those bridges were probably burnt for good.

'I wondered about asking Kash's brothers?' he said. 'They might need . . . help.'

'Dealing?' said Gemma. 'No fucking way.'

'It would be easy money, I reckon. They're well connected.'

'That's not the point,' said Gemma. 'If you get pinched again . . .'

'I know, I know . . .' He took a gulp of tea. 'I just don't know . . . I feel like I've let you down.'

Gemma reached across and took his hand. It was rare to see him like this, and she hated it. Normally he was happy-go-lucky, even when life was tough. 'You could never let me down.'

There were still oil stains on the inside of his long fingers. It was so unfair. He'd worked his arse off for Frank, covering for Tom on more than one occasion when he hadn't shown up for work after a bender. And it wasn't like Mark had had much of a start in life. He'd grown up in care. Everything had been a struggle.

He nodded up, towards the ceiling. 'What about your sister?'

The wedding invite had arrived a few weeks ago and stood on the windowsill upstairs, redirected quite fortunately through an old acquaintance at their last flat. It was Sarah all over – heavy, expensive card, silver lettering, formal.

Doug and Sarah request the pleasure of your company . . .

Gemma remembered Doug only dimly – tall, and clean-shaven, handsome, if you liked that sort of stiff, respectable look. Probably played squash after work. Perfect for Sarah – a life without problems or the unexpected. Gemma couldn't tell why she'd been sent the invite at all. Not after

40

the argument at Mum's funeral. They hadn't seen or spoken to one another in the five years since. Sarah must've felt they had to at least *post* an invitation, for old times' sake, even if was unlikely to reach her. Mark hadn't been offended there was no plus-one, but Gemma assumed it was a deliberate slight.

'I can't,' she said.

'Why not?' asked Mark.

'You know why. She hates me.'

'That was years ago. It's water under the bridge.'

Gemma laughed mirthlessly. Mark really didn't understand families. He'd been brought up by a succession of foster carers, and had little contact with the array of loose siblings he'd lived with over the years.

'I still owe her from last time.'

'It's got to be worth a try,' said Mark. 'Do you want me to talk to her?'

'No! Look, it's not an option.'

'All right, all right,' said Mark, a little petulantly. He sipped his tea.

There was a knock at the door, and Mark stood up. Sol's girlfriend who lived on the top floor was always forgetting her key.

Gemma had considered calling Sarah, of course, but it really seemed impossible. The hurdle of shame too great. Since their falling out, Gemma rarely gave much thought to Sarah or her perfect untroubled life. Not only was it painful, but it was pointless too. The bridge had been well and truly washed away that day at the pub.

Sudden shouts reverberated down the hallway, and before Gemma was out of her chair, Mark came stumbling back into the kitchen, catching himself on the counter. Two men followed, one in a hood, with a scarf over his face, the other bareheaded, and huge.

'Hey!' said Gemma. 'Leave him—'

The man – his bald head like an anvil, folds of skin over plates of skull – turned to her, pointed a stubby finger an inch from her face. 'Fuck off, or I'll knock your fucking teeth out.'

She backed away, driven by the sheer force of his presence as much as the threat. The man sweated potential energy, like a grenade with the pin pulled. He must have outweighed her by six stone.

The masked man stayed close to her while the thug advanced on Mark, who had nowhere to go and lifted his arms to protect himself. It didn't help. The attacker swung a paw-like open palm, smashing Mark's hands aside and sending him crashing into a small table.

'Please!' said Gemma. She tried to bustle past the hooded man, but he pushed her back easily. 'He didn't do anything!'

The giant man's chest was heaving. 'You think you can take my old man for a mug?' he said.

Gemma realised then what was going on, and who she was looking at. Tyler, their landlord's son, a man she knew by reputation only. He was supposed to be inside, having overstepped his responsibilities as a doorman three years earlier and killed a man. Evidently, he'd been released.

Mark wiped blood from his mouth. Already, the side of his face was swelling up from the force of the blow across his cheek. 'I can get the money.'

'Fuck off!' said Tyler, lifting a hand for another strike. Mark cowered.

'Please, we can!' shouted Gemma.

Des's son turned on her, eyes burning. 'You've got two grand?' he spat.

'We can get it,' she said, trying to sound calm.

'Can you fuck!'

He turned to Mark again, but instead of punching him, he grabbed at one of his flailing wrists. Mark tried to struggle. Tyler turned his back, threading the arm beneath his own armpit. He took Mark's hand and found his middle finger. His face didn't change expression as he snapped it backwards, the sound as crisp as a gunshot. Mark screamed and fell to the floor, hunched over. Tyler stepped away, looking at Gemma.

'It's his leg next,' he said. 'Get the fucking money. You've got a week.'

They were out of the house as suddenly as they'd entered, a whirlwind leaving the furniture awry and the door swinging open in their wake.

Gemma rushed to Mark's side. 'Let me see,' she said.

His head was beaded with sweat as he cradled his broken finger. 'I'm all right,' he said shakily. 'Are you okay?'

Gemma hugged him, and laid her lips against his forehead. 'I'm fine,' she replied. 'Let's get you to hospital.'

Mark let out a shuddering breath. 'I can do it,' he said. 'You get to work.'

'Don't be daft. I'll call in.'

Mark swallowed and looked up, smiling through the pain, but a scared smile. 'We need the money, babe.'

Chapter 6

SARAH

Doug's gone in early the next day.

As I make my breakfast in the kitchen, I take out two bowls before I realise my mistake. It's not something I've done for years. One for me, one for my sister. A tic from the past, muscle memory, a throwback to the mornings I knew it was up to me to get Gemma ready for school, Mum still sprawled on her bed, or the sofa, in yesterday's clothes.

I put her bowl back, with a small, private chuckle to put myself at ease. But I'm kidding myself. It must be on account of all the stuff from yesterday. It's an unnerving feeling to not be fully in control – for your body to work out of sync with your conscious mind. We're all prisoners of our past, I suppose.

While I eat, I scan the news on my iPad for anything about the car set on fire in the Pennines with a body inside. It doesn't take long before a story comes up from *The*

Darlington Gazette. The write-up is brief. It mentions the car, a blue Skoda Octavia, though not the identity of the man inside. There's no reference to the death being suspicious. It was discovered in the early hours of last Thursday – the second of September, on a stormy night, and apparently the fire mostly burnt itself out before the fire brigade arrived on the scene. There are no images. It says the vehicle was discovered on a country track, about a mile from the main road between a place called Hartsbridge and another called Ravenow. The police are appealing for witnesses or information. Gemma's name doesn't come up. That fact alone gives me hope she's not involved. It seems perfectly possible she was never anywhere near the north of England with Mark.

I try her number again, with the same result. The message I sent failed to deliver, which means her phone is switched off or out of service. Gemma has no social media profile that I'm aware of, so there's no other way to get in touch. I know Doug's right – that I don't owe her anything; somehow that doesn't put my mind at rest.

★ ★ ★

When I get to work, Nia tells me my client has arrived early, and indicates a pair of expensively dressed Japanese women seated on the far side of reception. I ask her to give me a minute. I feel her curiosity on my back as I head for the elevators. Even if she were discreet – and I doubt she is – I'm pretty sure it will have gone round my floor that the visitors yesterday were police officers.

On the fourteenth floor, I ask Katriona to find us a

meeting room, and sort out some refreshments, to get started in five.

The sergeant's card is still on my desk, and I close my door before ringing the number. He picks up.

'Sadler.'

'Hi, it's Sarah Kline. You came by yesterday.'

'Ms Kline. How can I help?'

'I was wondering, you said you spoke to Gemma's flat-mates. Do you have a number for them?'

A pause. 'We do, but I'm afraid I can't give it to you without their permission. Is there's something you want to talk about?'

'No, I just wanted to . . . well, I told you I haven't spoken to Gemma for years. I suppose I . . .' I don't know what to say, really. 'Do *you* think she was with Mark?'

'We don't know. I can give you the number of the lead investigator in County Durham if you like? We're just doing them a favour.'

'Thanks, that would be great.'

He gives me the number for a Sergeant Nelson of Durham Constabulary, then hangs up, like he's fairly pleased to be rid of me.

I'm about to make another call, when Katriona knocks on the glass partition, and holds up three fingers. Meeting Room 3. Nelson can wait.

* * *

The day is non-stop, mostly with prep for a hearing on Monday, which will be the last big piece of work before the wedding. One woman – a client we've already met

47

– doesn't want to come to the office at all, so we meet in a discreet hotel in Kensington. She fears her husband is watching her, and so has pretended to be coming for lunch with friends. It's probably not entirely paranoia, as he's worth close to sixty million, according to our preliminary investigation, and will seriously resent losing any of it when his wife formally files for divorce.

Over the years, we've had meetings like this in many odd locations – the back of taxis, a dog park, even a waxing salon. When I tell Doug the stories, he acts like it's glamorous espionage. Really, it isn't. Nor, more often than not, are the clients trophy wives out to make a quick buck – they're just women who thought they were marrying the right man and found out he wasn't exactly Prince Charming. Infidelity is normally the proximate cause, but there's plenty of emotional abuse and coercive control. Sometimes it's simply unhappiness borne of long days spent in big, empty houses with only staff for company. All we do is work out the equitable split, the fair share. And with very rich and powerful men, that can involve a lot of digging. You'd be surprised how many men driving round in Maseratis wearing five-thousand-pound tailoring claim not to have a penny in any bank account to their name.

The hotel where we meet provides a bowl of nuts we leave untouched, and I have no time for lunch, so by five I'm starving and light-headed. Then Katriona comes in with the news: the hearing we have on Monday has been delayed a fortnight due to the defendant's last-ditch request. It's frustrating for the client, but I'm relieved too. I won't have to take work home for the weekend. I ask Kat to inform the client, then I call ahead for Doug to order in takeaway.

I get an Uber home, I say hello to Raymond, the concierge, and retrieve the post from the box. In the elevator to the apartment, I flick through it. Bills, something from the RAC, a clothing catalogue, and there, nestled between them, a postcard. It's a Japanese print – red, black and white, a simple stork overlooking a pool. I turn it over, and my eyes catch on the back the familiar, messy handwriting I've not seen for probably twenty years, since the shopping lists we left on the pad by the front door, to make sure we didn't run out of essentials.

Hey, sis,

Saw this and thought you'd like it. Not sure what to say, really. I got the invitation, but I know you only sent it because you had to. I don't want to ruin another day. Enjoy yourself. All good with me. Maybe see you soon.

Love Gemma x

The postmark is second-class, but the word 'Hartsbridge' stamped at the top is what catches my eye. My heart sinks as I remember the place name in the news article. Gemma was with him then. If not in the burning car, she was in County Durham.

The elevator door has opened without me noticing, and begins to close again. I catch it just in time with the toe of my shoe.

As I enter the flat, the smell of Thai food makes my empty stomach twist. There's a thermal bag on the kitchen counter.

'You look pale,' says Doug. He's emptying crackers into a bowl at the table.

'I got a card from Gemma.'

He starts. 'That's good. So she's okay?'

'I guess so. Hang on . . .' I see now that the card was posted on the first of September. Nine days ago – a Wednesday. Less than twenty-four hours, then, before the car accident. She's got my address slightly wrong – no postcode, and the incorrect flat number. Typical Gemma. It's a wonder it reached me at all. 'Any idea where Hartsbridge is?'

'Rings a bell,' says Doug. He asks Alexa, and she informs us Hartsbridge is a town in the Pennines on the border between Northumberland and County Durham, with a population of approximately 418 souls. It grew from being principally a farming community in the early nineteenth century to a centre of iron smelting under the Brocklehurst family.

I explain about the connection.

Doug is holding two warmed plates in a tea towel and lays them gently on the table. 'It doesn't mean anything,' he says, but there's doubt rather than dismissiveness in his voice.

'It doesn't look *good* though, does it?' I reply.

He can't argue with that.

I should have an appetite, but I eat mechanically, with the postcard on the table. I don't touch my wine. Doug ignores the card, as if it's offended him in some way, and at one point, he places a foil container of noodles right on top of it, like he wants me to forget it too.

'I need to go up there,' I say suddenly, before I even think it through properly.

Doug laughs. 'You what?'

'If she's there, if something's happened to her . . .'

'You're kidding? It's the other end of the country.'

'Hartsbridge,' I say.

'Yeah, practically Scotland. It's two hundred miles, maybe two-fifty.' He starts to ask Alexa how long it will take to drive, but I interrupt.

'She's my sister, Doug.'

'And she's a fuck-up,' he replies.

'We all make mistakes,' I say, feebly.

'And we live with the consequences,' says Doug. 'Seriously, Sarah. What can you even do? The wedding's in a week's time. You can't go running off on a wild goose chase. Just tell the police and let them deal with it.'

Not a wild goose. My sister.

'It would only be for a couple of days,' I say.

He cocks his head, avoiding eye contact, and stabs at his food with a fork.

★ ★ ★

The rest of the evening is tense as we go through the motions. The argument isn't over, though now it's performed in mime – him lounging on the sofa watching a basketball match being played in the States, occasionally popping to the fridge for another beer, me at the table on a laptop, researching accommodation in Hartsbridge. I wish, not for the first time, that we had more space. We've talked forever about getting somewhere bigger, further out, but the flat's so convenient for both our offices. When we have kids, it'll change; at the moment, neither of us has the appetite for upheaval.

51

There's a pub in Hartsbridge, rather disturbingly called The Headless Woman, and there are rooms available. The only other place in the village is a hostel, and I don't much fancy that. Plus, the pub does breakfast. I make no secret of taking my card out of my purse to enter payment details for two nights, and I know he's *observing*, if not actually watching me. I can tell from the set of his shoulders that he's annoyed and bursting to say something.

Afterwards, I go to the bedroom and begin to gather few items together quietly. Then I catch myself and wonder why I'm keeping such a low profile. If this annoys him, so be it. He's an only child, so maybe it's hard to understand the complications of my relationship with Gemma. He knows about Mum, but he never asks me for any details. He treats that Sarah like she's a different person, not the successful lawyer who's got her head screwed on. Sometimes I forget her too.

I choose to stay in the bedroom and read, but it's hard to concentrate. By the regular clink of bottles coming from the other room, I'm aware he's getting through the beers at a fair lick. Not that I'm mentally keeping a tally, like I used to do with Mum. It's just not like him. He's got this marathon in a month, and he's training six days a week.

I should probably do the grown-up thing and go out and sit on the sofa too, just to show there are no hard feelings, but I don't have the energy and I don't want to make things worse. Better to leave things on a low simmer than risk increasing the temperature.

I get ready for bed and switch out the light. Doug comes in later, just as I'm dropping off. He trips over the edge of the chair, then undresses noisily, switching on the bathroom light and not bothering to close the door as he pees loudly. When he climbs into bed, the smell of toothpaste and stale beer wafts over me.

'I love you,' he mumbles. 'Sorry about before.'

'It's only for a couple of nights,' I say.

Just until I can find out where Gemma is. Make sure she's safe. And then, it's done. We're done, and I can get on with the things that really matter.

'You could come too, if you want?' I suggest.

Doug's already snoring.

Chapter 7

GEMMA

The hours passed quickly when things were busy at Elm House, and normally Gemma could lose herself in work during the daytime shifts. No two days were the same, and her job was varied – dispensing medication to the doctor's guidance, helping the residents wash and dress and eat, changing beds and cleaning. Sometimes it was just sitting with them for a chat, or playing a board game, or laying out jigsaw pieces. There were visitors to log in and out. The pace occasionally picked up when there were welfare emergencies, but even then they did their best to keep such urgent matters from the other residents. Mrs Panerjee prided herself on a calm and orderly operation.

Today had a different flavour entirely and it was nothing to do with her role at Elm House. The clock was a countdown. Each minute that passed brought them closer to their next encounter with Des's psychotic son. In a way, she blamed herself. They *had* taken advantage of the old man's kindness. And now they had to pay their debts, one way or another.

Towards the end of the shift, they welcomed a new resident at Elm House. Mr Christakis was an eighty-year-old man who'd been discharged straight from the local hospital having suffered a bad fall, but as yet was deemed unable to care for himself in his own home. The stay was meant to be temporary, and normally Gemma would have been under no illusions – very few of their residents ever left once admitted. However, Mr Christakis had no indicators of cognitive decline, so he had as good a chance as any of returning to normal life. He really should've been on the ground floor, with the more mentally agile residents, but all the rooms downstairs were currently occupied, so he was on the dementia wing.

He came dressed in a suit, wheeled on a chair, and was scrupulously polite, apologising for inconveniencing everyone, from the taxi driver to Mrs Panerjee. He was accompanied by his daughter, who was trying and failing to conceal her tears as her father was shown into the modest room on the upper floor.

'We hope to move him down soon,' said Mrs Panerjee, 'when there's space.'

Gemma wondered if the meaning of making 'space' was lost on Mr Christakis or whether he was putting on a brave face for his daughter. 'This looks quite *splendid!*' he said. 'I really can't thank you all enough.'

'Don't you worry,' Gemma said to the old man's daughter, handing her a tissue. 'I'll look after him.'

'Thank you,' said the woman. She reached into her handbag. 'I want to give you something . . . for your time.'

Gemma watched her take out the purse with a hunger that made her burn with shame. She placed her hand on the woman's wrist. 'Please, you don't have to.'

'No, I want to . . .'

'I can't,' said Gemma. 'He's in safe hands.'

★ ★ ★

As she left, just after 2 p.m., Mark texted, asking what time she finished.

She wrote back. 'Four x'.

A little deceit. A white lie.

She took the bus out towards Worthing, and the small estate of discreet, identical bungalows where her destination lay. Soon she was standing in front of 19 Trafalgar Crescent. She'd found the address through Sol upstairs, and he'd sworn he wouldn't tell Mark she'd asked.

There was no other option. She'd wondered about phoning the police, and dismissed the idea quickly. Even if it temporarily deterred Tyler, the repercussions could be more severe still. He didn't appear to be the sort of guy who let legal consequences affect his decision-making.

The door opened and Des stood on the other side. A small man of Caribbean heritage, his grey curls were thinning, and he was more bent over than the last time she'd seen him. A smattering of dark freckles covered his cheeks, and his forehead was deeply wrinkled.

'Hello?' he said.

He clearly didn't recognise her. Gemma had been prepared for that. She'd rehearsed the speech several times on the way.

'My name is Gemma,' she said. 'My boyfriend and I live in one of your properties on Windsor Drive.'

'Oh yeah?' he said. 'I'm letting ma boy take care of all that now.' He turned and called into the house. 'Ty! Got a visitor for ya!'

Before Gemma could say anything more, or turn away, the hulking figure of Des's son filled the hallway.

He did recognise her. His face darkened.

'You get back inside, Dad,' he said. 'I'll look after this.'

Des retreated, and Tyler took his place.

He lowered his voice. 'And what the fuck do *you* want?'

'I . . . I . . .' Gemma's speech left her. The words she'd practised weren't meant for a man like Tyler.

'Your piece of shit boyfriend didn't send you here to beg, did he?'

She shook her head. 'He doesn't know I've come.'

'But you *have* come to beg?' He was grinning.

'We're trying to get the money,' said Gemma.

'Trying?'

'He's been laid off.'

'Not my problem. Not my dad's.'

'I know that. We just need more time.'

Any light went out of Tyler's eyes, and she knew she was speaking to a brick wall.

'There must be some arrangement we can make,' she pressed.

'We've made an arrangement. Money, or I hurt him.'

'We can't get it that quickly. There's just no way.'

Tyler's gaze went from her face, southwards. It travelled over her body, and lingered there. 'Tell you what, sweetheart. I'm having a get-together with a business associate later. Whitehawk way. Why don't you come along?'

In the silence that followed, plenty was spoken without words.

'Don't think too long,' said Tyler. 'I might withdraw the offer.'

Gemma's mouth was dry. 'And if I do, that's it?' she said. 'You won't hurt him?'

Tyler's eyes returned to hers. 'If you do what I say – *exactly* what I say – the debt is cleared.'

He spat in his meaty palm and offered it to her.

Though her mind was screaming, Gemma's body didn't hesitate. This was the way out. The only way.

She shook his hand.

'Nine p.m. Twelve Empire Drive,' he said. The door closed.

On her way back to the bus stop, Gemma was shaking. She wanted to be with Mark, to lie next to him, his arms around her, and to pretend that none of this had ever happened. Even imagining it made her gut squirm. How could she look him in the eye after what she was planning to do? She knew he could never understand, even if she said she was doing it for them.

The surge of vomit came almost without warning, and she had to throw out a hand against a shuttered shop window, before her stomach ejected the lunch from Elm House over the pavement.

Chapter 8

SARAH

It takes ninety minutes just to get out of London, even leaving early, and the satnav's telling me it's another three and a half hours to Hartsbridge. Though Doug's not with me, I can hear his voice in my ear telling me 'I told you so'. This morning, he was outwardly civil enough and didn't try again to dissuade me from making the trip northwards. I could tell there was still resentment simmering, though, and I didn't reiterate last night's offer for him to accompany me. He let me get the case down myself from the storage space, though he knows I hate going up there and sticking my head through the cobwebs. I skinned my knuckles on the ladder too, but was too proud to make a sound. He came into the bedroom dressed in his running kit while I silently packed. He told me to drive carefully, and call him when I got there. Then he was gone, with the briefest of kisses goodbye.

It's a deathly dull journey up a traffic-clogged M1. I eat at a grim service station and carry a strong coffee back to the car. Before setting off once more, I try Gemma's number again.

'*This phone may be switched off or disconnected . . .*'

Were my sister and I ever really connected? Maybe, though such memories are dim. Though we shared a room for fifteen years, there are no photos of us together that I know of, because Mum never took any. What I remember are the arguments. First over toys and the TV remote, then over wardrobe space, later over more serious things, like who was going to make sure Mum had eaten or wouldn't choke to death in the night. That mostly fell to me.

I resented it, but I've often thought afterwards that I wasn't being entirely fair. I was, after all, the older sister. I became aware of Mum's problems sooner. And I probably tried to shield Gemma from some of it, when she was too young to understand that not every parent was slurring their speech when their kids arrived home from school. Maybe I didn't let her understand.

We had moments of harmony of course – when we weren't at each other's' throats. There was a period, I remember now, when we were young, maybe six and eight. Gemma had started having nightmares that she was being chased, the sort of dream that made her thrash around in bed, wake up screaming and sometimes even wet herself. When it happened, I learned to spot it, and I'd climb out of bed and go to hers, wrapping her body up in mine and stroking her head to comfort her. The strangest thing was, she told me the next day that I'd appeared in her dream, taken her hand and led her to safety. When she was older,

Gemma rarely slept at home at all. Only two years separate us in age, but it might as well be twenty. A therapist could suck us dry.

Past Leeds it thins out, down to two lanes each way. The landscape becomes more desolate, with hills of dark peat lurking like purple smudges on the horizon. I've never been to this part of the country before – it never seemed like much of a destination. The times we've been up to Scotland, we've flown or taken the train. This country is the sort to sleep through. The view gets prettier though, when I leave the motorway. The land undulates, with new vistas opening up along the soft contours of the Yorkshire Dales. No hedgerows here, just drystone walls.

After an hour or so, I'm passing through villages strung along a river every few miles, but there's a sign about a flood ahead, with a diversion. I keep the satnav running, and turn off, taking a higher road, single track at times, through rolling farmland with grubby, stoical sheep dotted in the fields. It's nice enough now, but it must be a hard life up here when the weather closes in.

The diversion drops me back into the valley, and I arrive at Hartsbridge, five and a half hours after leaving London. I slow down, taking it in. First impressions are that it's quite a pretty village, and in the summer I imagine it must attract its share of tourists. There's a teashop, closed today, which advertises ice creams too, a fireplace store, a small grocer cum post office, and an upmarket photography studio or gallery. A path runs alongside the river under trees, and there's a spot with picnic benches by a weir. A large and unkempt village green. The houses are all Georgian and Victorian, at a guess, built of dark stone and opening onto the narrow pavements. It's almost impossible to imagine Gemma, or Mark, in a place like this.

I park up in front of a The Headless Woman, on the edge of the green. It's a typical country pub – maybe seventeenth century, the blocky stones rendered white, two-storey with small mullioned windows and a roof of thick slate. Two chimneys are belching smoke, and there are only a couple of cars in the car park to one side, plus a sad-looking children's playground with a rusting climbing frame and a tilted swing. The sign shows the torso of a woman in Elizabethan dress, her neck a faded red slice. It's not as sinister as I expected.

I get out and stretch my legs. It's only three o'clock, but the sky is already getting gloomy, like dusk is impatient to fall, and I can't get an idea of where the sun might be behind the uniform grey cloud. The air smells fresh, with a not unpleasant tang of distant manure, and it's a good few degrees colder than back in London. I fish my thick coat from the back seat. I can check in to the pub later, so I leave most of my stuff in the car.

My first port of call is the post office – it's the one place I know for sure my sister visited, ten days ago. What they can possibly tell me, I have no idea.

There aren't many people about on a cold September afternoon – an old woman making her way bent over and pulling a trolley bag, a couple of stout, red-faced hikers marching along looking at a map. On the green, a man hurls a ball to an eager Labrador.

My heart sinks when I see the 'Closed' sign hung on the post-office door. I should've checked that before I left, because I see it closed at midday and it's shut on Sunday too. There's a bell though, and I ring it, just in case someone's inside. No one comes. I look through the window, pointlessly. There's no sign of life and there's a shutter up over the counter. The shelves look half-stocked, with large gaps. There's a fridge selling booze on offer, with a selection of less-than-freshly-made sandwiches.

'It's closed, love,' says a voice with faint scorn.

I turn around to see a slight young man, early twenties, in a baggy black tracksuit with a rodenty face and a few wispy hairs on his upper lip and chin. His dark hair is cut short and prematurely receding, leaving him with a widow's peak.

'Ah, yes, I was just hoping to speak to someone.'

He nods. 'You want Mary. She don't live in the village. Back Monday.' His eyes linger on me, measuring me up, and it's not an entirely comfortable feeling.

'Thanks,' I say. I'm about to beat a retreat when I have another thought. 'Actually, maybe you can help. Do you live here?'

He twitches. 'Yeah. Why?'

'I'm looking for my sister,' I say. I take out the envelope from my bag and carefully withdraw the photo inside. It's the last one I have of Gemma, taken when she was nineteen or twenty, and I found it in an old box at the back of the wardrobe. It shows us both, together, at a fortieth birthday party held for Auntie Phyllis. We're in a pub garden, arms around each other, with me doing a better job of looking happy. We honestly couldn't look more different in the way we dressed for the occasion. Me in smart jeans, a white halter and blue cotton blazer with silk scarf, Gemma in a charity-shop hippy dress. Maybe there's something in our faces that

65

declares us related – people used to say we were similar when we were at school – but I can't see it. Gemma's wearing a tonne of dark eye make-up and shocking red lipstick. One side of her hair is shaved, the other side long, dyed black, with a fringe cut severely across her forehead. She was always changing her look, and it strikes me that I've no idea what hairstyle she'll have now.

When he sees the photo, he barely glances before looking away. But his protruding Adam's apple unmistakably bobs in his throat before he shakes his head. 'Nah, don't think so.'

'Are you sure? She was here a bit over a week ago. Maybe with her boyfriend.'

He shakes his head again and smiles. 'Sorry. Can't help you.'

I'm not convinced at all. He knows something, I'm almost certain.

'My name's Sarah Kline,' I say. 'You are?'

His head moves backwards on his shoulders, like he's surprised by the question. 'Look, sorry, all right,' he says. 'I never seen her.'

And then he's off, in an uneven gait, striding down the pavement.

I think about heading after him, grabbing him and spinning him round. However, the sober, sensible me watches helplessly as he disappears around a corner without looking back. I wish Doug *were* here, because I don't think he'd just let the young man walk away.

I feel a bit stupid, but this isn't defeat. In fact, it's progress. I knew she was here, at this post office, and there was always a chance she was just passing through. But if this guy *did* see her, that probably means she was here for longer, and I reckon others could well remember her too. There's still the pub. In this sort of place, it's the heart of the community, and there's a very good chance indeed that Gemma's photo might stir a few memories there.

I walk back towards it, past the art studio, which is open. It contains all sorts – photos and painting, ceramics and the occasional metal sculpture on a plinth. Something catches my eye. A rack of postcards just inside the window, and a particular design that makes my heart jump. I stop dead, turn around and go inside.

There's a man leaning over a large design table with a metal ruler. He looked up, and says, 'Be with you in a moment,' then takes a scalpel and carefully slices through a piece of thick card.

I cross the shop, past a rolodex of poster prints, to the postcards and pick up the Japanese stork. It's exactly the same as the one Gemma sent.

'Just looking, or can I help you with something specific?' says the man. He's come out from behind the desk. He's small, with an affable round face, and corduroy trousers, with a checked shirt. Maybe mid-forties. His hair is curly and messy, laced with silver. He makes me think of a well-fed scarecrow, part farmer, part country gent. His glasses hang around his neck on a cord.

I hold up the postcard with one hand and scramble in my pocket for the photo again. 'I'm looking for my sister,' I say. 'She bought one of these postcards, about ten days ago maybe.'

The man reaches out for the photo, perching his glasses with his free hand. His hands are large but well looked after, with beautiful nails. I have the impression he must be an artist of some sort. He holds the photo at a distance, then brings it closer.

'She's missing,' I add.

There's a longish pause, then he says, 'Yes, I remember her. Can't remember the exact day. She asked to borrow a pen too – wrote out the card right over there on the desk.'

I feel suddenly light-headed. It's not a breakthrough really, just another crumb on the trail. There's a thrill, though, at standing in almost the same spot as my sister, and further vindication for the trip. Yet there's a darker anxiety building too. If she was here at some point, what happened between then and her boyfriend's car burning on a hillside?

The phone rings, and the man excuses himself to answer it. 'Neil speaking.' After listening a few moments, he puts a hand over the mouthpiece and whispers, 'Just be a minute. Do have a browse.'

'Thank you,' I mutter.

As he returns to the call, which seems to be about picture framing, I follow his advice and wander around the rest of the shop. I walk between several black-and-white landscape photographs, moody vistas, framed by skeletal trees, or fore-grounded with crumbling dry-stone walls. They're beautiful, in their own way, if a little foreboding. The photographs don't have titles, but there is a small notice on the wall which gives them a copyright of N R Packer and a small biography.

Neil Packer was born and bred in County Durham, the son of a village vet. He takes inspiration from the rich landscape, weather, people and culture of the Pennines to catalogue life and the seasons. He also runs photography courses for beginners – please ask in the shop for more details.

He comes off the phone.

'These are yours!' I say.

He nods modestly. 'That's right. Not to everyone's taste . . .'

'They're amazing.' I even wonder about buying one for Doug, as a sort of peace offering – a wedding present for when all this is over. Any of them would look great in the apartment.

'Well, thank you very much,' he says. 'Now, you were asking about your sister?' He picks up the photo again. 'Yes, I'm sure it was her. Missing, you say?'

'We think so,' I add. 'It's a bit of a mystery. She was here, in Hartsbridge.' I don't mention Mark's demise. Seems senseless to bring it up when I've no real evidence Gemma was involved. Plus, Neil seems like a sweet man and I'd rather not alarm him. 'Do you remember anything she said, or how she was?'

'In a rush, I'd say,' remarks the owner. 'Agitated. They were in and out like a whirlwind.'

'They?'

'She was with a young man. He didn't actually come in. Just poked his head through the door and told her to get a move on.'

'Do you recall what he looked like?'

Neil shakes his head and sighs. 'Not really. Tall though. Skinny fellow. They looked like they were off hiking.'

Tall and skinny would be pretty much anyone's description of Mark, but hiking doesn't sound like Gemma one bit. 'What makes you say that?'

'Their clothes, I suppose. He had a big rucksack. I only remember because it looked heavy on him. I guessed they were staying up at Dale Grange, because I'd seen her a couple of days earlier too.'

69

'Dale Grange?'

'Just over the bridge and up the hill. The hostel.'

'She didn't seem scared?'

'Oh, no,' says Neil, looking troubled. 'Just that she had to be somewhere, maybe.'

I gather up the photo. 'You've been *so* helpful – thank you!'

'No bother,' replies Neil. 'I hope you track her down.'

I turn to go, then stop. 'One more thing – are you open Monday? I'd love to come back and look properly at your work?'

'That we are,' he says. 'Pop back whenever.'

Chapter 9

GEMMA

The room where Gemma had been told her to wait stank of fags, like the threadbare curtains had been rubbed in an ashtray. She hadn't seen Tyler yet, but her arrival had been anticipated.

It was dark outside – the back of the house overlooking a tiny yard and an alley filled with rubbish. Music thumped through the floor as she sat on the far edge of the bed from the door. She wondered if she should just lie down, maybe even take her clothes off and get under the sheet. That, at least, looked clean. But she didn't want to give him the wrong impression, that she was in any way eager for what was about to happen. She just wanted it to be over, as quickly as possible.

She'd been up here an hour already, waiting. Though the door wasn't locked, she felt like a prisoner in a cell. Maybe, just maybe, he wouldn't come, and the door would open with Tyler telling her she could go home – that this was all a wind-up to teach her a lesson.

She checked her phone, to see if there were any messages from Mark. She'd told him she was working an extra shift, and hoped he believed it. She thought he would, because he trusted her. It brought tears to her eyes to think of his sweet, simple, believing face. She wiped them away quickly. Crying wouldn't help, and nor would feeling sorry for herself. This had to be done, or worse things would happen.

The door handle turned and a man walked in. She stood up. It wasn't Tyler, but another guy. Not quite fat, more solidly built, wearing jeans and a leather jacket over a white vest. Swarthy, with a receding hairline, what remained combed backwards in thin strands that showed his scalp beneath. Whatever aftershave he was wearing actually smelled nice. He looked at her for a moment across the bed, eyes travelling from her face to her waist, as if appraising a used car. Then he looked around the room with the same expression.

'Cold,' he said. He walked to the electric heater and turned up the dial. 'Your name?'

For some reason she didn't want to tell him. Maybe it was easier to pretend she wasn't Gemma Kline at all, just another, disposable person wearing her skin for however long this was going to take. Her mouth betrayed her and she muttered, 'Gemma'.

'Miroslav,' he said, touching his chest. There was a hint of a foreign accent that she couldn't place. Russian, maybe, or Eastern European, but mixed with thick East London. 'Take off your clothes.'

It took a second or two to process the words, because they were uttered in such a dispassionate tone, he might

72

have been asking her to do something as innocuous as pass him salt over a dinner table. As the reality of the command sank in, she couldn't move. 'I don't want to,' she said. As if that mattered.

He looked at her, with pity but not kindness. She could tell from his cold eyes that he had no guilt about what he was asking her to do. His sympathy was merely a recognition of her own shame – that her life had brought her to this point. It was a look she'd seen before, in her sister's eyes, on the day of her mum's funeral, and it had filled her with rage. Today, though, she had no recourse to anger. She was too numb.

'Take off your clothes,' he said again, this time gently but with an edge of insistence.

She wondered what he would do if she refused again. Maybe get violent, or maybe simply threaten it. He might get Tyler, to ask what the fuck was going on, but she doubted it. He looked like a man who solved problems himself. And, either way, the result would be the same.

She looked wistfully across at the closed door. She knew she couldn't reach it before him, and even if she did, Tyler was downstairs. There was only one way out of this situation, and she'd known it from the moment she entered. They owed what they owed, and they had no money. This was a reality from which she couldn't escape.

She kicked off her shoes. As she pulled her sweater up over her head, her top underneath came too. She tugged it back down, preserving her modesty for as long as possible. He watched, and didn't rush her.

As she unbuttoned the top of her jeans, he took off his jacket. His arms and shoulders were matted with thick, dark hair. Underneath were faded tattoos that looked very amateur.

She removed her top and folded it over the bed's headboard. Then she reached to unhook her bra.

'Can we lock the door?' she asked.

He looked at it and gave a shrug. 'No one is coming in,' he said.

She took off the bra, then her jeans, and stood in her underwear, exposed to the cold of the room.

He waited, smiling now, like it was a game. Then he pulled down his own jogging pants, keeping his trainers on. He wore white boxer shorts beneath. He was barrel-chested, with the slight bulge of love handles. He reached into the pool of his clothes and took out a condom packet.

'On the bed,' he said.

She pulled back the duvet and slipped inside the sheets. They felt dank. With her head back on the pillow, she looked at the ceiling, where a single bulb hung from a frayed wire. In her peripheral vision, she saw him removing the rest of his clothes, but she didn't look. Then the bed creaked as it took his weight. He seemed to fill the room.

'This will be okay,' he said. 'Do not be scared.'

Scared? The word seemed too small for the moment. Fear was part of it, but it was much more. There wasn't a word for what she was feeling. The sadness and shame, the guilt and disgust, the helplessness and sheer despair that her world had come to this.

Thick fingers hooked inside the elastic of her underwear. She froze, trying to find some way out of herself. Some crack in the ceiling through which her consciousness might escape. She couldn't. And so she closed her eyes.

Footsteps pounded up the stairs, a voice shouting, 'Where is she? Gem?'

A voice she knew.

The door crashed open, and Mark was standing there. The flood of emotions was almost too much to handle. Sheer relief and terror. She had no idea how he'd tracked her here, but she was glad he had. She pushed at Miroslav's shoulders. He was immoveable.

'Who are you?' he said sullenly.

The sound from Mark's mouth was a roar as he advanced and swung a fist that caught Miroslav on the temple. The big man grunted and rolled off Gemma, tumbling from the edge of the bed and hitting the carpet with a thump.

Then another man was there too, standing behind Mark, eyes taking in Miroslav's naked form with a look of horror.

Mark came to her, scooped her out of the bed. She gathered her clothes to her body. The third man didn't try to stop them, and stepped aside. They descended the stairs.

'My shoes . . .' Gemma said.

Mark didn't seem to care. The party was in full swing on the ground floor, with astonished guests turning to stare as they passed. Fortunately, among the sea of faces, there was no sign of Tyler.

Outside, Mark's car was running on the pavement. He opened the door and practically shoved her in. Then he walked around the other side and threw himself into the seat too, slamming the door. As she shut hers, he was already driving away. He didn't speak until they were several streets away, heading back to the seafront.

'What the fuck, Gem?' he said. 'What the fuck?'

'I had to,' she said, finally breaking into tears. She couldn't look him in the face. 'I had to, for us.'

He punched the side of the door with his fist. Until five

minutes before, she'd never even seen him angry. 'No, you fucking didn't!'

'We owe them money.'

He pulled over, hitting the brakes hard, and they both jolted in their seats. Then Mark turned and drew her to him by the back of the neck, fingers pressing into her skin until their foreheads were touching. She couldn't tell what he was feeling, because she guessed it was the same as her, and Gemma wasn't sure what that was either. Relief. Uncertainty. Fear.

Tonight was done. But it wasn't over. There was still a debt to be paid, and it had probably just got bigger.

Chapter 10

SARAH

The pub can wait. With a spring in my step, I follow Neil Packer's directions to the hostel, crossing the street towards what looks like a packhorse bridge spanning the river. It's when I get close that I sense a prickle of the hairs on the back of my neck and turn to see the young man from outside the post office. He's between two buildings, leaning against a wall smoking, and is looking in my direction. He does so shamelessly, as if daring me to avert my eyes first.

'What are you looking at?' I call.

He simply continues to smoke, then casually turns away and disappears down the alley.

The buoyant feeling goes out of me. I wonder then about calling the police. I've got the Durham number – for this Sergeant Nelson – in my phone. But what could I tell him? There's a guy in a tracksuit who's a bit of a creep. They're hardly going to bring him in for questioning on those grounds.

The hostel is a grim-looking gothic building. The doorway is a dark stone arch and a plaque above reads 'Dale Grange'. Underneath, in a porch area, there are several pairs of muddy walking boots drying off. The door inside is glass, filled with notices and posters.

I've not stayed in a youth hostel since my uni days, when, with a group of friends, we booked out a bunk room for a weekend away, and the smell as I open the door takes me back. Outdoorsy, damp and a little stale. There's a foyer with a vending machine, a rack of leaflets about local beauty spots and attractions, and a front desk. The pictures on the walls are maps and aerial photos of the Pennine moors, valleys and fells.

A man with long ginger hair is sitting on the other side of the desk, earphones in, playing some sort of game on a phone.

'Hello?' I say. He doesn't seem to notice me, so I move closer and give a wave. 'Hi!'

Now he looks up. His eyes are very blue, and red-rimmed. He smiles but doesn't say anything. A name tag reads 'Reuben'.

'My name's Sarah,' I plough on. 'I was wondering if I could ask you some questions about—'

The man reaches to a bell on the desk and rings it, still smiling unnervingly at me. I'm starting to think I've done something to offend him.

There's a noise from another room and an athletic young woman comes out of an internal door behind the desk. I catch a brief glimpse of shelving with cleaning products and a washing machine She's dressed in walking trousers and a fleece zipped up to her neck, and she wears a snood pulled up over her head and ears. Her long red hair spills messily over the top. If the colour wasn't a giveaway, the freckles and the shapes of their faces makes me sure they're brother and sister, maybe even twins.

'I'm Carla,' she says. 'This is Reuben, my brother. He doesn't speak, but he understands what you're saying and he likes making friends.'

Reuben smiles, so I grin back, now that I know I haven't offended him.

'Hey, Reuben.'

'Do you need a room?' asks Carla, pulling the monitor towards her.

'Ah, no.' I go through the introductions about my sister and Mark, and she nods immediately when I show her the photo.

'Yeah, they were here. Week before this. Up here hiking.'

'That's what I heard.' I see no reason to spare her the grisly details, but Reuben's presence gives me pause. There's something childlike about him, though I'm acutely aware I don't know what his condition is.

Carla seems to sense my indecision and turns to her brother, tapping her watch. 'You should get ready for work, Rubes,' she says. 'Van'll be here in ten.'

He nods enthusiastically and wanders off through the rear door.

When he's gone, I continue. 'Mark — Gemma's boyfriend . . . he was found dead near here, in a burnt-out car.'

Carla backs away, drawing her elbow off the desk. 'Jesus. On the moor high road?'

'You heard about it?'

79

She blows out her cheeks. 'Yeah. Didn't know it was the same guy though. We heard someone came off the road on the tops. The ice can be lethal up there. Fuel tank must have been punctured.'

'Was it near to here then?'

'Sort of,' she says and points to the map on the wall. 'About four miles as the crow flies. Middle of nowhere.'

'When did you last see them?'

'Would've been Thursday, I *think*. Hold on . . .' She turns her attention to the book on the desk, flicking back a page, running a finger down. 'No. Wednesday. They stayed for two nights. Wait, what did you say your sister's name was?'

'Gemma. Gemma Kline.'

'That's not the name she gave.'

She turns the book around, and I can see Gemma's handwriting has inscribed two names – Doug and Sarah Thomas. Is that some sort of joke? It's unmistakeably her writing – just the same as on the card. The phone number isn't the one I have for her either, and the address has been left blank.

'Weird,' I say. 'Did they book in advance?'

Carla shakes her head. 'Just showed up, paid in cash.'

'And how did they seem?' I ask.

'They kept themselves to themselves,' she says. 'We ask if people want to log their routes with us – you know, in case they get into trouble. They weren't interested.'

'Were they arguing?'

'I didn't see or hear anything,' she replies. 'They had a dorm to themselves.'

'And when they left – nothing untoward?'

'I don't think so,' says Carla.

'Not upset at all?'

Carla holds up his hands, palms facing me. 'Hey – I don't want to get involved in something that's none of my business.'

Reuben is back – he's changed into a thick jumper, and gives her a thumbs-up, before settling with his phone again.

'I'm sorry. I know I'm coming across as pushy. It's just she's—'

'Missing. Yeah, you said.' Her tone is cooler. 'Look, maybe it's the police you need.'

Maybe it is. The false name thing has really thrown me.

I thank Carla for her time, and ask if I can leave my number. She looks unsure, casting a worried glance at her brother.

'I don't think I can help. I've told you everything I know.'

'I'd like to leave it anyway.'

Somewhat reluctantly, she swings the book back to face me and lays a pen on top. I scribble my name and number a few lines below Gemma's writing.

'If you remember anything else, even if it's small, I'd appreciate it. I'm staying at the pub.'

'Of course,' says Carla. She offers me a commiserative, tight-lipped smile, like she knows it's a long shot. I guess she's pleased to be rid of me too.

I say goodbye to both of them and leave the reception, trying to make sense of what the false names are all about. Gemma was here, but for some reason she didn't want anyone to know that.

A nasty wind has kicked up as I leave the hostel and

head towards The Headless Woman. Darkness is definitely coming too, and there's no one about.

So what do I know, other than that my sister was here, pretending to be someone she wasn't? I don't reckon she was up here hiking, whatever she claims.

'So what the hell were you doing, Gem?' I mutter.

Chapter 11

GEMMA

It didn't seem an exaggeration to say they were living under a death sentence. There'd been no word from Tyler since the events of the party in Whitehawk. Somehow that made it worse still. As a precaution, they'd moved out of the house on Windsor Drive – Kash was letting them crash at his, but he'd been clear it could only be a couple of nights. Sooner or later, they'd have to raise their heads above the parapet and face the consequences.

Gemma was still going to work – she was fairly sure their enemies didn't know where she was employed – but she found herself looking over her shoulder and occasionally taking detours from her usual route to and from Elm House.

She'd just come back from the shops, and entered through the back door. She found Mark and Kash seated on the battered sofa in the living room, looking at a phone between them, held by Mark.

'Hart*bridge*,' Mark was saying. 'Not Hart*ford*.'

'Whatever, fella,' said Kash. 'Tom-ay-to, tom-ah-to.'

'What's up?' asked Gemma.

Both of them looked up, a little guiltily.

'Nothing much,' replied Kash. 'I've gotta split. Catch ya later.'

Mark and Kash shook hands in an elaborate series of synchronised moves, and Kash went out on one of his many trips to see his various clients.

'What was all that about?' asked Gemma.

Mark took out the phone again. He seemed in a good mood, with his leg bouncing under the table as he opened up a map.

'Fancy a trip up north?' he said.

'Why?'

'Could be the answer to our problems,' he replied. His features took on a lively, cunning look. There was danger there too, in the way he licked his lips.

'What are you talking about?' asked Gemma.

'This place,' said Mark. 'This house where they grow the stuff. Kash seems to think it's a big thing.'

'Okay . . .' She didn't know what he was getting at.

'It's a big secret, right?' said Mark.

'Well, yeah.'

'Well . . .' he continued. 'Bet they'd pay to keep it that way.' His eyes were wide, as he waited for the penny to drop.

'Wait. You want to blackmail them? That's stupid.'

Mark's excited expression dimmed a fraction. 'Is it?' he said.

'Yes,' replied Gemma. 'You don't even know who *they* are.'

'And they don't know who we are. That's why it works.'

Gemma shook her head in dismay. 'You hadn't heard of this place until five minutes ago. It's probably bullshit anyway.'

'No harm finding out, is there.'

His mind seemed set, his confidence undented. 'Mark, listen. *If* it's true, they're criminals. If we get caught, they'll kill us.'

'We won't get caught.'

Gemma shook her head again, firmly. 'You don't think they'll try to find the person who blackmailed them? They'll track us down. You're not this stupid, babe.'

Mark looked cross. 'No, I'm not. Listen, Kash only knows because he overheard his brother letting it slip. They don't even know that he knows. If we cut Kash in, he's good.'

Gemma couldn't believe what she was hearing. It made her angry that he'd even dreamt it up as a possibility, after everything they'd been through already. Tyler would be the least of their problems if they managed to get on the wrong side of some serious organised criminals. 'Stop it,' she said. 'They'll find Kash. And then they'll find us.'

'How?' said Mark, tossing the phone aside and spreading his hands.

'I don't know *how*,' she replied. 'It's not worth the risk, is it?'

'Easy for you to say.' He lifted his hands, where two of his fingers were taped together, and there was bruising across the ligaments on the back of his hand. The noise of the break was something Gemma would never forget. 'What do you think Tyler's going to do to me, when he finds me?'

She didn't have an answer for that. Or, rather, the answer didn't need to be expressed. The consequences would have moved on from a broken leg.

85

'If you don't come, I can do it on my own,' he said softly.

'You'll get yourself killed.'

'I'll be careful,' said Mark. 'I'll keep my head down. No one knows me up there.'

He stood up from the table and took her face between his hands softly.

'I can do it,' he said. 'I know I can. Trust me. You trust me, right?'

'Of course I do,' replied Gemma. 'I just—'

'Two or three days,' Mark interrupted. 'I go up, get the lie of the land, get paid. In and out. Invisible. Like the wind.'

'And then what?' She was struggling to keep her voice down. 'You think they won't look for you?'

'How would they find me? I'm at the other end of the country – their product must go nationwide. If I play my cards right, they won't even see me.'

'You sound crazy,' said Gemma. 'This isn't a game. They're drug dealers. Dangerous people.'

Mark shrugged. 'They're drug *growers*. They probably sell it on wet to a distributor. They'll want to keep their hands clean.'

'Now you sound desperate.' She pulled his hands away.

'Babe, I am desperate. We both are. Listen, I get this done, and it could mean a fresh start, for both of us.'

'I've got to go to work.'

'And I'm going to Hartsbridge,' said Mark coldly. 'With or without you.'

Chapter 12

SARAH

My fingers are cold as I stand in the lee of the pub wall and dial the number for the Durham police contact. I'm not convinced Sergeant Nelson will be able to help me, but I obviously know things the police don't, so it's only right to share if we're both trying to find my sister. I hover over the call button. There's a good chance I'm going to get her into trouble here, if and when we track her down. This could even end up with her in custody, and it will be my doing.

No, that's getting carried away. There are worse things than getting arrested. She's my sister. God forbid she ends up in prison, but it's my duty to look out for her. I press the call button.

The phone is picked up almost at once.

'Dewer speaking.' A thick accent, voice a bit sleepy, like I've woken him up.

'Hi – my name's Sarah Kline. Sergeant Sadler gave me this number, in London, for Sergeant Nelson.'

'That's my boss. Sorry, what's this about?'

I explain that it's about my sister, Gemma, who's missing, and the car that was found.

I hear a rustle of movement, and I have the impression I've got his attention. 'Oh, right. Gotcha. Has your sister been in touch?'

'No, but I'm here, in Hartsbridge. I've found where she was staying.'

'In Hartsbridge?' He sounds surprised.

'Yes. She was at the hostel here, with her boyfriend.'

'Right. Right.' Another pause. 'Perhaps I could come and talk to you in person?'

'Of course. I'm staying at the pub tonight. Tomorrow at nine-thirty a.m.?'

'Excellent.'

'Do you want my number?'

'Better do, yes.'

I let a sigh ease out, then give it to him. We hang up. I've not got great hopes for the constable, but first impressions can often be wrong.

As I put the phone away, a van is coming down the hill, and I see Reuben is in the passenger seat, with another man driving. The side of the vehicle reads 'McAllister's Meat Processing', with a phone number and picture of a smiling cartoon pig. I give him a wave, and he waves back enthusiastically.

The interior of The Headless Woman glows with warmth, and I'm immediately comforted to walk through the front doors into a bar area. There is a fire burning at one end, and a few of the tables are occupied, mostly by couples. There's a family with two young kids also. Two middle-aged men are drinking together on stools at the bar. One looks like a farmer, wearing a sleeveless padded jacket and wellington boots. The other is in a fluorescent work jacket, and a hard hat lies at his feet. In front of them on the bar are two half-finished pints of bitter. At the other end of the bar, by a fruit machine, sits the young guy with the tracksuit and the widow's peak from outside the post office. One long-fingered hand rests around a short mixed drink, while he scrolls through his phone with the other. He looks at me briefly, and I stare back defiantly until he returns his attention to his phone. I need to find out his name before I speak to Constable Dewer tomorrow.

I inspect the menu written up on the board. The usual pub fare. Behind the bar, beside a mirrored wall under the optics, hang packets of crisps and nuts. A large jar filled with yellowing pickled eggs stands next to a chopping board covered in lemons. It's hardly my typical hang-out, but at the moment I'd take anything that's dry and warm.

A woman, fifty or so, with bleached blonde hair and a pinched face emerges, drying her hands on a towel.

'Hello, love,' she says. 'What can I get you?'

'I've got a room booked,' I reply. 'Sarah Kline.'

'Right you are. We wondered if you were going to make it. Let me get you a key. You come far?'

'London,' I say.

She nods, and I detect the smallest flinch from the man by the fruit machine, paying attention to my words.

The woman ducks around the side of the bar, out of sight, before emerging shortly. 'This way,' she says, then leads me through the back, past the loos and up a set of creaking stairs covered in a threadbare carpet.

On the upper floor, there are several doors saying 'staff only', but at the end of the corridor, she opens one into a double room with a beamed ceiling. It's pleasant enough, a bit chintzy, with woodchip walls.

'Watch yourself on this,' she says, tapping the low door-frame leading into an en suite. 'Any idea what time you want breakfast?'

I suggest about eight-thirty, and she smiles. I can't tell if that's early, or late; I feel judged anyway.

'Are you serving food now?' I ask.

She nods and tells me to come down when I'm ready.

Something touches my ankle and I let out a scream, only for my heart to slow when I see it's a black cat.

'Oh, sorry, love,' says the barmaid. She lets out a hiss, and the cat scrams for the door. 'Bloody thing's like Houdini,' she adds. 'I swear she sneaks through the keyholes.'

'It's all right,' I say. 'Just gave me a shock.'

When she's gone, I lay my case on the bed and go over to the small window, drawing back the curtains. The view is over fields backing onto the pub. The hills rise in the distance. It feels a long way from London.

I don't know what to think about the man downstairs. Should I try to speak with him again, or dig a little more discreetly?

My eyes are starting to itch. I didn't want to make the barmaid feel awkward, but I'm allergic to cats. I go to check my washbag, just in case I've got some antihistamines. No joy. I wash my face in cold water – depending on how long the cat's been in here, I could be in for an unpleasant night's sleep.

I think about calling Doug. Instead I opt for a message.

Here safely. Sadly there's a cat. Not started sneezing yet. Hope you're okay x.

To be honest, I'm annoyed to be the one making the first move towards rapprochement, but Doug can be stubborn.

He writes back almost immediately. *Glad to hear it. Bless you xx.*

There's no point trying to parse any meaning from that – he's never been one for expressive communication over text. It used to wind me up in the early days, but it's just his way.

There are pictures on the walls, mostly farming scenes past: stoical, unsmiling workers sitting atop old threshers and another leaning on a stick with a dog lying at his feet. There's a mirror, speckled and a little warped with age, hanging from a narrow chain. I look knackered, older than my thirty-five years, and I can see the unmistakeable shadow of Mum in my features. Gemma always used to say I resembled her – it was an insult she saved for when we were really going at it.

Heading back downstairs, I pass what looks like an office of sorts, with a computer, and box files on shelves. There's a pint glass with dregs in the bottom beside the keyboard, and several certificates for food hygiene. The image on the monitor is split in two, showing the feeds from two security cameras, one on top of the other. One shows the bar, the other overlooks the front door of the pub. If Mark and Gemma were here, there could well be footage. It's probably a bit presumptuous to ask straight away. I'll find a moment.

The clientele have thinned out downstairs, with only one couple still at their table and the two men at the bar. Tracksuit man is hanging around too, but he's playing the fruit machine with his back to me.

I go to look at the menu as the barmaid drops glasses into a washer.

'Is the chilli spicy?' I ask.

'Spicy as you want it,' comes a voice from the fruit machine. I'm not sure if this is meant to be an innuendo, so I pretend not to hear. But the barmaid adds: 'Archie's cooking.'

He turns. 'Do you want it hot?'

'Oh – yes, please. Thanks.'

He detaches himself from the fruit machine and lifts a folding section of the bar and goes through. The thought of him preparing my food puts a dent in my appetite.

'And to drink?' asks the barmaid.

The men at the bar are staring at their drinks, but I can feel their attention is on me. I see myself as they do, or so I suppose. City girl out of her comfort zone.

I'd normally have asked for a wine list with no shame, but I go for a pint of Guinness instead. Doug got me into it, years ago, on a week-long rainy trip to the west of Ireland.

While it settles, the man in the work jacket catches my eye.

'Evening,' I say.

He nods back.

I'm about to retreat to a small table with my drink, when my eyes are drawn to the fireplace. I'd clocked the object as a bull's head on the way in, but now, to my astonishment, I can see it's actually a rhinoceros. I chuckle, and the man in the wellies looks at me with faint annoyance.

'Do you get a lot of those round here?' I ask, gesturing with my glass.

'It's from the manor,' he says, as if that explains everything.

'Brocklehurst Hall,' the barmaid adds, covering a dish of sliced lemons. 'The house above the village.'

'They kept rhinos?'

'No,' says the barmaid. 'I reckon he shot that one.'

I blush, feeling a bit dim.

'They had plenty of other animals up there though,' says the man in the fluorescent vest. 'Private collection. Have a look behind you.' He nods towards another picture, hanging just inside the door. It shows a grand, symmetrical three-storey country house, spanning a dozen or so windows in width, with ivy snaking across the façade. In front of it is a dapper-looking gentleman standing beside an ostrich which towers over him. There's a boy sitting on the bird's back.

'And this is nearby?' I ask.

'It was,' replies the barmaid. 'House is abandoned now.' She shoots a glance at the farmer nursing the end of his pint. 'The boy you see there, Alexander – he still owns it. He must be, what, seventy, Bill?'

The man with the wellies grunts out, 'Something like that.'

'What happened to the animals?'

The man – Bill – plants his empty glass down hard enough it's a wonder it doesn't smash. He pushes back his stool and grabs his flat cap. He's a big guy. Even though he's a little stooped, he must still be six three, and his many layers, despite the heat radiating from the fireplace, magnify his physical presence. One of his eyes is partially closed, and there's a scar running from his temple across his eyelid and ending at his nose. With a glowering expression, he marches past me and out of the door into the night.

'Did I say something?'

'Don't mind Bill,' says the remaining man. 'He's touchy about the house.' I let him continue, because it's pretty obvious from the knowing look in his eye that he wants to. 'He's the custodian,' he explains. 'Still lives in one of the wings.'

'God knows how he can stand it,' the barmaid remarks. 'I couldn't. Place gives me the creeps.'

I take a sip of my drink, looking at the picture. It doesn't look creepy at all. It must be worth a fortune. I'm surprised it's not a country hotel or a conference centre catering for outdoor team-building.

'It's beautiful,' I say.

'It was,' replies the man. 'Not any more. After Alexander left, it went to ruin. Mostly boarded up now.'

'What a shame,' I comment. 'Why did they leave?'

The barmaid and the man share a conspiratorial look, and then she says: 'You really don't know?'

I shake my head.

'It's got a history,' she adds. 'Alexander's fifteen-year-old daughter, Alice. She went missing. Sixteen year ago. It were all over the news.'

'Missing as in ran away?'

'That's one theory,' says the man, sounding unconvinced. 'Went out one day into the fells and never came back.'

'That's horrible.' In the back of my mind, the tenuous connection forms: two missing young women. I resist the comparison. Sixteen years is a long time. 'Was there a search?'

'Was there?' repeats the man. 'I'll say. Most of the village turned out, me included. We combed the whole estate. Not a sign. Vanished without a trace.'

Just like Gemma.

'Her poor mother couldn't cope at all,' the barmaid continues. 'Not surprising they packed up really.'

It sounds like something from a gothic novel, and I wonder if they're pulling my leg. This could be a story they tell any punter gullible enough to fall for it. But when I watch their faces, there's no hint they're having me on. Still, it seems odd I never heard about it. I guess I'd have been in uni at the time, and I didn't read the news much then.

'You think . . . someone took her?'

'She was beautiful,' says the man. 'A real stunner.'

I suppose that's a maybe. 'And the police? They investigated?'

'Of course,' replies the barmaid. 'Questioned anyone with any connection. All the local lads. Bill Farrah too. He worked at the house back then.'

'But . . .'

'Nothing,' she says. 'They closed the case in the end. The parents moved abroad. Elizabeth – that was Alice's mum – they say she died of an illness, but I wouldn't be surprised if it was by her own hand. She was fragile mentally anyway.'

'How tragic.' I recall the glowering figure who quit the bar a few minutes before. He's left an inch of amber beer in the bottom of his glass. 'So Bill is alone up there now? It must be lonely.'

'Bill's a chap content in his own company,' says the man. 'The place is falling to bits and he's the only one holding it together. Plus, you need someone up there to ward off any nosey hikers. A hundred keep-out signs aren't half as effective as one bloke with a shotgun. Especially if he looks like Bill Farrah.'

I can imagine. He's still formidable enough, even though

he must be pushing seventy. Sixteen years back, he would have been a real force to be reckoned with. Overpowering a fifteen-year-old girl wouldn't have posed a problem.

Not the sort of a man you'd want to cross paths with in the middle of nowhere.

Chapter 13

GEMMA

Gemma stirred from her slumber as Mark pulled up on the creaking handbrake. They were in a small car park in front of a looming dark building she guessed was the hostel. 'We're here?'

'Told ya,' said Mark, tapping the dashboard. 'Never in doubt, babe.'

Gemma had been worried the car wouldn't make it on the journey up north at all – part of her had hoped it would break down and put an end to the plans – but Mark had worked miracles on it over the last year, after hours at Frank's garage. Frank himself used to joke it was held together with burned oil and blind hope.

It had been Mark's plan to sleep inside the vehicle, to stay off the radar. Then the heating fans had gone on the journey up, so she'd put her foot down on that. And he could hardly argue now they were up here. She could see her own breath, even with the doors shut. They'd catch hypothermia if they tried to use the car overnight. So it was a hostel in Hartsbridge – the cheapest place they could find close to the country house.

Still shaking off sleep, Gemma had a curious sense of being dropped into another country entirely. She'd never been north of Manchester before. Hartsbridge was a tiny village, so far as she could see, nestled between hills of purple heather and massive skies. Through scattered trees below, on the other side of a small bridge edged with stone, she saw a country pub that looked closed.

A woman walked past with two sheepdogs, off the lead, trotting obediently at her heels. She caught Gemma's eye and waved in a friendly way. Gemma nodded back.

Mark leant across and laid a hand on her knee. 'It's going to be fine. Relax.'

She had a sudden flashback to the very first time they'd met. He'd used the same words, or something very similar, then. It was the last day of a festival on the outskirts of Eastbourne. A downpour had turned the field to a quagmire, and the car she was sharing with mates, stuffed to the gills with damp camping gear, had only just made it out before a puncture stopped them in their tracks. They were blocking the rest of the exiting traffic. No one in her party had a clue what to do, and the hundreds of other tired festival-goers waiting in the queue were quickly getting impatient. It was Mark who'd come to the rescue, soaked through with rain himself, bringing a jack and fitting a spare tyre in the space of five minutes. Gemma had chatted as he worked, holding an umbrella over him, horns beeping and expletives filling the air. They both lived in Brighton, as it turned out, though different sides of the town. She hadn't thought of him afterwards. Then, a few months later, she was looking for a room in a shared house and happened to walk into a living room to find him there. If it wasn't fate pushing them together, it was something close. The generosity he'd shown that day in a muddy field was typical. Mark would help anyone, whether it was an old woman with her shopping, or a stranger looking for a lost dog in the park. He'd once spent a whole Saturday tiling a bathroom for their neighbour, just because he was at a loose end.

They climbed out of the car, and Mark grabbed the rucksacks – one small and one large – from the boot. He said they needed to look the part, but Gemma felt like a complete fraud. She walked awkwardly to the front door of the hostel. The walking boots were at least two sizes too big; they were all she'd been able to find at short notice in the charity shop. Mark assured her they wouldn't be doing much actual walking. He had his regular army boots, laced high up the shins.

A man with ginger hair was on his knees by the front door, hand down a drain scooping out leaves. He watched them with a blank expression, but smiled when Gemma did.

Inside the porch, a woman was filling a rack with leaflets. 'Can I help you?'

'All right, love,' said Mark, absently looking at a map on the wall. 'We're looking for somewhere to stay.'

'Just for a couple of nights,' added Gemma. She hoped it would be no more.

The woman walked behind the counter, to a computer monitor. She tapped the keyboard.

'No problem. Two nights in a dorm will be forty pounds.'

'Nah, we don't want a dorm,' said Mark quickly.

The receptionist looked sympathetic. 'It's all we have, I'm afraid,' she said. 'You'd be the only guests in there, at least for the first night. We've got two other dorms already at capacity. You might be on your own tomorrow too – we're not booked up until the weekend.'

'A dorm is fine,' said Gemma.

The woman asked for a credit card, but Mark stepped in and said he'd pay by cash, by the day.

'Normally we ask for a card, in case of damages.'

'We promise not to damage anything,' replied Mark.

Gemma thought the receptionist was close to asking them to leave.

'Sorry,' she said, 'we don't carry a card. Off the grid, you know?'

The receptionist smiled, and opened a ledger. 'No problem. Would you mind filling in your details for me?'

Mark looked about ready to argue, and Gemma silenced him with a glare. So much for keeping a low profile. She fished for a name and wrote down the only thing that came into her head, then a phone number made up on the spot. If the receptionist checked, they could be in trouble, but that seemed unlikely.

'So you're up here walking?' asked the woman. 'If you need any route recommendations, just let me know.'

'Thank you,' said Gemma. 'We will.'

The receptionist found their key and told them to take the second door down the hallway. Mark shouldered the rucksack again, and followed Gemma.

They walked down the corridor, past a party of a two

men and women coming the other way loaded up with climbing ropes. They gave nods and greetings – Gemma wasn't used to everyone being so friendly, but it made her feel better to know there were plenty of other people around. She opened the door to the room. The dorm had four bunk beds along two walls. As promised, it was empty. She could hear laughter from the next room over.

They dumped their stuff on the bed furthest from the door.

'Nosey, wasn't she?' said Mark.

'It's her job,' replied Gemma. 'I thought we weren't drawing attention to ourselves. You're Doug, by the way. I'm Sarah.'

'Ha! Nice one. Did you see the map on the wall?' said Mark. 'It was right there – Brocklehurst Hall. There are loads of paths going close.'

'If Kash was even right.'

'That's what we're here to find out,' he said. 'We'll head out there tomorrow.'

Gemma wondered again about objecting. Back in Brighton, Brocklehurst Hall had seemed like another country; now it was a short walk. The chances to turn round and go back were shrinking.

Mark began to roll a cigarette – he looked giddy, like a schoolkid.

This whole idea didn't seem smart to Gemma in any way. She'd tried arguing about the plan a dozen times or more in the car. Mark had an answer for every objection. Tyler had no connection to whatever was going on at the country house. All he cared about was the money. And besides, Mark assured her, they'd be careful every step of the way. If it looked like the plan was going tits-up, they'd bail. 'The last thing I'd do is put you in danger, babe. I promise.'

And though it was a promise she knew he couldn't keep, Gemma believed he meant it.

Chapter 14

SARAH

The young man called Archie reappears, holding a steaming bowl on a plate and some cutlery. 'Where'd you want this?'

I take myself to a table and he deposits it in front of me, avoiding eye contact.

'Thanks.'

'I was just telling our guest about Alice Brocklehurst,' says the barmaid, as Archie heads towards the kitchen doors.

He pauses, grins and shakes his head, before disappearing into the back. I can only guess he's twenty-five at most, so he must have been a young kid when Alice Brocklehurst vanished. No point grasping at straws.

The chilli is just what I need. Hot enough to give my mouth a slight burn, quenchable with the Guinness. I find I'm famished, and hunger overcomes my reluctance to eat something Archie's had a hand in. Afterwards, I order a large Shiraz.

The final couple leave, so it's just me and the barmaid and the man with the hard hat. He downs his drink and asks for a Scotch 'for the road', before adding, 'If you ask me, it was the cat that got her.'

'Oh, shush yourself, man,' says the barmaid, waving an arm dismissively as she lifts a glass to the optic.

'What?' he protests.

'Sorry, "the cat"?' I ask.

The barmaid rolls her eyes. 'Don't get Nige started.'

I smile. 'Too late for that. Come on – spill the beans.'

The man turns on his seat, manspreading impressively. 'It's how Bill came by his scar.' He points to his face. 'Alex's father, James – he was the one with the animals. He had a couple of big cats – jaguars, they said.' His eyes narrow. 'Or was it panthers, Tara?'

'I don't bloody know,' says the barmaid over her shoulder.

'Bill's father was head warden on the estate, going right back to the war. Bill grew up there, running around with Alex. One day, one of the cats got out and it finds little Bill – he can't have been more than six or seven. He was lucky it wasn't hungry, I suppose – just gave him a scratch.'

Some scratch, I think, recalling the gouge through the big man's face. 'That must have been terrifying. What happened to the cats?'

'Nowt,' says the man called Nige. 'The Farrahs were loyal, and the Brocklehursts kept them well. He got stitched up and was back home a couple of days later. I remember the first time I saw him after the bandages came off. Didn't want to go near him, but my ma made me.'

'Were the police involved?'

Nige shakes his head. 'Mebbe money changed hands. Who

knows. Anyway,' he continues, 'a few years later, in the seventies, the laws changed, so Alex had to get rid of most of the animals. Problem was, there were plenty of other rich landowners in the same boat – too many for the zoos to take. A lot of them just took the easy way out. Both barrels to the head, you know? There was a rumour that Sir James couldn't do it.'

'A daft rumour,' says the barmaid.

'I'm sorry, I don't understand,' I tell them.

'Because it's a nonsense,' says the barmaid.

Nige puts up his hand to silence her. 'So what does old Jimmy do?' He pauses theatrically, before extending his arm in front of him and spreading his fingers. 'He just lets the bloody things go!'

I grin. It does sound pretty far-fetched. Not to mention, the timings are *way* off.

'Hang on,' I say – and I can hear the alcohol in my raised voice – 'you said Alice was fifteen. She can't even have been born when the cats were released.'

Nige chips in. 'Yeah, but they bred, didn't they? There could be dozens of 'em up there, right now? Paddy Draper's been saying for years there's one up there.'

'Oh, well, if Paddy said so . . .' says the barmaid.

'Who's Paddy Draper?' I ask.

'Local crackpot,' the barmaid replies. She side-eyes Nige at the bar. 'We've got a few of them.'

'All I'm saying,' adds Nige, 'it's not beyond the realms of possibility. Paddy swears blind he saw one. And they never found her, did they?'

He tips the shot down his throat, gathers his hat, then wobbles out, wishing us both a good night, leaving me and the barmaid alone.

I wait a few more minutes, before making my move, standing and walking over to the bar with the remains of my red wine, where the barmaid is cleaning up with a cloth. Archie must be back in the kitchen, and I wonder if he's listening. 'This is going to sound odd,' I say, 'but I'm up here looking for my sister. She's sort of missing too.'

'Is that right?' says the barmaid, frowning.

'Well, I'm just trying to piece together her movements. I know she was staying up at the hostel, and I wondered if she'd come here. She was with her boyfriend.'

I pull out the photo again, and lay it on the bar.

The barmaid peers at it. 'Face rings a bell. A week ago, maybe. I think she wanted to use the loos. A lot of walkers do. Used to have a policy – customers only. Not that anyone pays any attention.'

'I noticed you had security cameras,' I add. 'I know it's a lot to ask . . . perhaps I could have a look?'

She draws back, and I think she's going to say no.

'I don't see why not,' she replies. 'You want to wait till tomorrow, or now?'

I smile. 'Let's do it now . . .' I scan the empty pub, 'if you're not busy.'

She deposits the cloth in a sink under the bar, then walks to the main door and slides the bolt across. I finish the wine with a gulp.

We go back upstairs to the office, and the barmaid takes the only seat. She makes a few clicks with the mouse. 'Do you know what day it would have been?'

'Sometime between Monday and Thursday. Sorry – can't be more exact.'

She sighs. 'It must have been Tuesday or Wednesday. We're

106

closed Monday, and I wasn't working Thursday. I think it was the middle of the day she came in, so Tuesday I reckon.' She looks up. 'Tell you what, do you want to have a look yourself.'

'If that's . . . okay?' I say.

'She's your sister,' she says, and pats my arm. 'And for Christ's sake, ignore Nige. He's full of it. I'll be downstairs if you need me.'

I thank her, then sit down. I wait until she's out of earshot, before quickly familiarising myself with the system, adjusting the cursor until the time stamp reads eleven. The two camera feeds run synchronously, one showing the activity in the bar and the other the road outside, and the couple of tables there. If I drag it, everything moves too fast, the people a blur, but there's a way to nudge the fast forward until a minute is passing by every ten seconds or so.

The pub gets a reasonable amount of traffic, with deliveries and punters coming in. At the front, walkers pass by, some taking the seats with hot drinks, checking their maps, peeling off layers, or making calls. Looks like Hartsbridge can be a busy place at times. I pause in a couple of places as a woman of the right age slips into view, but each time it's an anticlimax. Then, at 12.15, I see him. I see Mark.

He enters the shot, carrying a rucksack, his languid gait unmistakeable. He looks back, and a couple of seconds later, she jogs into view. My sister. I stop the footage to be sure.

I knew she'd been here, of course. The postmark, the man in the art shop, the handwriting in the guest book at the hostel – they all told me that. But until now – and really seeing her in digital form – she's seemed little more than a ghost.

The resolution is poor, and the image is sapped of colour. From the looks of it, she's no longer wearing a ring through her nose, and her hair is longer. She has big boots on her feet and wears some sort of thick, padded jacket, buttoned up to the neck.

Before I can stop myself, I reach out and touch the screen. It's weird – the stir of powerful emotion. Just seeing her moving about – *alive*. It opens up a sea of dread ahead, something that's been lurking, which I'm really only just acknowledging to myself now. She might not be alive anymore. That's wild speculation, of course. I push it away, and hit play once more, at normal speed.

She's talking to Mark briefly, then they both place their bags on a bench, and she goes inside the pub, where the second feed picks her up walking to the bar, then disappearing out of sight. It's just as the barmaid said.

Outside, Mark is pacing, coming in and out of shot. For a second, he looks up at the camera. There's a group of walkers, sprawled out across both tables. They look relatively old, a mixture of the sexes.

Three minutes or so pass, and Gemma reappears. She and Mark shoulder their bags again and leave. It was tantalisingly short. They seem to be heading to the left of the pub. Where they were going is anyone's guess, but it certainly appears they were planning to walk somewhere. Maybe they were hiking, after all.

I rub my eyes. It's getting late. I rewind the footage, watching the whole thing through again, desperate to glean any further clues. Less than forty-eight hours later, Mark was dead and my sister vanished from the face of the earth.

Maybe I'm imagining things, reading too much into the

108

images, but both of them seem a little cautious. Gemma's head jerks around, in a way that seems unlike the carefree sister I grew up with.

Once they've left, it's just the walking group, drinking cups of tea and chatting. I will my sister to come back, to reveal something else. She doesn't.

'What the fuck are you doing?'

The voice makes me leap out of the chair. Archie is standing in the doorway to the office, hands on the frame. He looks wild-eyed.

'Oh . . . er . . . the barmaid, Tara — she said I could.'

He walks in, reaches across and switches off the screen. 'Said you could what? Snoop around?'

Though I probably shouldn't, I get angry at his tone. And I'm not going to be intimidated. I stand up and face him. There's not much room in the little office, so we're too close for comfort. He's blocking the way out. I can smell his sour sweat and the kitchen stink on his clothes.

'Get out of my way,' I say firmly.

He takes a moment or two, then moves aside, enough to let me pass. He doesn't deserve an explanation. I know I wasn't doing anything wrong.

I worry, for a horrible moment, that he's going to follow.

'Talk to Tara,' I say, then head back to my room and lock the door.

Chapter 15

GEMMA

'You sure this is the way?'

'I can read a bloody map,' said Gemma, play-hitting him with the folded map they'd bought at the hostel. Every step of the plan involved spending money they couldn't spare. She just hoped it was a price worth paying.

They'd reached a gate that led up a steep farm track. There was a footpath sign – something called the Salter's Way, marked with a horse silhouette. They passed a sprawling farmhouse on a track. A dog was barking out of sight. The track veered off up a path alongside a field of bored-looking cows, before reaching a stile. It was bog on the other side. Gemma did her best to tread on the drier bits, but Mark sank up to his ankles.

'Fuckin' hell!' he said, dragging his feet out and looking at the dripping boots in dismay.

Gemma laughed. 'This was your idea, remember?'

'Whatever,' he said.

There was a road which approached the house directly, but they'd decided it was far safer to approach via paths, on foot, if they were trying not to be seen. She'd no idea what they'd find at the house, though it was safe to assume there wouldn't be a garden full of cannabis plants on full public display.

The rocky footpath continued, running parallel to a babbling stream hidden by dense fir trees. At the top, the path split into three beside a small waterfall. Gemma consulted the map, and pointed to the central one. Here, the path they wanted veered off the main Salter's Way and basically followed a watercourse uphill into the moorland. They found themselves crossing and recrossing the same stream across muddy ground. The path disappeared at times – it was hard to tell the track from areas of natural erosion – but they'd pick it up again when they found the boot-prints of walkers who'd gone before.

'You know, I've been thinking?' she said. 'About the wedding . . .'

'Oh yeah?'

'Maybe I should go?'

Mark's face twisted. 'You've changed your tune.'

'I know. But she invited me. She didn't have to.'

Mark stumbled and almost fell into a bank of heather. Gemma stepped more carefully over the same spot.

'We both said stuff we shouldn't.'

Mark paused. 'Not being funny – do you think she really wants you there?'

Gemma shrugged. 'Hard to know with Sarah. It's complicated.'

'Sounds it.'

She could tell Mark wasn't really interested in the conversation, and she couldn't blame him. Her relationship with her sister wasn't really a topic they'd ever discussed much since Mum's funeral, and she'd no doubt given the distinct impression it wasn't something that troubled her much at all.

'I don't think she ever forgave me for moving out,' she said, as much to herself as her walking companion.

'Your mum was an alky, right? You were only young.'

When he put it like that, it sounded like a simple decision. And, at the time, it had felt like a no-brainer. She'd flunked her GCSEs, and split from her boyfriend. Mum was just another layer of hassle and hopelessness. So when a friend had said she had a spare room for the summer, Gemma had jumped at the chance. She never really thought it would be permanent, until suddenly it was. And as time moved on, it became easier simply to call her mum rather than actually visit. On the phone, it wasn't hard not to dwell on the sort of life she was living. Or indeed what her sister might be going through. When Sarah had answered the phone, their conversations were short and to the point. Her sister never asked her to come back or gave the impression Gemma's absence made the slightest difference. Gemma figured she was one less person for Sarah to worry about, even that she might be glad Gemma had gone. But when she thought about it now, it didn't seem quite so clear-cut.

By the time she and Mark reached the high ground, she was breathing hard. It wasn't much to look at – miles and miles of rolling heather, tufty yellow grass and peat bogs. A wilderness. In the distance, some sort of telecoms mast punctured the horizon. The wind was gusting and filled

113

her hood. The low cloud blew in ghostly shreds across the landscape.

'The map says it's another couple of miles,' she said.

They plodded onwards. Here, the path was clearer, marked every hundred metres or so by small piles of rocks. When the mist really closed in, she imagined it would be hard to see them though.

Gemma didn't mention the wedding again. Mark had made his feelings about her sister clear – she was 'snooty', as far as he was concerned. And whereas once Gemma would have agreed, the last few years of complete separation had made her think again. That day at the funeral, they'd both been on edge; looking back, a bust-up had been almost inevitable. She'd been broke, as always, and even getting the train to London and a taxi out to the crematorium had been cash they couldn't spare. It was stupid to have brought up Mum's house, she could see that now, but she was desperate, and it was only her remaining shreds of pride that had made her lose it with her sister.

After another half an hour, they found themselves looking down into a shallow valley.

'There she is,' said Mark.

The house – Brocklehurst Hall – was perhaps three hundred metres away. It was larger than Gemma expected – massive in fact. Three storeys high, and ten windows across, three quarters of them boarded up. It was built in dark stone, with four sets of chimneys and a few steps leading up to a front door surrounded by a portico, supported by columns.

Mark shrugged off the backpack and fished inside, taking out an ancient pair of binoculars they'd got from the charity shop too, for five quid. One of the lenses was cracked. He lifted them to his eyes.

A bird shrieked and burst from the heather below with a cracking flap of wings. Gemma watched it skirt low over the ground, before resettling out of sight.

'It's perfect,' said Mark.

'What can you see?'

'Nothing much. You reckon we can get closer?'

Gemma checked at the map. 'There's one path that's nearer. It goes round the back.' She reached out. 'Let's have a look then?'

He passed her the binoculars and she raised them to her face. The house snapped into view as she panned across the landscape. Twisting the lenses for better focus, she tried to keep her hands steady. Despite the crack, they worked fine. The building looked even more grim close-up – the lower boards on the windows were scrawled with graffiti and it looked like one of the grand chimney stacks was crumbling away. The gravel at the front of the house was overgrown with weeds.

'It looks abandoned,' she said.

'Course it does,' replied Mark. 'That's the point. Can't imagine a copper out here, can you?'

'I think Kash was having you on,' said Gemma. She hoped he was. Now they were here, Mark's plan seemed even more preposterous.

Mark snatched the binoculars back. 'Nah,' he said. 'They'll have it all hidden somewhere. Underground, he said, in the cellars. Come on.'

They continued around the head of the valley for another twenty minutes, the house dipping in and out of sight, until the path followed a barbed fence with occasional signs about private property.

'See,' said Mark. 'They don't want nobody getting close.'

Gemma checked her watch and saw it was already after two. The autumnal sun was trying its best to penetrate the thin cloud but only succeeded in creating a diffuse glow.

Through the binoculars, more of the estate was visible from their new vantage. The side of the house was less grand, with a modern extension overlooking terraces of what might have been an ornamental garden and a small lake. Beside the house stood a stone barn and other, more modern brick outbuildings around a yard with old stables lining the other side. There was a Land Rover parked up too. It looked pretty battered, and possibly abandoned.

'Now what?' asked Gemma, lowering the binoculars.

'We wait,' replied Mark. He sat down on a patch of heather and pulled a can of lager from the side pocket of the backpack. 'You want one?'

'No thanks. What are we waiting for?'

'We need a contact,' said Mark. 'Someone must work down there. We just have to find out who.' He tugged the ring pull and foam exploded, pouring over his wrist. He held it away from his body until it subsided. 'Cheers, babe!'

Gemma didn't feel like celebrating. There was something about the house that made her uneasy. It might have been grand once; now it looked grim and forbidding. She imagined empty rooms, trapped in time. She'd never believed in ghosts, but a place like that had to have its fair share. And who knew what other secrets it would be hiding?

Chapter 16

SARAH

I wake to the muffled buzz of my phone, vibrating somewhere nearby. For a moment, I'm trapped under something heavy, and I reach out blindly, struggling against the weight. My hand finds the phone in folds of copious feather duvet. The shapes of the room and the furniture take on hard edges and I remember where I am. The pub. Hartsbridge.

The caller ID is withheld. I'm surprised to see it's after eight already.

'Hello,' I answer.

'Sarah Kline?'

It's a woman. She sounds serious. I push myself upright. The morning light is a faint line sneaking under the curtains. I can't believe I slept so heavily, and my head has a dull ache from the red wine.

'Hello?'

'I'm Sergeant Nelson,' she says. 'You spoke to my colleague yesterday.'

I thank her for calling back, trying to get my thoughts in some sort of order, then tell her I've been looking into my sister's movements, and that I've found out where she and Mark were staying. 'A place called Dale Grange, in Hartsbridge,' I say. I don't mention the assumed names, or anything about Archie. That seems premature.

After a pause, Sergeant Nelson says, 'Well, thank you. That's helpful. Are you still in Hartsbridge?'

'At The Headless Woman,' I tell her.

'How long are you planning on staying?' I can hear she's intrigued. I suppose it might seem odd, me travelling all the way here.

'Another night at least.'

'Listen, Ms Kline, I just want you to know we appreciate your assistance. There are still several unanswered questions about your sister and her companion.'

'You don't have to tell me that.'

'We have reason to believe she might be hiding.'

I was coming to the same conclusion, I suppose. Hiding, or on the run. Or worse.

'Hiding from what?'

'It's hard to say. Her associates from Brighton reported she owed money. They weren't keen to say to whom.'

'Right.' I can't say it's terribly surprising, given her past financial woes.

'We're still looking into it. In the meantime, it's very important: if you hear from her, contact us at once. We don't want you putting yourself in danger. I'll give you my personal number.'

I thank her and take it down.

'I understand my constable is coming to see you shortly?'

'That's right. Dewer.' To be honest, I'd rather be dealing directly with the sergeant, who seems to have her head screwed firmly on. But something she said snags my attention. 'What did you mean, *danger*? Is there something I should be worried about?'

I hear a heavy breath. 'Oh, I'm sure it's nothing, but you're on your own, and we don't really know what we're dealing with yet.' Her tone turns lighter. 'Better safe than sorry, eh?'

After we've hung up, I take a shower, feeling more awake. This feels like progress. Clearly the police are taking things seriously. It was always going to be tricky to find Gemma on my own; with the local police as well, there might be a chance.

The room is stuffy, so I open the window. Then I call Doug. He doesn't pick up and I remember he'll be on a long run Sunday morning. It's a ritual as reliable as the tides. Often, he'd answer anyway, and I hope he's not smarting still. So I leave a message saying everything's fine, and I miss him, and that I've found where Gemma stayed here in the village with Mark. I keep the business with the fake names to myself – his opinion of my sister is low enough already.

Then I open my laptop and quickly check there's nothing from work that needs my attention. I booked Monday off in a bit of a hurry – a vague excuse about personal reasons – and there's an email from Kat asking if I'll be back in time for a general team catch-up on Tuesday. I reply quickly that I will, hopefully. I figure by then I'll either have found Gemma or have exhausted the avenues of inquiry.

The first sneeze of the morning takes me by surprise.

119

Maybe I could politely ask Tara to give the room a vacuum, explain about my allergies. The booze seemed to quell the worst of it the night before. Who knows where the nearest chemist is?

Outside the bedroom door, I can hear the sounds of cutlery clattering in the pub below and steel myself as I head down the stairs. I hope it's not Archie, but if it is, I'm assuming he'll have spoken to the barmaid and realised me being in the little office was completely above board.

Thankfully, it's Tara herself, and she's setting a table for me. The pub has that slightly unwashed smell of last night's woodsmoke and old beer, which is actually comforting. But it's noticeably cooler without a fire in the hearth, and I guess the heating's slow to come on in the morning.

'Take a seat!' she says cheerfully. 'Breakfast's coming up.'

I remember now what I ordered, and regret it. The chilli's sitting heavy from the evening before, and really I fancy something simpler. Before I can say anything, she's bustled away, back into the kitchen, and soon I can smell the bacon frying. She emerges again, and enquires what I'd like to drink. I ask for coffee. As she prepares it behind the bar, she asks if I found what I was looking for.

'Sorry?'

'On the CCTV,' she says. 'My lad said he must've startled you.'

My lad. Archie's her son. There goes any chance to make a complaint about him. Maybe it's a good thing there's someone to keep him in check though.

'Oh, yes, thanks – she was here, you're right.'

'Good, good,' she replies. 'But you said she was missing?'

'It's a long story.'

120

She carries over the coffee. 'One you want to tell?'

I smile to myself, surprised she's so willing to bluntly stick her nose in. It's hard to take offence, and she's been more than helpful so far. So I explain, about the police coming to my office in London, about how I've not seen Gemma for quite a while, about the car set on fire.

Her hand goes to her mouth. 'Oh, my God! That's awful.'

I nod. 'So, you see, I'm worried about her.'

'Course you are, treasure.'

As I tackle the huge breakfast, my eyes wander back to the rhino's head hanging over the fireplace, surveying the room. In need of a break from the food, I stand up, crossing the room with my coffee cup to look again at the picture on the wall, showing the former inhabitants of Brocklehurst Hall. The story of fifteen-year-old Alice has got me thinking.

Tara's still milling about.

'You think it's easy,' I say, 'for someone to just disappear?'

'Up there?' says Tara, jutting her chin in the vague direction on the hills. 'Of course. Look at Alice.'

'They never found *anything*?'

'Not even a hair.' She pauses. 'It's a wilderness around the estate – all sorts of gullies through the peat bogs. Tunnels too.'

'Tunnels? For what?'

'Old mine workings. Small quarries – the house is built from local stone. The Brocklehursts worked the ground for almost four hundred years.'

'So what do you think happened to her?'

'If I had to guess, she took a fall from her horse. She was quite the rider. Olympic hopeful, they said. Maybe she was knocked out, or hurt, crawled until she couldn't. Ended up in a deep bog. It happened a couple of years ago – a runner broke his leg and the ground swallowed him up. Wasn't found for three weeks, and it was only because we had a dry spell someone saw his running shoe sticking out of the ground.' She looks at me with sympathy and adds hurriedly, 'Of course, that doesn't mean anything about your sister.'

'The police must have had suspects,' I say. I want her to tell me more about Bill Farrah, the man with the not-so-dashing scar who left in such a hurry the night before.

'They went hard on all the local boys. She was a popular girl, but her family were strict, and she was at a girls' boarding school in the term. She went missing in the holidays, and there was a theory she might have been seeing someone behind her parents' backs.'

I take a seat again at the breakfast table, cutting into a sausage.

'Nothing came of it, though? No arrests?'

'Only one.' She nods towards the door. 'Reuben Fletwick, poor lad. Same year as her at primary school. He used to draw her pictures. Besotted, he was. Plus, he always was one to wander off on his own.'

As I chew, I think of the mute young man up at Dale Grange. I've no idea of his condition, but he didn't strike me as dangerous or malicious. If anything, he was childlike.

'They obviously released him?'

'No real evidence,' says Tara. 'He and his family got some stick for a while afterwards – wasn't nice.'

'I saw him yesterday, driving off with another man.'

'That's right. He's got himself a job at the meatpackers over in Ravenow. His uncle runs the place.'

There's a knock on the window, and on the other side I

see a man in police uniform. Tara goes to open the door and he steps in, clutching his hat to his thigh.

'Apologies!' he says. 'I'm early. You're having your breakfast, I see.'

Constable Dewer is slim, five foot ten, with a handsome, boyish face and very dark features and olive skin that makes me think there's something in his ancestry distinctly Mediterranean. I'm guessing thirty-ish. He hovers awkwardly in the doorway.

'No, it's fine,' I say, standing up again. Then to Tara – 'I'm sorry – it was lovely, but I don't think I can finish it.'

'No problem,' she replies.

I'm not sure I want her listening in, so I point outside. 'Let's get some fresh air, if that's okay?'

Dewer moves aside to let me pass. His eyes light on the half-eaten breakfast as Tara carries it back into the kitchen. 'How's business?' he says, in a friendly way that tells me they know each other well.

'Can't complain,' she replies.

I head outside and Dewer follows. We cross the road and settle at one of the picnic tables above the weir.

It's a beautiful morning, the sky a high blue saturation, the trees undisturbed by even the gentlest breeze. Dewer takes out a notebook as we sit opposite one another.

'I was surprised to hear you were up in our neck of the woods,' he says. 'Long way from home, isn't it?'

I nod. 'For Gemma too. It's not like her to . . . Well, this isn't her sort of place.' I worry he'll take offence. 'She's a city girl, you know?'

He doesn't say anything, and I wonder if it's a tactic, or just because he's a bit clueless. In arbitrations at work, it's sometimes the most illuminating strategy just to let the other side talk. And I do, obligingly – I ramble on with the same story. That Gemma and I weren't close. That we drifted apart. I can hear myself, and see him waiting for an explanation of why exactly I am here and what I hope to achieve. Problem is, I don't think I really know myself. I want to find her, of course, even though I'm getting more anxious by the hour about what it is I'll discover. I tell him about the postcard, and the fake names used at the hostel.

'When I heard what happened to Mark, I had to come.'

'You knew him?' asks Dewer.

'We only met once, briefly – at a funeral.'

Dewer turns his attention to his notebook, flicking back to a page with writing that I can't read. I wonder if he's testing me, or simply lost for something to say. It annoys me, considering how much I'm giving him.

'Do you think it was an accident?' I ask. 'The car?'

He looks at me, very directly, and is silent a moment. 'We're keeping an open mind. Why do you think they'd used the names of you and your fiancé? That seems quite a deliberate choice.'

'I have no idea. Some sort of joke?'

He frowns. 'Is it funny?'

I have the feeling again that this isn't quite the courtesy I was expecting – that maybe I've been drawn away from my breakfast on false pretences, that I'm the one being interviewed here, and that he's actually the one in control.

'I just want to find Gemma,' I say. 'If you think Mark's death wasn't an accident, I need to know.'

Dewer closes the book again, and his shoulders relax a bit. 'The post-mortem has been inconclusive,' he says. 'The body was badly burned, but the initial exam detected no smoke in his lungs.'

'So he was dead prior to the fire.'

Dewer nods. 'It looks likely he might have died in the crash itself. The car was on its roof. It came off the road and rolled several times, ending up in a shallow stream. It appears he wasn't wearing a seat belt.'

I can't see why he mentions that at all. Is it to suggest Mark in some way got what he deserved, or is it to imply there was no foul play? In any case, I don't see how it's relevant to my sister's fate. 'Gemma could have been with him though. She might have escaped the wreckage.'

'We've no evidence of that, I'm afraid.'

'She was his girlfriend. They were staying up here together.'

'Maybe they argued. Maybe he was angry, or intoxicated, or both? Took the road too fast for the conditions.'

'Did he have anything in his system, from the post-mortem?'

'We couldn't ascertain that. But he had a history of drug offences.'

'I . . . I didn't know.' Although I'm not entirely surprised.

Dewer raises his eyebrows in a condescending way that reminds me immediately of one of the more despicable barristers who crosses my path occasionally. I can almost hear his nasal whine, 'So why *did* she stay with him so long, if his behaviour was so intolerable?' I need to keep my temper in check.

'I don't get it. *You* were looking for Gemma. Police came to *my* office. Now I'm here, it's like you're not interested.'

'I'm sorry if I'm giving you that impression, Ms Kline,' says Dewer, 'and we do appreciate your help. It's just . . . we have to proceed from evidence. We don't know your sister, or her boyfriend. We can't chase shadows based on hunches, and especially when there's no evidence that a crime has been committed.'

'She's not the first young woman to go missing round here though, is she?'

His eyes widen. 'What do you mean?'

'I hear it was the same with Alice Brocklehurst,' I say. 'She went missing too.'

He snorts. 'About twenty years ago.'

'Sixteen, wasn't it?'

He takes a deep breath and exhales more calmly through his nose. 'That case has nothing to do with this.' His face and his tone are suddenly not at all friendly. I've hit some sort of sore spot, and it gives me a flash of triumph.

'I read about it – no one was charged back then. She was never found. Two young women, both missing, in the same village. Bit of a coincidence, isn't it?'

He pulls the hat on, like he's getting ready to leave. 'Look, I want to help find your sister, I really do, but if she was up to something, isn't it likely she's done a runner?'

'It's possible,' I say. 'But she's not answering her phone.'

'People have perfectly good reasons not to want to speak. Did you speak regularly before now?'

'No, but I'm her sister. She'd answer if I did call.'

'Her sister, who she's not close to?'

He's got me there. I can't help feeling he's doing his best to keep me at a distance.

'Can't you at least . . . I don't know – trace her phone? You've got the number.'

Dewer shakes his head, sadly. 'We can't authorise that, I'm afraid.'

'Can't, or won't?' I ask.

'Ms Kline,' he says, like I'm stretching his patience close to breaking point. 'I realise you're upset, but you have to recognise that we're doing our best for you. We don't have the resources to expend on finding someone who doesn't want to be found. It's a question of privacy.'

'Sorry – I'm not telling you how to do your job.'

'I understand, Ms Kline.' He's standing now.

I stand too. 'Have you spoken to anyone in the village about it?'

'Until yesterday, we didn't know your sister had stayed in Hartsbridge.'

Quite, I think. I bite back the retort that I've managed to establish more than the police in less than twenty-four hours.

'But you will now?'

He looks perplexed. 'Who particularly should we talk to?'

'You could start with the hostel. Carla.' I pause. I don't want to get Reuben into any trouble, but it's the one place I know for sure that Gemma spent time.

He looks at me. 'What were you saying about my job?'

He turns and leaves. I watch him walk back towards his car. What now? Maybe I am chasing shadows. For the first time, I'm actually angry with Gemma. If she's hiding somewhere, maybe even content, then I've come up here for nothing. Like Doug said – a bloody wild goose chase.

Chapter 17

GEMMA

The sun was bathing them in late afternoon light, hovering over the horizon. It wouldn't be long before it disappeared completely behind the slope of the western hills and the temperature dropped considerably. The last thing Gemma wanted was to pick their way back to the hostel in the darkness.

'We should go,' she said, hugging herself.

Mark, three cans in, was kicking at stones on the path. He looked deflated. Gemma had only had one beer, but coupled with the lack of food, her stomach was an uncomfortable knot. She needed to pee, and didn't fancy doing it au naturel. Mark lifted the binoculars again and stared down the hillside.

'Maybe we should get closer,' he said. He didn't sound convinced. They'd been here about three hours. There was no reason to think anything would break the monotony.

'It's not worth it,' replied Gemma. 'If we're seen, we're fucked, right?' She was clinging to her suspicion about Kash's claims, and from Mark's face, she thought doubts must have been creeping into his mind too. It wouldn't be the maddest thing in the world if the whole story had been blown out of proportion, a game of Chinese whispers between potheads about a mythical weed farm in the middle of the hills. Looking down at the old house now, it really did appear to be abandoned and devoid of life. 'Come on,' she said. 'I'm hungry. We can come back tomorrow.'

'All right,' said Mark.

They gathered their things and began the plod back the way they'd come. Gemma's limbs were stiff, pins and needles in her feet. They'd only travelled a couple of hundred metres when Mark turned and jerked up the binoculars hanging around his neck.

'Hello, sunshine, what's this?' A smile spread over his lips.

Gemma saw it too. Coming along the road in the distance, beyond the house, was a single rider on a low-cc motorbike. Whether it was the atmospherics, or the acoustics of the valley, the growling sound of the engine seemed to be coming from a different direction entirely, decoupled from the bike. Gemma crouched and whispered, 'Get down!'

'He can't see us,' said Mark, eyes glued to the optics.

Gemma guessed he was right. The sun was at their backs after all. She could see the bike only dimly – yellow and black – and the rider himself was just an anonymous figure in a red helmet, with blue-and-white checked trousers that seemed familiar. There were panniers slung across the bike's rear end, making her think of a bee loaded with pollen. The bike turned around the side of the house, before slowing into the yard and stopping. The rider dismounted, then a distant, muted horn reached Gemma's ears.

The barn door opened, and another figure appeared – just a stick man at this distance. Gemma guessed they were talking, and the rider wheeled the bike across towards the open door. He went inside.

'You think he's picking something up?' asked Gemma.

'What else?' replied Mark. He laughed, a short 'Ha!'

Sure enough, it was only ten minutes later that the second man emerged and walked across to the Land Rover, climbing inside.

'Get the plate,' said Mark, scrabbling in the bag to find a biro.

Gemma, who had the binoculars now, wasn't sure what good it would do them, but recited it anyway. The Land Rover disappeared off down the track. Mark was still scribbling on his hand with the pen.

'What are you going to do with that?' Gemma asked.

'I dunno,' he replied glumly. 'There must be a way we can track it.'

'We're not the Feds,' she said.

She looked back towards the house, where there was more movement. The rider emerged too, pushing the bike, with the panniers bulging, and the helmet hanging from the handlebars. He slung a leg over the saddle and turned briefly in their direction. A young man.

'Oh shit,' she breathed. Now the trousers made sense. 'I recognise him.'

Mark snatched the binoculars from her. 'You do?' he said.

Gemma nodded. 'I saw him in the village. He was at the

pub when I used the loo earlier. Collecting glasses. He must work there.'

Mark turned to her, eyes sparkling. 'We got 'em, babe. We fucking got 'em!'

Chapter 18

SARAH

Fresh from the disappointment of my little chat with the constable, I drift back towards the pub.

'Any joy?' Tara asks. She's on her knees, by the fireplace, brushing ash from the grate onto newspaper laid on the hearth.

'I'm not really sure.'

'That's a pity. They'll keep looking,' says Tara.

I force a smile, hoping it conceals my low opinion of Constable Dewer.

I pause. 'This is going to sound really silly, but could I borrow your vacuum cleaner?'

I mention my allergies and she looks surprised, then straightens up, holding her lower back.

'You should've said! I'll take care of it. And I'll change the bedding too.'

'You don't have to do that!'

She tells me it's no problem, and she'll get to it as soon as she's finished down here.

I return to my room. As soon as I'm in there, I have a feeling that *something* is different. A charge in the air, a . . . presence. The bathroom light is on, but I'm fairly sure that could've been my oversight. Still, I'm tense as I peer around the door. There's no one there. My things are on the side of the sink, as I left them.

I let my eyes sweep the bedroom, looking for anything out of place. Yesterday's underwear is lying beside my case, on the stand beneath the open window. I'm *almost* convinced I dropped them on top the night before, but they could've slid off. Or maybe a gust from the open window? Approaching, I can't help wonder if it was Archie. He'd have a key, wouldn't he?

I open the case, and check the contents. If anything's been moved, it's not clear. I close the window again, staring outside. Nothing but the empty hills look back. Tara is carrying out a crate of bottles to a large wheelie bin. I don't think she'd have come into the room in the brief time I've been outside, and I can't think of a way to ask her without sounding accusatory. It's quite possible I'm being paranoid. Or that it's the cat again, somehow sneaking in.

On the bed, I open my laptop, googling Alice Brocklehurst. There's actually a reasonable amount of press from the time about the missing girl, but nothing like what there would be now, in the age of social media and twenty-four-hour news. Opening up one of the articles, I have a mild shock. Alice Brocklehurst looks a little bit like Gemma. Well, Gemma if she'd been born with a silver spoon in her mouth, and given a shit about her appearance. One picture is repeated across several of the news articles, that of an English rose in dressage uniform, standing proudly beside a large brown horse with a braided mane: 'Talented equestrian, Alice Brocklehurst, and her horse, Castor'. The stories seem to span about a week, and then stop. The detail in each is roughly the same too and much like what I've heard down-stairs: speculation that Alice hurt herself while out walking, the failure of the search party, the promising riding career cut tragically short. Oddly, there's nothing that I can see from her family – not a single statement – but the pieces all end with a Durham Constabulary appeal for information. There's nothing, either, about any arrests or suspicions that foul play might be involved.

There's one article that seems to focus more on the rumours about the big cat, from a trashy magazine and only available as a PDF link. The publication itself looks to have folded. The article, imaginatively titled 'Beauty and the Beast', seems to consist of few actual facts, other than a colourful history of Alice's ancestors at the house, with its menagerie of creatures. It quotes an unnamed local source claiming there have been several sightings of a big cat roaming the moors, but counterbalances it with a zoologist from Chester, who declares in no uncertain terms that the survival of a family of felines in the area is highly improbable and that such sightings tend to be the result of overactive imagina-tions or large dogs or deer seen from a distance.

One article has a different image of Alice, this time as 'fourth from top left' in a school photograph from 2003, when she can only have been ten or eleven, then blown up at the side. She does indeed look younger here, though still striking, and she's one of the few kids not smiling. She's wearing some sort of cast on her lower leg. At the side of the class, beside a female teacher, stands Reuben.

It feels wrong to even think it. His life must have been hard enough already, with bullying and prejudice and misunderstanding. I've got to believe the police did a thorough investigation sixteen years ago and he had nothing to do with Alice Brocklehurst's disappearance, just as he has nothing to do with Gemma's. At the same time, I wonder, am I letting my own discomfort preclude a thorough investigation? If he didn't have a disability, would I be so ready to dismiss the possibility – however unlikely – that he might know something more about Gemma's movements a week ago? Though the constable might ask a few questions, I wouldn't trust him to be forensic about it. He didn't seem to have a lot of urgency about him.

Which leaves me back at square one, with a day to kill.

Is there really any point in staying in Hartsbridge at all? Maybe it's time to beat a retreat back to London, tail between my legs and full of apologies, and focus on the biggest day of my life next weekend.

For the first time, I ask myself, would Gemma have done all this for me? The honest answer is, I don't know, and maybe it's not fair to ask. I'm the big sister, not her.

I look around the room. Even without the lurking suspicion that Archie's been in here, I wouldn't be sad not to spend another night with the scuffed woodchip wallpaper, lumpy mattress and creepy photos. The barometer on the wall, as if it senses my mood, tells me there's rain coming too. If there's evidence out there, that can't be good for preservation.

Dewer really did seem keen to wash his hands of me, and

I'm sure it wasn't my imagination that his attitude changed as soon as I mentioned Alice Brocklehurst. I don't know why I can't drop it. Like he said, she probably has nothing to do with this. Maybe it's just the mystery of it, or the macabre thought of a young girl lost and alone, crawling across a hillside until she collapsed. I can't shake the idea that Gemma was in that car with Mark when it crashed. And if she was, and she somehow survived, maybe she didn't even get that far. If it happened at night, there's no reason the police would have carried out a particularly thorough search of the area. At the time, they didn't even know about a potential passenger at all. Gemma could be a hundred metres from the car, and nobody would even have a clue.

I jump at a knock on the door. Opening it, I see Tara, vacuum cleaner in tow.

'I was wondering,' I say. 'Can you show me where exactly the crashed car was found?'

Tara looks surprised. 'On the top road?'

'I'd like to go up there. Have a look myself.'

I take out my phone and place it on the bureau. After a little bit of orientation, Tara shows me the road, which threads a lonely path across empty landscape. 'Somewhere on that stretch,' she says, indicating a section. 'Not sure exactly.'

I drop a pin and switch to a satellite view, which confirms there's not so much as a farm building up there. It's hard to see why there's even a road at all. My app tells me that it'll take almost thirty minutes to get up there, and the route skirts in a wide loop across the moorland.

'If you wait another half-hour, I can get Archie to go with you,' Tara offers.

I can't think of anything worse, so I tell her that won't

be necessary. 'I'm a big girl,' I say. I don't want to sour things, but I have to know more about him. 'Is he your only child?'

Tara smiles. 'I've got a daughter too, but they're chalk and cheese. She moved out years ago – works in Newcastle now. Archie's more of a mummy's boy.'

'It must be nice to have him around.'

'When he pulls his weight!' she says. 'He helps Bill out at the house too.'

'Oh yes, with what?'

'They've got a veg patch,' she explains. 'Well, more than a patch. Sells things to the local farmers' markets. Green-fingered, you know.'

'Very wholesome.'

'His dad's in the nick,' she says wryly, 'so anything's a bonus.'

I want to ask more, though I can't see a way not to make her uncomfortable. All sons are the apples of their mother's eyes, aren't they?

Besides, maybe I'm reading more into Archie than is fair. It's a cliché that apples don't drop far from trees, and it's certainly not his fault his father was a criminal.

'I can sort the room now if you're heading out?' says Tara.

I thank her, asking for a minute. On my own once more, I tuck my laptop in its case, and zip up my bag, arranging a few items on top in a specific configuration. I'll know if anyone else has been poking around.

Back outside, the crisp morning is already starting to fade. The comms mast in the distance has been obscured with low cloud.

I walk to the car, but draw up a few metres short.

'You're kidding me!'

Down the driver's side, from the front wing to the petrol cap, are several deep, roughly parallel scratches about two centimetres apart. I have no idea what's made them. The fact there are five and they follow an undulating scored path indicates this was no accidental collision – someone reversing out clumsily from the car park.

I look out to the main road, as if the culprit might miraculously be around and looking sheepish, but I'm alone. My first thought, again, is Archie, and my anger flares. He'd only have to step out from the back of the pub, commit the act of vandalism and slip back inside. However, I can hardly call Dewer and demand his interrogation based on a gut feeling. I've already pushed too hard, and there might come a time I need the police on my side.

My second thought, maybe unfairly, is what Doug's going to say when he sees it. *Told you it was a bad idea going up there . . .*

I run my splayed fingers along the gouges, and it strikes me that they could almost be made with someone's nails, if nails were capable of cutting into metallic paint.

'You all right there?'

I turn and see Nige, the chatty bloke from the bar the night before. I gesture to the car. 'I'm not sure. Maybe someone's taken a dislike to me?'

He ambles up to me, limping. It looks like a chronic injury of some sort. His expression is troubled. 'Oh, that won't do at all!' he says. 'It happened last night, did it?'

'Must have, I think.'

He rubs his chin, then looks at me sheepishly. 'Listen, I hope you don't mind, but I was just up by the hostel. Carla

139

told me it was someone you knew up in that car. And that your sister's missing.'

'That's right. Sorry I didn't mention it yesterday. I don't know what to think at the moment.'

'Agh, no bother,' he says, with a wave of his hand. 'Thing is, I was up there, that night.'

'Really.'

'I'm volunteer fire service,' he explains. 'Couple of nights a week. Keeps me busy.'

'I read the fire mostly burned out,' I tell him.

'That's right. Thing is, we'd already had one hoax call, the night before, at Brocklehurst Hall. Sent two engines out for nowt. Not saying we didn't rush, but . . .'

'I doubt it would have made much difference,' I reply.

'Well, that's what I thought,' he says. 'Anyway, I thought you should know.'

'I'm actually going to go and look now,' I say.

'Oh, is that right? Nowt much to see, I wouldn't think. I'm pretty sure there was no one else besides the man. To be honest, there weren't much of *him*.'

I grimace. 'So the police said.' I lower my voice, glancing briefly at the pub, 'I know we've just met, but if you do hear anything that you think might be relevant . . .'

'Of course!' he says. 'You'll be the first to know.' He looks about ready to say something else, but gives me a nod. 'Anyway, be careful up there.'

Chapter 19

GEMMA

It was definitely him. The same black and yellow bike was parked at the back of the pub, between the glass bin and a woodshed. From what Gemma could see, he worked in the kitchen mainly, and occasionally behind the bar too. She wondered who else at the pub might be in on it.

Back at the hostel, she watched as Mark wrote out a message on a piece of paper.

We know what you've got at the house. We know what you're doing. Pay us and we'll be quiet.

'What's the number again?' he asked.

She read the digits off the slip that had come with the phone. The cheapest model bought from a service station. Another up-front cost to their scheme.

Mark wrote the number at the end of the message, then underlined it.

'What if they don't call?' asked Gemma.

'They will,' said Mark. 'Even if it's to tell us to fuck off.'

'And they definitely can't track it?'

'It's a burner. That's the whole point. Why'd do you think drug dealers use them?'

She admired Mark's confidence, even if it scared her. It was a world he knew more about than her, even if he was long out of it. A knot was growing in the pit of her stomach. There was still time to forget all this, to leave Hartsbridge without upsetting anyone. Brighton was impossible if they didn't have money to pay Tyler, but that didn't mean there weren't other places they could go. They'd find work. They'd manage somehow. She'd said as much to Mark, several times. 'Who wants to manage?' he'd said. 'I'm fed up of managing. We deserve better.'

He folded the note.

'How much are you going to ask for?' she said.

'Ten grand.'

'Seriously?'

'You think we should say more?'

'We only owe Des two. Let's not get greedy.'

'Ten grand's nothing to them,' said Mark. 'They need to think we're serious. You ready?'

'Now?'

'Why not. The pub looked busy.'

They'd spoken about how they'd deliver the note. As far as they could tell, the pub had CCTV at the front and another camera inside, but the car park at the back was unmonitored, and that's where the bike was parked. There were a couple of horses in the field behind, which seemed to attract people to the fence. Mark would probably draw more attention if he tried to get close, so the plan was for him to keep a lookout, away from the cameras, and Gemma to slip round and leave the note somewhere on the bike. If she saw anyone, she'd backtrack. If confronted, she would say she was looking for her boyfriend who'd come out for a smoke. It was simple really, and Mark kept saying it couldn't go wrong.

Gemma suddenly needed the loo very badly.

'Give me a sec, okay?'

'Sure, I'll see you out the front.'

She sat on the toilet and held her hand in front of her. It was shaking.

When she'd finished, she washed her hands in the mirror and stared at her own face. 'You can do this,' she whispered.

She put on her coat and opened the door of the room. Standing on the other side, right in her way, was the guy with red hair. She screamed, and he in turn stumbled backwards into the wall behind, dropping the towels in his arms and putting his hands over his ears.

Mark came bundling through from the reception, eyes taking in the scene.

'What are you doing to her?'

He advanced on the man, who started picking the towels up off the floor.

'No,' said Gemma, getting in between them. 'It's just a misunderstanding.'

Mark put his arm around her shoulders and escorted her out into the corridor. 'I don't like the way he looks at you,' he said.

Gemma wanted to go back and check the man was okay, but Mark seemed determined to leave. Together, they exited the hostel.

'Honestly,' she said. 'He didn't do anything. There's something wrong with him.'

'Yeah, he's a weirdo. I bet he's got a spyhole, or something.'

Gemma didn't have the strength to argue.

Across the road from the pub, Mark took a position under the trees by the bridge, and lit up a fag. He handed her the note. 'You ready?'

Gemma nodded. She didn't feel ready at all.

Mark kissed her on the forehead. 'You got this, babe.'

She crossed the street, towards the car park, under the sign of a decapitated woman. As she approached, a couple of young women came through the door, laughing loudly. They paid her no attention. Gemma rounded the back of the pub through the car park, then walked as confidently as she could towards the back. The horses were in the middle of the field, and no one else was about. She approached the motorbike, pausing briefly to check the rear of the pub. There was some movement behind the frosted glass of an illuminated window of the kitchen or perhaps a toilet, but she knew she couldn't be seen.

A helmet was hooked over the bike's handlebar. With her eyes glue to the back of the building, Gemma slipped the note inside the helmet itself. Then she wondered – what if it were to fall out, unseen on the ground? So, instead, she tucked it firmly between the dashboard and the small windshield. He couldn't miss it there.

Something touched her knee, and she drew back, stifling a gasp. It was just a cat, black as night with green eyes. Gemma bent down to stroke it, and it purred softly. Then she hurried back the way she'd come, crossing over to where Mark was waiting, smoking under the trees. He turned as

144

soon as she reached him, and together they walked back up
the hill towards the hostel.

'Now what?' she asked. Her heart was pounding.

'Now we wait,' said Mark.

Chapter 20

SARAH

My mind won't move on from Archie as I drive out of Hartsbridge, passing several quaint-looking cottages and what looks like an old chapel. He knows something, and he doesn't want me here. I try to consider other possibilities for his shiftiness. Maybe he does remember Gemma and simply doesn't want to be involved. Perhaps he's been in trouble with the police before. I wonder if there's a way to find out his shift patterns at the pub, to find out what he was doing the night Mark's car went off the road. It would be hard to get the information out of Tara without raising a major red flag, but if I could look at the CCTV of the bar area again, he might be conspicuous by his absence.

Then again, this all might be my paranoia. The scratches would be a petty way to try and get rid of me, more likely to raise suspicion than throw me off the scent. They really could've been anyone.

Leaving the village behind, I'm back alongside the river, near the valley floor, alongside open fields dotted with livestock and the occasional barn or feeding station sprouting hay. The landscape is distinctly sectioned by drystone walls and intermittent barbed-wire fence, but it's noticeable that the fields only extend to a certain altitude, after which heather and moorland take over and it all looks far less hospitable. There are rocky gullies cutting north to south, presumably watercourses draining from the ground above.

The car's navigation system takes me a different route to the one on my phone, promising to shave ten minutes off the journey, and I turn up a single-lane track, winding through a thick forest, with tight bends and little space to manoeuvre around the odd pothole. I hope I don't meet anything coming the other way.

Almost as soon as I think it, a Land Rover appears on the road ahead, coming at speed. I slam on the brakes, and feel the wheels skid. The car's rear end slides out, off the tarmac, and I'm heading for a tree. I close my eyes and grip the wheel, waiting for the thump.

It never comes, and I open my eyes again to see the trunk right in front of the bonnet. It takes a second or two to remember the mechanics of breathing. I unclip my seatbelt and get out, legs shaking. I check the car, hardly able to believe there was no impact. Sure enough, there's half an inch between me and the tree. The Land Rover has remained on the road, exhaust pumping out grey fumes. Its reverse lights come on, and it backs up casually until it's alongside me. Despite the cold, the window is wound down and sitting behind the wheel is the grumpy man from the night before at the pub. Bill Farrah.

'What the bloody hell are you doing out here?' he growls.

I'd been expecting a polite enquiry about my well-being, given my car is slewed off the road, and my immediate reaction is outrage.

'You almost killed me,' I said. 'Ever heard of speed limits?'

He climbs out of his car too, big leather boots hitting the road. He looks up and down the track, as if watchful for anyone else nearby. My anger is gone in a second, replaced by fear. I'm on my own out here in the middle of nowhere. Last night's speculations on gothic murder mysteries suddenly feel a lot less amusing.

'This is a private road,' he says. 'There's a sign.'

'I didn't see it,' I reply, and my tone is annoyingly querulous.

Farrah reaches back inside the Land Rover and pulls out a long-barrelled shotgun.

'Maybe you weren't looking,' he says.

I take a backward step, almost tripping over a tree root. This has to be a joke.

'I don't appreciate you threatening me with a gun,' I say, mustering any semblance of defiance I can.

'Round here, we don't take kindly to trespassers,' says Farrah.

He's just a bully, I tell myself. He's getting off on this. 'Do I need to call the police?' I ask, trying my very best to maintain my composure.

He guffaws, the lifts the shotgun to his shoulder and points it right at me. A sensation I've never had before – like cold liquid – creeps through my legs. I want to move, but I can't. The two barrels skewer me to the spot. 'Go on then,' he says.

My phone is in my pocket. There's no way I'm going to reach for it. I can't believe this is happening, but if he's willing to point that thing at me, what else could he do? No one else knows I'm here. As far as Tara is aware, I'm driving to the top road.

'I suggest you go back the way you came,' says Farrah. His aim hasn't shifted.

There's no good way to answer his challenge. I don't think he's going to be interested in my excuses about my satnav. It's not the first time it's given questionable advice. Sent Doug down a one-way street in rush-hour London two years ago, which provided him with a fun dinner-party anecdote.

'Gladly,' I reply.

I move back to the car, and he follows me silently with the barrel. Only when I start my engine does he lower the gun, then climb back into his vehicle. I'm shaking, almost uncontrollably. How dare he? As soon as I'm away from here, I'm going to call the police. How fucking *dare* he?

I assume he'll drive away, but he doesn't. He glowers from his seat as I'm forced to perform a seven-point turn under his watchful eye, then we drive back towards the main road. He follows close behind, like a bouncer escorting a rowdy punter from a nightclub. At the bottom of the hill, I indicate left, and he goes the other way, back towards Hartsbridge. I pull over once he's out of sight in the rear-view mirror. The adrenaline slowly drains from my blood, and I realise that calling the police is probably pointless. What can I say that won't be contradicted by Farrah himself? It'll be my word against his. Outsider vs local. Hysterical woman vs no-nonsense bloke.

Why was he so angry though? I've only met him once, and we barely said a word to one another. The reaction seemed disproportionate to someone accidentally straying up a private road – unless there's something at the end of it he wants to hide. I use the satnav to explore and see that the road I've just left actually heads directly to Brocklehurst Hall itself. It's hard to believe Farrah is so protective about his vegetable patch.

Before I really know what I'm doing, I call Doug.

He doesn't pick up, and after the beep tone for his message, I'm a bit stuck for words.

'Hey, sweetheart. I . . . I just wanted to speak to you. I think I'll be back later. Maybe. Talk later hopefully.' Only when I've hung up do I think that was a really weird message.

The satnav wants to take me back the way I've just come, so I ignore it, driving on until it reroutes me. The country I cross is shallow rolling valleys, more scattered farmland, but as often as not it looks empty, with only the occasional crow flapping across heather. The cloud has thickened over the morning, and a telecoms mast on a distant hill becomes intermittently visible through the low fog. Drystone walls and the odd crumbling sheepfold tell of forgotten practices. There are signs warning of deer crossing.

I'm gradually gaining height though, and the car's thermo-meter shows the dropping temperature. Condensation starts to blur the windscreen, without any actual rainfall. I cross a river over a clanking metal bridge, then follow the contours of a hillside. The landscape to the left seems to be desolate moor, and to the right it drops away to what must be a stream. There's no barrier above the slope, so I play it safe and stick to the middle of the road, travelling slowly to avoid a repeat of my near-miss earlier. I somehow doubt I'll bump into anyone though, and certainly not travelling at the reckless speed of Bill Farrah.

After a few miles of seeing no one, a chevron sign looms ahead from the mist. It's bent over, twisted out of shape as if something has collided with it. A strand of blue police tape tied to one side is flickering in the breeze. I pull level and stop, leaving the engine running with the hazards on. This must be the spot.

I take the umbrella from the footwell in the back seat and climb out, hitching it up.

Then I walk to the slope side of the road. The umbrella does nothing – the damp comes in from every direction anyway.

The car, I'm surprised to see, is still there, lying in the water, on its roof, a charred mess. Its black undercarriage is exposed to the elements, and the boot and the driver's door hang open. It reminds me of some giant, dead flying beetle, flipped onto its shell. The path it took from tarmac to resting place is obvious from the flattened chevron barrier, and the damage to the heather on the slope. I see at once that it was coming from the other direction – further into the moorland – rather than the way I've approached. It must have been terrifying, especially at night. And maybe it's not such a mystery why the vehicle has been left where it crashed. Hard to see how anything except a large crane could retrieve it from down there. Presumably the local council will come to get it at some point.

On the road, there are dark skid marks, twisting across the tarmac for about twenty metres back from the damaged sign. It looks like he saw the turn too late and slammed on the brakes, losing control. If it was icy, like the woman at the hostel said, that would only have made it worse.

I'm not sure what I'm doing, or what I hope to find, so I fold the umbrella and climb over the remains of the barrier. I pick my way between the sprouting heather and thistles, steadying myself first on the twisted corner sign, then by gripping the soaking heather with my hands while using the brolly as a stick for balance. My Converse trainers aren't meant for these conditions, and my foot slips out from beneath me. I slide down a few feet, hands scrabbling, before managing to gain purchase again, but the impact with the ground sends a painful jolt through my hips and knocks the breath partially from my chest. I gather myself, soaked already.

With more care, I reach the base of the slope, where the ground is spongy and saturated. The river isn't wide – maybe three metres, cutting deep banks through the peaty ground. The car is twenty paces away.

I make my way to it, shoes sinking with each step. Closer, and I'm sure it's not just my imagination, there's a smoky tang in the air, even though the fire was extinguished days ago. The driver's side is closest, and it's been severely crushed, so the car lists slightly in that direction, towards me.

I don't want to look inside, but I force myself. It's just metal – the seats scorched to their frames, the steering wheel gone, the dashboard melted away. No windows or windscreen. Glass is scattered on the banks in a thousand tiny pieces, and more sparkles under the babbling stream. The back end of the car is a gaping, open wound in the chassis, like something's taken a bite out of the vehicle. I'm relieved there's no sign of any human remains.

I walk around to the other side, where the door has been

153

separated from the passenger side and propped on the ground – from the way the metal has been sheared through in a clumsy line, I guess they must have cut it away to get at Mark, or whatever was left of him. I can't envy the poor sods given that job. I never cared for Gemma's boyfriend, never really knew him at all apart from our brief, unfortunate encounter at Mum's wake, but I couldn't wish this end on anyone. At least he wouldn't have suffered long, if the post-mortem was anything to go by.

To look into the rear seats of the car, I have to step carefully into it and drop into a crouch. Only metallic skeletal fittings and framework remain.

I'm not sure what I was expecting by coming up to this place – some signal, obvious or subtle, that my sister was here. But there's so little left, I realise the hope was forlorn – the ground around the car is black and grey with ash.

Backing away, my eyes are drawn to the blackened bodywork. *Hold on* . . .

There are scratches.

I swallow.

Five of them.

Or, at least, they might be scratches. With the outer paintwork completely stripped, they're really only pale lines.

I run my fingers along them, trying to feel relief in the markings, and I'm not sure if my mind is deceiving me or not. Only a few inches appear on the rear side door, so it could easily be something that happened in the chaos of the accident.

I straighten up and turn to the separated door. The inner side is exposed, and the glass has gone, but I knock it over flat. Sure enough, on the other side, there are matching markings, the continued trails of the same gouges. Just as on my car, the full scars must extend a couple of feet at least. Like someone's dragged some sort of tool along the side of the vehicle.

Or – and I know this is silly – a claw.

I chuckle, self-consciously. Legends like the Beast of Brocklehurst Hall are all very well in the comfort of a warm pub, but out here, alone, there's a wholly different feel. Now I've travelled out of the village and seen how wild and uninhabited it is up here, it's not *quite* so hard to believe there might be something roaming the pathless hills.

Of course, that makes no sense. My car was vandalised in the car park. And it's quite probable it was the act of the same person. Perhaps simply a bored delinquent kid, the sort that exists in every town and city. Still, I *will* pass this onto the police. I don't care that it's not what the reluctant constable might term evidence; it's not nothing either.

I start to walk downstream. If my sister *was* here – if she did somehow escape the wreckage, she might have gone in any direction. Downhill makes the most sense. Back towards civilisation. Images of her crawling and bleeding won't be chased away, but I know it's just my overactive imagination. Since seeing her on the CCTV, she's a ghost. She might be anywhere in this vast landscape, or nowhere – a theoretical needle in a haystack. Still, I scan the ground as I go, looking for prints of any kind.

There's nothing, my feet are soaked, boots mud-clogged. I've gone less than a hundred metres, slim hopes fading, and my practical brain telling me to turn back, when I spot something in the water a few metres away, distorted through the ripples. Stepping closer, my initial suspicions are confirmed.

It's money.

I have to use stepping stones to reach it. Not just any money. The note – a fifty – is curled over, lodged against some rocks by the current. Reaching into the freezing water, I fish it out. It's soggy but not yet disintegrated, and I know it came from the car because one corner is black and charred.

New possibilities arise, things that make me feel more uneasy than before. Fifty-quid notes aren't common currency – and surely not for my sister. I don't think I've seen one myself for a few years. I slip it into my pocket, and walk a little further, scanning for more. I don't see any.

I head back to the slope and climb carefully up to the road, my legs heavy, a leaden feeling in my gut and profoundly depressed. I've one hand on the car door when I have the uncomfortable feeling that I'm not actually alone. It's just a prickle, and I spin on the spot. It's the 'claw'-marks I'm thinking of, but it's a person I see.

Standing on the other side of the river, the figure is hard to make out in the shifting mist. I'm certain it's a man. He's completely still, dressed in a hood and long coat. There's forty metres and a river between us. I'm not exactly scared – I could get into the car and drive away before he got anywhere close – but it's unnerving nonetheless. The fear from the encounter with Farrah lingers, and the possibility occurs to me that this person too might wields a gun, concealed under his outdoor garb. He's looking in my direction, completely still.

'Hello?' I shout.

There's no reply, and I wonder if my voice has carried over the wind. I fumble in my coat pocket for my phone. If he can see, he probably thinks I'm calling the police, but there's no signal anyway. Instead, I point the phone towards him, selecting the camera. He turns and starts to move away as I press the shutter several times. I get a few shots before he disappears behind the hill as if he was never there at all.

Chapter 21

GEMMA

The phone rang at close to 8 p.m., a low buzzing on the windowsill of the hostel room. Mark and Gemma both stared at it, but he moved first and snatched it up.

'You got the note?' he said.

Gemma studied his face, trying to work out what was being said at the other end of the line. He lowered the phone from his ear.

'They hung up,' he said. 'Why'd they hang up?'

'Is there a number?'

Mark looked at the phone and pressed a couple of buttons, then shook his head. 'Withheld.'

'So we can't call back?'

'It's okay, babe – they'll call back.'

'So what do we do now?'

'Nothing,' replied Mark, nodding as if to convince himself. 'We've got them on the hook, babe. They know it. We've just got to be patient before we bring 'em in.' He mimed himself with a fishing rod, manipulating the reel.

Gemma swallowed. Did he really believe that? Were they really in control here? Mark loved going fishing, and he'd even persuaded her to go with him a couple of times, early in their relationship. Hours spent on the quay, watching for a twitch on the line, starting at the leaden, opaque surface of the sea. She hated the water. Partly because, to her shame, she'd never learned to swim. But also because you never knew what was down there, lurking.

'It's going to be okay,' he said, for the hundredth time.

She put her arms around him from behind, laying her cheek against his back. The reasoned words, the familiar objections, were all queued up in her throat. It was pointless to give them voice again. So instead she squeezed him and tried to imagine a point in time when this was over, when they'd be back in Brighton, their debts paid, maybe sitting on the beach on a sunny day with ice creams in their hands. The sort of thing they'd done in the early days of their relationship.

The vision was fragile, and she clung to it.

Chapter 22

SARAH

Back in my car, I use my finger and thumb to expand the photo of the stranger of the hill. The quality is terrible. There are six photos, catching him in the process of turning. Whether it's the fact he was moving, or the mist was interfering with the camera-phone's focus, his face is a smear under a dark hood. I'm left with little other than a vague impression of a slight figure, medium height, in a long green or brown coat. His hands are thrust into his pockets. His age is impossible to gauge. It wasn't Bill Farrah — he's too small for that.

On the face it, it's not really suspicious. Why shouldn't there be a walker out there? Or simply someone else taking a curious look at the sight of a well-documented local accident? And maybe he wasn't actually watching me at all. He may not have heard my voice calling to him.

Still, on top of all the other weirdness — the scratches, and now the money — I can't dismiss it.

Driving back into Hartsbridge, I think about pulling over to ring Dewer then and there. Or maybe his boss, Sergeant Nelson. I'm passing the old chapel-like building again, only this time there's someone outside, on the narrow pavement, standing on top of a small stepladder wearing a high-vis tabard and inspecting the top of a sprawling bush. It's the guy who runs the art studio, Neil something. As I slow down, he raises a pair of secateurs in greeting. I'm not sure if he actually recognises me, or if he's just being friendly. I wonder though . . . maybe I don't have to trouble the police just yet. I've got this far on my own, and the more information I can gather independently, the better my case will be.

I pull over on the stretch of road just beyond and I put on the hazards.

Climbing out, I walk back towards the man on the ladder. He watches me, and his raised eyebrows suggest he's surprised.

'Howdo?' he says, climbing down. 'Any joy with your sister?'

'Afraid not. Actually, I could use your help again.'

He pulls off the gardening gloves he's wearing. 'Do you want to come in?' He gestures towards the building. It's his house, then, I assume.

'Oh, no, I don't want to disturb you! It's just, I've taken this photograph, and I hoped you might recognise the person in it?' I take out my phone.

He squints. 'I'd need my glasses. You're sure I can't interest you in a slice of cake? My mother's been baking. She bakes like there's still three of us, and I'm diabetic, so most of it ends up on the bird tables!'

After the breakfast, I'm not hungry, but he's being so nice, I can't say no. 'You've convinced me.' I look back towards the car and lock it.

He leads me in, up the path between more roses. The whole garden is immaculate – with borders and sculpted hedges and an apple tree. The building itself is single storey, with arched windows, though there's an extra section at the end, making a L-shape. A small engraved plaque above the door reads 1798.

'It's a beautiful place,' I say, as we enter the open porch area. 'What's the history?'

'Methodist chapel,' replies Neil. 'I bought it years ago for a song. It was a hell of a mess, but we got there in the end.'

'I thought you were local,' I say.

'We are,' he replied. 'We were over on the Ravenow side before, when my father was alive. He worked for all the farms, providing veterinary services. Now it's just me and Mum, and she was starting to struggle with the stairs. So when this place came up at auction, I decided to move.'

He leads me into an entrance hall, with an uneven polished parquet floor. A short corridor leads off into the house, and a set of double doors are open on a large, double-height kitchen, which I can only guess used to be the main hall. There are photos on the walls of the landscape, many of which look similar in style to those in his shop. There are some more figurative paintings too. The smell of sweet baking fills the air.

He keeps his shoes on, so I do the same, as he leads me into the kitchen. There's a large range in the centre, its chimney rising through the ceiling. The rest is an old-fashioned country kitchen, hand-crafted from wood. In a living area beyond, a tiny elderly woman sits in an armchair, eyes closed, with knitting on her lap.

It's when I see the configuration of the windows inside that I realise I recognise this room from a photo.

'Did this used to be the school?' I say.

'Indeed,' says Neil. He takes a knife from a drawer. 'Sunday School first, then the local primary. It shut down – what? – maybe ten years ago.'

'So Alice Brocklehurst went here?'

He cuts into a loaf of fruit cake on a cooling rack. 'You've heard about poor Alice then?'

'Just a small bit for me,' I say. 'Did you know her?'

'Of her, really. The family were a funny lot. Kept her indoors most of the time. I suppose she might well have come here though. This place used to cater for all the village kids. Came here myself as a nipper! Isn't that right, Mum?'

He's talking to the old woman, but she doesn't say anything.

'I think she's asleep,' I say.

'Oh, so she is,' he chuckles. 'Anyway, this photograph . . .' He deposits a substantial piece of fruit cake on the counter in front of me on a small Willow-pattern plate. Then he reaches to a shelf and takes a pair of spectacles, resting them on his nose.

I take out the phone again and show him the photo. 'It might be nothing, but I'd like to know who this is.'

He looks a moment, then asks, 'Where is this?'

I tell him that I was on the 'top road', as Tara called it, and add it's where the car accident happened a few days before. I bite into the cake. 'This is delicious, by the way.'

Neil smiles warmly. 'What were you doing up there?' he asks.

It seems wrong to keep him in the dark, when he's being so helpful, so I explain that the man who died was my sister's partner.

He looks at me sympathetically. 'Now I see why you're so worried for your sister.' He sighs. 'I couldn't say for certain, but I have a feeling it's Patrick Draper.'

The name rings a bell. I heard it before, at the pub. 'The man who believes the legend of the big cat?'

Neil laughs. 'Believes? He'd swear it blind.'

'And you don't?' I take another bite of cake.

Neil smiles again, this time in a withering way, and hands back the phone. 'No, I don't.'

'Does he live nearby – Draper?'

'Other side of Hartsbridge. The old mill-house. I'd steer clear though.'

'They said he was harmless in the pub,' I say. 'I'd very much like to talk to him.'

Neil shrugs. 'I can't stop you. Just take what he says with more than a grain of salt.' He lowers his voice, 'Back when the Brocklehurst girl went missing, he was telling everyone it was the cat.' He gives air quotes. 'Even went up to the house and pestered the family. He and Bill Farrah came to blows over it one night at the pub. Bill gave him a hiding.'

'Why?'

'Because it's claptrap. The family were grieving; the last thing they needed to hear was his mumbo-jumbo.'

'I had a run-in with Bill Farrah earlier today,' I tell him. 'He seems to have a problem with me.'

'Bill's got a problem with the world,' he says. 'Don't take it personally.'

'He actually pointed a gun at me.'

Neil's eyes widen. 'You should tell the police. That's not right.'

'I think I probably will,' I say. 'Someone scratched my car last night, too.'

'Oh dear – I am sorry. It doesn't sound like a typical Hartsbridge welcome!'

'I . . . I can't help thinking that people know more than they're saying, about Gemma.' I pause. 'What's up there, at the house?'

Neil shrugs. 'Nothing much, that I know of. It's sad, really. In its day, it was rather grand.'

'So what does Farrah actually *do*?'

'Stops the place falling down,' laughs Neil. 'Have you seen it?'

I shake my head. 'Why don't they just sell it?'

Neil smiles sadly. 'Maybe it's not that simple, when you've got a connection to a place. The family left after Alice went missing, but I think that was more Lady Brocklehurst's decision. The house has been in the male line for hundreds of years. Tradition is hard to break.'

'And is there no male heir now?'

'Not a direct one, but I wouldn't know the ins-and-outs of the family tree,' he says. 'You're asking the wrong person, I'm afraid.'

I wonder if I should tell Neil about the money, or the scratches on Mark's car, but I've burdened him enough, and he's been more than helpful already. 'I'd better be going,' I tell him. 'Thank you for the advice.' I look past him, at the old woman. 'Thank your mother for the cake too!'

Neil shows me back to the door.

166

On the threshold, I ask him, 'I know the cat thing is far-fetched. Is it absolutely impossible though?'

He looks at me quizzically, like he actually doubts my sanity. 'Anything is possible, I suppose. But, no, I think it's very unlikely. Apart from Paddy Draper, there've been no sightings. No livestock deaths. I've spent as many hours in those hills over the years as anyone with my camera, and I've never seen a thing.'

'But there must be rabbits up there? Creatures like that. Food.'

Neil takes a deep, patient breath. 'Hold on two ticks – I want to show you something.'

He retreats through another door into what looks like an office. I see him reach up to a shelf for a box file, which he carries back out to me. He places it on a phone table beside the door.

'Dad didn't have a great deal of time for the Brocklehursts in the first place.' He opens the file and takes out a stack of photos, leafing through. 'Thought they were mad keeping all the animals they did. He was more of a sheep and horses man.' He turns a photo around to show me a picture of a man in a tweed suit, standing in front of a cage. On the other side is a black panther, staring fiercely at the camera too. Even though the quality is poor, the size and presence of the big cat are astonishing.

'Is that your father?' I ask.

Neil nods. 'This was before I came along. Dad never liked to talk about it, but my mother told me later. When old Thomas couldn't get rid of all the animals, it was my father he called on to do the business for him.'

'He euthanised them?'

Neil nods. 'Don't get me wrong. My father wasn't senti-mental. Far from it, in fact. Couldn't be in his line of work. And I'm sure they paid him handsomely. But it must have been a hell of a thing to kill something like that, don't you think?'

Chapter 23

GEMMA

'What do you want?' said a voice on speaker. It was muffled, electronically distorted. Sexless. It creeped her out, because it meant that whoever was speaking wasn't taking this lightly at all. It was just before nine.

Mark stood over the phone. He had toothpaste round his mouth, because he'd dashed straight through on hearing the ring. He glanced briefly at Gemma.

'You know. Money.' He paused. 'Twenty grand.'

She widened her eyes in surprise.

A laugh. 'We don't have that sort of cash.'

'You'd better get it then, or the police will be banging on your door.'

There followed a few seconds of silence, the phone's speaker muffled. Gemma imagined whoever it was talking to somebody else.

When the voice spoke again, it was direct and untroubled. 'Who are you?'

'Doesn't matter,' replied Mark. 'We know who you are.'

'I don't think you do,' said the voice.

'Listen,' said Mark. 'Enough talking. It's twenty thousand.'

'I told you, we don't have it.'

'Get it, then,' instructed Mark. He reached down and hung up. As he straightened, he let out a long breath. Gemma could see his hands were trembling and pale.

'Twenty thousand?' she asked.

'Why not?' said Mark.

'Do you think it was him, from the pub?'

'Who knows? There was the other guy at the house too.'

'What if they've really not got the money?'

Mark didn't answer, but she could see the first signs of defeat in his features. In turn, she felt a trickle of relief. This could be over at last. It broke her heart a bit too, though. He'd got them this far, against the odds. She knew what it meant to him to make it work.

A door slamming somewhere made them both flinch. It was followed by the sounds of raucous laughter in the corridor outside. Other guests coming back from a few drinks, perhaps.

'I think we should go to the pub,' said Gemma.

'Are you crazy? He might be there.'

'Exactly. They'll be looking for us now. And the best way not to draw attention is to fit in.'

Mark sighed. 'You're right. But what if they call back?' Gemma picked up the phone, and switched it to silent. 'Hey, what are you—'

'Let them sweat a bit,' she said. She pushed it under a pillow.

'But they might—'

'If they call back, they're on the hook, like you said. They'll call again. We can't seem too desperate.'

'I guess so,' Mark replied, though he looked uncertain.

'Trust me,' she said. 'Come on – just an hour. I need a drink.'

It was only the young man at the reception desk, and he gave a smile as they left.

Music drifted up from the pub. It was busy inside, considering it was only a Tuesday night, and all the tables were occupied. At one end was a low-key karaoke set-up. A fat guy in Crocs was belting out the crescendo of an Ed Sheeran hit. There were two young women in the bar, and no sign of the motorbike rider.

'I'll get drinks,' she said.

She pressed forwards towards the bar while Mark hung back. While she waited, she surveyed the other people in the room. It was a mixed crowd, and from their clothes, a mixture of locals and outdoorsy types. The busyness made it seem safer somehow. Maybe they weren't in such danger as she'd feared. The people from the house would more likely suspect it was someone who knew the area, maybe from one of the other nearby villages.

She ordered a pint of lager for Mark and a double vodka tonic for herself.

The singer finished to much applause and calls for an encore. 'Sorry, ladies and gentlemen!' he said through the mic. 'I've got places to be.'

Gemma took the drinks and headed over to where Mark was standing near the door. He was peering at a picture on the wall.

'Kid's riding a bloody emu,' he said. She handed him the pint. 'Ta, babe.'

She turned her attention to a framed photo. It took a second or two to realise it showed the country house they'd visited earlier, from much better days. A man was standing outside, beside a young boy sitting on a giant bird.

'I think it's an ostrich,' she said, sipping from her glass.

Mark looked at her and grinned. 'Oh right. Makes *much* more sense.'

She laughed, almost spitting out the drink. It was good for the act, yet it felt wrong, given the circumstances, to find amusement in anything.

There'd be time for laughter later, when they'd left Hartsbridge behind.

Chapter 24

SARAH

The Old Mill is right on the water, about three hundred metres from the pub. The river actually appears to flow under an outbuilding, and from the name of the house, I wonder if there might once have been a waterwheel there, before the Industrial Revolution brought steam to power such operations. The house certainly looks old enough.

As I drive past slowly, there's no sign of life inside. Under a carport, there's an ancient red Volvo with no hubcaps and an interior of pale tan leather. If it was Patrick Draper up there at the crash site, on foot, there's no way he could be back here yet. Unsure of quite what I will say if he does come to the door, I knock. Inside, a dog barks loudly.

I wait a couple of minutes, then knock again. This time, the dog is silent, but no one else seems home.

Returning to the car, I feel utterly deflated. Short of buying a pair of walking boots and heading into the hills, combing back and forth, I don't see what else I can do here. And even then, what would be the chances of finding Gemma? If she did somehow crawl out of that wreckage, I could be ten metres from her body and not know it.

As the myriad possibilities vie in my fevered thoughts for attention, I have mad ideas. Could I hire a helicopter pilot to sweep the area? It might cost a few thousand, and Doug would think I was insane. But if she's out there, somewhere . . .

No. What really would be the point? If my sister is on those hills, miracles don't happen. She's dead by now, just like the runner who went missing. Like Alice Brocklehurst, if that's what happened to her. Swallowed by the earth.

There is still something I can do, though. It occurred to me from the very moment I tried to call Gemma back in London and it wouldn't connect. I think I pushed it to the back of my mind for one very obvious reason – I don't break the law. Not first and foremost because I have a moral problem with it, but because of my job. I've seen enough lawyers think they're bending the rules, who end up getting disbarred. The legal press revels in such incidents – minor frauds usually. Incomprehensible schemes to get a few extra quid, which ends up crashing a career.

But the police won't help me, so I can convince myself I don't really have a choice.

As I scroll through my contacts, the ID I land on is Felicity Grace. I'm fairly sure that's not her real name. I think she might once have been a police officer, or connected to the Met, though I'm not sure.

We use Felicity for the trickier electronic surveillance work – and we don't question her methods. She's a genius whom I've never met in person, but who never fails to get results. If there's a trail of ones and zeroes, she can sniff it out. Yet I'm acutely aware that what I'm about to ask her isn't typical at all. This is personal.

She picks up straight away.

'Ms Kline?' There's music in the background – a thumping bass.

'Hi, Felicity. Odd job for you, off the books.'

'Sounds intriguing.'

'Can you track the last-known location of a mobile phone? If I give you the number?'

'Does the phone belong to you?'

'No.'

'Your child?'

'Er . . . no.'

'Then it's against the law. Hey, aren't *you* a lawyer?'

'I am.'

'That's what I thought.'

She doesn't say anything else for a few seconds.

It's the next bit that could get me into trouble, and I'm struggling to find the right words. So instead I use the wrong ones. 'I'm trying to find my sister. She's gone missing, and the police have given up. I don't know what to do.'

'I'm sorry – I can't help you, Ms Kline.'

She hangs up.

I look at the phone despondently. So much for that plan.

I'm about to start the engine, when my phone rings. It's an unknown number.

'Sorry about that,' says Felicity. 'Couldn't speak on that line. So, what's your sister's number?'

'You can do it?'

175

'Almost certainly.'

'I can pay you.'

'Oh, I know that. Just add it to the next bill.'

And just like that, I'm one of the rule-benders. I'll find another way to pay her, when the time is right. Doing so through the firm is unthinkable.

I give her the number and she asks me to leave it with her for a few hours. I thank her profusely and unprofessionally, and I can sense her unease with my outpouring of emotion. But the elation of finally, perhaps, getting somewhere quickly drains. There's a very real chance, isn't there, that the information I'll get back will be a grid reference in the middle of the moors? It's not hard to imagine I'll find the phone I'm looking for in Gemma's cold dead hand.

I drive back towards The Headless Woman feeling like I've at least done something useful, and telling myself that really it's Felicity who's breaking the law, and I'm just doing what's right. I'm pretty sure the other partners wouldn't see it that way. That's beside the point though. No one need ever know.

The car rings through the hands-free, and it's Doug. I feel another lift, like I'm emerging from a black hole. I answer straight away.

'Hi!' I say, and it probably sounds far too bright and breezy given we haven't spoken for almost forty-eight hours, and we're getting married in six days.

'Any luck?' he says. To my disappointment, his mood doesn't match mine. He sounds sullen and uninterested. It punctures my buoyant feeling.

'Not really,' I tell him.

'So you're coming back?'

'Tomorrow,' I reply. Even if Felicity does come up with a conclusive answer today, I don't fancy the long drive back in the dark. 'Definitely tomorrow.'

'Good,' he says. 'I miss you.' His tone, however, is less than reassuring.

'Are you okay?' I ask.

'Just tired,' he replies.

I get the impression there's something more he wants to talk about, but he just says goodbye and hangs up.

When I pull into the car park at The Headless Woman once more, Tara is walking along the wooden fence at the back of the pub, rattling a bowl and whistling.

She smiles at me. 'Any news?'

'Wasn't much to see up there,' I say. I consider showing her the photos I took, but she seems preoccupied, looking out over the fields.

'You've not seen Blackjack?' she asks.

I guess she's talking about the cat. 'No, I'm afraid not. She's wandered off, has she?'

'Since yesterday evening. Not like her.'

'I can help you look if you want?' Tara's been more than helpful to me in my search.

She waves a hand. 'Oh no, don't you worry. I'm sure she'll show up sooner or later.'

I offer again, but she insists, so I go inside.

Up in my room, the bedding has been changed; the things on my case are as I left them. Maybe I was being paranoid after all.

I've no idea how long Felicity might take to dig out the phone details – if she even can – so I log onto my work emails on the bed, trying to slip back into some sort of normality. There's one from Katriona, with a red flag. It's titled 'Apologies!' and I assume it's something she's overlooked at work, but reading on, she says she can't make the wedding reception next weekend. Her brother is making a surprise visit from New Zealand and there's a family meal planned. She's devastated, and guilty, and feels terrible, because she was looking forward to it. I feel bad for her. She probably had it on her mind last week but couldn't tell me face to face. I message her back, telling her not to worry *at all*, and that her family is far more important. I mean it, of course. It would be lovely to see her on the wedding day, but there will be over a hundred and fifty other guests. We'd probably barely have spoken.

I'm finishing up the note when I have the urge to sneeze. Dammit. Blackjack's presence is still not fully exorcised. If I'm going to spend another night here, I'll need some anti-histamines. A quick search on my phone tells me there's a chemist in the neighbouring village of Ravenow, which is closed today. However, there's a supermarket five miles away with a pharmacy. I've time to kill.

Tara's on the phone downstairs. It sounds like she's talking to her daughter from the fond tone, so I just give her a wave and mouth 'Back in a bit'. I don't want her feeling guilty about my issues.

I drive out of Hartsbridge, past the hostel this time. There's a minibus standing in the car park, the driver smoking. I wonder how many other people were staying at the same time as Gemma and Mark – and if any of them might remember something. If this were a TV show, the lead investigator would charge her hard-working subordinate to track them all down and get statements. All I've got is the reluctant Constable Dewer.

The road is narrow in places, so there's some slowing down and easing alongside other traffic. I pull into a lay-by to let two cars through, and the second is a police car, driven by Constable Dewer himself. He catches sight of me as we pass, and as I drive off, he puts on his blue lights. I tap on the brakes, and he parks up behind.

'What the . . .?'

I watch in my mirrors as he climbs out, and positions his hat on his head in an overly formal manner.

He approaches, and I try to read his face. It's grim and pale. My stomach drops, because I think it can only mean one thing.

They've found Gemma.

Chapter 25

GEMMA

Gemma could feel the alcohol fizzing through her veins as she and Mark left the pub just before midnight, his arm around her. He was still humming along to Guns N' Roses, the song he'd murdered quarter of an hour before. She leant against him, as she had a hundred times before as they walked along the Brighton seafront when they used to talk about the future.

Back when they were first together, it was all about getting a campervan. Mark would fix it up, and they'd take it across Europe, living on food bought from street markets, sleeping where wanted, getting occasional work in tourist areas. Neither of them had ever even crossed the English Channel before, but it seemed more than possible they could achieve it. Just a case of saving up a bit of money, quitting their jobs and saying goodbye.

It had never happened, of course. Their financial situation

was always a mess, living from pay cheque to pay cheque. Mark mostly worked for different mechanics, as and when they needed an extra hand. She did bar work, before a couple of shifts at a care home had given her more satisfaction than she'd expected. It turned out that most of the residents just wanted someone to talk to, and many of them had lived absolutely fascinating lives. There was a woman who'd been a nightclub dancer who knew the Krays. And old Mr Denny had been a fighter pilot at the end of the Second World War. They were all dying, one way or another. The longest resident had been in there for six years, but most lasted fewer than eighteen months. Gemma attended a funeral about half a dozen times a year at the request of Mrs Panerjee – representing the home. She sang the hymns and said the right things, reassuring the family that their dearly beloved had been happy in their final days and weeks, even if the truth was more banal.

'How much is a camper?' she asked absently as she and Mark climbed the hill towards the hostel.

He squeezed her tighter to him. 'That's freaky, babe,' he said. 'I was just thinking the same thing.'

'We could though, couldn't we?'

'Yeah, we could.'

They entered the brightly lit foyer of the hostel. The front desk was empty.

Back in their room, the high of the booze drained from her blood, as did any fantasy of the future. The dorm, their meagre belongings – it all brought her squarely back into the present.

Mark took out the phone and cursed. He turned it to face her.

182

Five missed calls.

He rubbed his cheeks nervously. 'I knew we shouldn't have—'

The phone rang again, a gentle buzzing, in his hands.

'Answer it!' she said.

Mark brought the phone to his ear.

'Hello?' Gemma couldn't hear the other side of the conversation. 'You think we're thick? . . . You're not hearing me . . . No, you calm down.' Mark's voice had raised, and Gemma motioned to keep the noise down. 'If you don't, we're done and you can kiss it all goodbye.' He frowned and looked at the phone, then spoke to Gemma. 'They hung up.'

'What did they say?' asked Gemma.

'Wanted to meet at the house. Fuck that.' Mark ran a hand through his hair. '*Fuck!*' Ten minutes passed, and Gemma too began to feel anxious. Not that they'd be caught any more, but that the man from the pub, and his associates at the house, weren't taking them seriously.

'Okay, give me that.' She reached for the phone and Mark let her take it.

'What are you doing?'

'Showing them we mean business.'

'We don't have a number for them.'

Gemma dialled 999. Mark made a grab for it, and Gemma held it out of reach.

'No!' he said.

'Trust me,' she replied.

The operator answered and asked what service she required.

'I can see a fire. It's coming from Brocklehurst Hall, outside Hartsbridge. Looks like part of the building is burning.'

183

'What's your name, please?' asked the operator.

'Sorry, the line's breaking up,' said Gemma. 'Please, send a fire engine. It looks bad. I don't know if there's anyone . . .'

She ended the call, then switched off the phone.

'What did you do that for?' asked Mark.

'To scare them,' she said. 'To let them know this isn't a game.'

Chapter 26

SARAH

I'm glued to my seat as I watch Dewer approach, though I manage to wind down the window. His eyes are mostly fixed on me, but he takes in the scratches on the car briefly. As he reaches the side of the car, he removes his hat.

'Ms Kline?'

I nod. My mouth is dry. 'Have you got news about Gemma?'

The briefest of frowns crosses his forehead, before vanishing. 'I'm afraid I need to speak with you about something else.'

He looks into the car, at my phone resting on the seat beside me. Even though I know it's completely illogical, I have a sinking feeling this is to do with the contact I've had with Felicity. There's no way he could know about it, but I can't prevent the blush flaring across my cheeks.

'We had a call this morning from a local resident, at

Brocklehurst Hall,' he continues. 'Complaining about a trespassing incident.'

It clicks into place. *He* phoned the police. 'You've got to be kidding me. That nutter pointed a bloody shotgun at me!'

Dewer doesn't look impressed by my indignation. 'Mr Farrah explained that you were aggressive.'

I take a deep breath, trying to stay calm, like we tell our clients prior to any courtroom appearances. I'm a lawyer – I can handle this if I stick to the facts. 'That wouldn't be my recollection of events,' I say to him. 'I took a wrong turning due to my satnav. He was driving too fast and I had to swerve off the road. Then he pointed a gun at me and told me to leave.'

The constable nods distantly. 'The family are very particular about their privacy,' he says.

His tone is distinctly sceptical, and I just shrug. 'Seems a bit of an overreaction, doesn't it?'

'They've had a lot of trouble over the years. Criminal damage, graffiti, that sort of thing.'

'Well, my graffiti days are behind me,' I reply, trying to lighten the tone. 'I just took a wrong turn.'

There may be the slightest smile on his lips. Have I won him over? He must see that Farrah's complaint has little merit.

'I was going to call you actually,' I continue. 'As you can see, I've been the victim of some vandalism myself.'

He looks at the car door again. 'Do you have any idea who was responsible?'

'No, but the car on the top road has similar markings.'

His eyes latch onto mine. 'I'm sorry?'

'I think the same person made scratches on both cars.'

His brow folds in the centre. 'Why would anyone do that?'

There he goes again, withdrawing.

'I was being watched too. I think it was Patrick Draper.'

'Paddy? Where?'

'Right up there, in the hills. He was at the site of the accident. I think he knows something.'

Dewer's face tightens, but as he's about to say something, his radio crackles. '*Respond for Hartsbridge.*'

He presses a button. 'Dewer here,' he says. 'Go ahead.'

'*We've got something. Partial remains. IC1 female.*'

Dewer's eyes find mine, then he quickly turns away, putting distance between himself and my window. I struggle with the seat belt, then leap out after him, following him as he speaks into the radio in hushed tones.

'Wait!' I shout.

I only hear 'on my way'.

As he reaches his own car, I grab him by the elbow and yell to stop at the same time. He turns to me, swallowing, looking very boyish. I withdraw my hand quickly, shocked at what I just did. 'I'm sorry,' I mutter. 'It's Gemma, isn't it?'

He places his hand on top of his car. 'Ms Kline, I don't have all the details yet . . .' He can't meet my eyes, and I think to myself he's not equipped for this.

'Where?'

He looks torn. Like he wants to get into the car and go, but can't.

He nods past me, towards the village I've left. 'Downriver. Part of a woman's body has been found in the water.'

I have the feeling of my consciousness trying to abandon my own body, like I no longer have the willpower or the strength to hold it up. My knees actually buckle a little.

'Ms Kline, I can escort you back to the pub if you wish. I think you should stay there until we have more definite answers.'

I'm shaking my head. 'No. No way.' I spin around, and stare down the road. 'That way? How far?'

'Ms Kline, please . . .'

I start walking towards my car.

'Ms Kline, you're not in a fit state to drive.' It's like his voice is coming at me underwater. Now it's him catching up with me. 'Sarah . . . let me take you.' There doesn't seem to be enough oxygen in the air I'm breathing, and a pain is building under my sternum. 'Please, it's not far,' adds the constable softly.

I manage a shaky breath, breathe out slowly. There are tears in my eyes at the sudden kindness in his tone.

'We can get your vehicle later.'

Still numb, I grab my phone and lock the car. We walk side by side to his, and I sink into the leather passenger seat. I realise I'm shivering. 'Cold,' I mumble.

'It's shock,' he says. He starts the engine and then flicks a switch on the console. As we drive, I can feel my seat warming in my lower back and under my thighs.

We drive back into the village and out again, along the looping road. We pass Mill Cottage. The river comes intermittently into view below. Neither of us speak.

It isn't more than a couple of minutes until we come to a small stone bridge, nestled in the valley. It's an idyllic spot, the sort of place you'd stop for a picnic. There are two police cars and another vehicle. A group of three walkers is standing to one end of the bridge. They look numb, and one is crying into the shoulder of another.

188

There are two officers on either side of them, and another is further up the road, holding up a queue of cars, and a tractor has pulled up.

Dewer comes to a gentle halt. 'You can stay in the car if you want.'

And, Christ, I want to. I really do. I want to shrink into the warm leather and never have to confront what those ghoulish spectators are ogling over the bridge's edge. But my hand is already on the door release, then my feet are on the tarmac.

One of the bystanders turns to me, but absently. She doesn't know who I am, and I want to scream at all of them to go away, to leave my presence, and Gemma's – I want them to understand, from my face, that this is a private moment and they're not welcome.

Dewer is beside me, his hand on the small of my back. He doesn't try to stop me, or talk. We walk to the edge to the bridge, and I almost step in a pool of vomit spattering the bridge's wall. I look over the side. Another uniformed male officer, with a grizzled older face, is standing below, and beside him on the ground he's laid out a fluorescent jacket. Whatever's beneath is small.

'What's under there?' I say quietly.

One of the bystanders looks at me in bewilderment, like they too are coming to terms with it.

Then, almost on cue, a gust blows through, catching the edge of the jacket below and lifting it off the ground. The officer makes a lurching grab to catch it. It's too late.

A single arm, white and lifeless, one end an angry red and black, from which a pale bone joint emerges. The man manages to cover it up again, but the hand is reaching out from the side like it's waving, or groping for help. And there's a ring on its finger I'd know anywhere.

It's too much. Too much. The blood seems to drain from my toes and fingers, rushing to the hot ball in my chest.

'Woah!' says a voice. 'Hey, help her.'

They can't be talking about Gemma, so they must be talking about me. The day darkens at the edges, shrinking like two giant hands clasping over my eyes.

'She's fainting.'

I've never done so before, yet there's something strangely pleasant about falling into the arms of a stranger. Letting someone else take the strain, at least for a while.

Chapter 27

GEMMA

'What the hell are you playing at?'

The digital distortion on the voice couldn't conceal the anger. Gemma could feel the rage emanating from the phone's shitty speakers. She had the impression it wasn't the same person they'd spoken too before. Something about the tone was different – a desperate edge.

'Next time, it'll be the police,' said Mark.

They were still in the hostel room – they'd heard the fire engine storm through the village about an hour before, sirens blaring. They'd agreed that Mark would do the talking, even though the plan to send the emergency services had been hers.

'You shouldn't have done that.'

'You know what you have to do,' replied Mark. 'Twenty K.'

'We told you before. We don't have that sort of money.'

'Then get it. Enough fucking about.'

'We can get five.'

'Are you deaf? Twenty.'

A pause. 'I'll see what we can do.'

'You can do ten.'

'And then you'll come back for more.'

He had a good point, thought Gemma.

'Cross that bridge later,' said Mark. 'We're not greedy.'

The man gave a harsh bark of laughter. 'And then what?'

Mark punched the air and beamed. Gemma couldn't help smiling too. It hadn't actually worked, but it was work*ing*. 'We'll give you a location.'

'Got this all worked out, haven't you?'

'You'd better believe it,' said Mark. 'Call tomorrow at seven p.m., or the Old Bill will be paying you a visit. It's that simple. You understand?'

'I understand,' replied the man.

'This is just business,' added Mark. 'No hard feelings.'

'This isn't business. When we find you, we'll cut you into fucking pieces.'

The call ended.

'He's pretty pissed off,' said Mark, with a wry smile.

'It's not funny,' replied Gemma. 'Anyway, how are we going to get the money?'

'We need a drop site.'

'A drop site?'

'Yeah – somewhere they leave it and we pick it up.'

'They'll be watching.'

He rolled his eyes. 'You don't say. It needs to be somewhere they can't watch.'

'Like where?'

'We'll have a look tomorrow. Let's get some sleep.'

Gemma didn't know how he could even consider it.

Chapter 28

SARAH

The door to the briefing room opens and Constable Dewer comes in holding a steaming mug. 'Tea,' he says, offering it. 'I didn't know if you'd want sugar. I put one in.'

I take it. 'Thank you.'

Cupping the mug, it burns my hands, but I keep my grip. There's something about the pain that I need to feel. Dewer hovers.

I'd wanted to stay at the bridge, but he insisted there was no point to it. He explained that an ambulance would take the arm to the nearest hospital, actually in Bishop Auckland also, like the police station I find myself at.

I can't get it out of my head. How could *that* be my sister. It was just . . . meat.

'We've got a dozen officers on the scene,' says Dewer. 'They're searching river downstream and up. As soon as they find anything, we'll let you know.'

Anything. Any more pieces of Gemma, he means.

The door opens again and an older woman in uniform enters. She must be in her late forties at least, with cropped grey hair. She has blue eyes and no make-up.

'Good afternoon, Ms Kline. It's good to meet you at last, and I'm sorry it couldn't be under different circumstances.' She reaches out a hand. 'I'm Sergeant Nelson.'

I take the hand. Her grip is surprisingly steely, or maybe mine is especially limp today. No wedding ring. Despite her stature, I get the impression of a woman who's worked her way up by not taking any shit.

She flashes a polite smile at Dewer. 'I can take it from here, constable.'

He looks pleased to be out of the room. I wonder how many murders he's dealt with in his time. They can't get many this way, and it's probably the usual, miserable catalogue of domestic killings and punch-ups that get out of hand. Cut and dried stuff that doesn't make the headlines.

I know this isn't that. My sister didn't die in an accident. Someone killed her and chopped up her body. I want to escape my own skin, to flee the myriad possibilities of Gemma's final hours, but I can't. I'm trapped with them, chained to a seat and forced to watch the horror movie procession of my thoughts. Someone did that to her.

'Ms Kline,' says Nelson. 'I need to ask you some difficult questions. Do you think you're up to it?'

I nod.

She opens a case and takes out a small, transparent plastic bag with a tag attached. I can see right away it's my mother's ruby ring.

'Do you recognise this?'

I nod. 'It was my mother's,' I say, with a croak. 'Gemma had it.'

It belonged to my grandmother too, and her mother before. At least that's what Mum always said. It certainly looks old enough, like a piece of Edwardian costume jewellery. I'd never have been able to carry it off, but Gemma would have managed to pair it with her own, eclectic style. I'm touched she still wore it, and my bottom lip starts to go. I fight it.

'We're going to do a DNA test on the arm we found,' says Nelson. 'As part of that investigation, we'll also need a biological swab from you as a reference. Is that okay?'

'Yes, of course.'

I like Sergeant Nelson. She's not old enough to be my mother, but there's something maternal about her, alongside the calm professionalism.

She settles back a little. 'Did your sister have any distinguishing features on her body? Any scars, or tattoos, or birthmarks?'

I take another sip of the tea and nod. I remember the day she showed it to me. She must have been fifteen, a week or two before she left home. A black rose at the top of her pelvis, disappearing under her underwear, the skin around red and inflamed where the infection had set in. She wanted me to get antibiotics from the doctor without Mum knowing.

'Not on her arm. Why are you asking?' I say. 'I mean, it's her.' I gesture to the evidence bag. 'You have that.'

Nelson. 'It's important we carry out an accurate identification.'

I try to picture Gemma in my mind, and all I see is her the day of Mum's funeral, staring angrily from under an umbrella. 'She might well have had more tattoos in the last few years that I don't know about . . .'

'There are some scars . . . Does that mean anything to you?'

Again, I'm struck by the gut-wrenching possibilities. She was unhappy as a teenager, but I never saw her harming herself. 'What sort of scars?'

Nelson's eyes flick briefly to the case again, and I know what's in there.

'You've got photos,' I say numbly.

She doesn't deny it.

'Can I see?' I say it before really thinking.

'I don't think that's necessary,' she replies.

Fuck what's necessary. I need to see. It feels like the least I can do, to bear witness, given that I'm the one sitting here, alive, and she's not. 'Please.'

Slowly, clearly reluctantly, Nelson opens the case again and takes out an iPad. She keeps the screen averted from me while she taps in a code. 'The arm was photographed in situ, but this image is from the hospital.' She turns it towards me.

The image is no more shocking that what I saw by the bridge. In fact, seeing it on a screen, caught in a harsh, unforgiving light rather than in the flesh, is much easier than I imagined. A section of the arm shown in close-up on some sort of blue sheet, like a surgical drape, extending from the few inches above the elbow to the delicate fingers. The ring has been removed. The scars are clear though. Not what I was envisaging, telltale marks on the wrist, but two long silvery streaks, some almost a centimetre across, along the outside of the arm. They look more like an injury of some sort than anything self-inflicted.

'I never saw these before,' I say.

I reach out and touch the screen, only for the image to change. This one is a wider shot. I stifle a gasp. The blue drape lies on a stainless-steel surface, and the top of the arm is visible. It looks like something from a butcher's slab, cut just beneath the shoulder. It's fairly neat, with a circle of white bone visible. The flesh is pale and bloodless.

Nelson whips the tablet away. 'I'm sorry, I—'

'It's okay,' I say.

'We'll find who did this,' she says. She puts the tablet back in the case. 'Will you give me a moment? I'm going to ask Constable Dewer to take the samples we need. Then I think it would be best for you to get some rest. We can also find a trauma specialist, if you want to speak to a professional.'

Her offer momentarily flummoxes me. Compared with Gemma's trauma, mine seems insignificant.

'I'll be fine,' I reply.

'That's good,' she says. Standing up, she leaves the room.

I'm finishing the tea, when my phone rings, and I fumble for it. It's Doug. I tried to call him on the way to the station but only got his answerphone and couldn't find the right words to leave a message. How exactly can I even begin to explain all this?

'Any joy?' he says breezily. It's only when I hear his voice now that I at last break into tears. 'Sarah?'

'She's dead, Doug. Gemma's dead.'

'Oh my God. How?'

'We don't know yet. They found her . . . her body in a river.'

I hear him exhale. 'I'm so sorry. I . . . I don't know what to say. Listen, I can be there in a few hours.'

'There's no need,' I say automatically.

'Don't be silly. I'm coming right now.'

'You haven't got a car.'

'I'll rent one from the place up the road. Hang tight.'

There's nothing he can do here, but I'm grateful nonetheless. 'Okay. Don't drive fast.'

'Of course not.'

'I mean it.' I'm feeling protective. Paranoid. If something were to happen to him as well . . .

'Where are you now?'

I tell him I'm at the police station, but he should come to the pub in Hartsbridge. We part with *I love you*s.

After we've hung up, I consider phoning work to tell them I definitely won't be back tomorrow or likely the following day, but I don't have the strength. In fact, I need food. There was a vending machine on the way in, so I get up and walk out into the corridor. It's colder here, with no heating, and I head back towards the entrance where the dispenser is situated. There's a break room of some sort off to one side, the door open, and as I choose a chocolate bar, I can hear men's voices on the other side.

'. . . you say that, but that bridge is right on the county line.'

I freeze, finger on the selection pad. They're talking about Gemma.

'So who'll take it?'

'Arm was the west side of the bridge. Gotta be Nelson. She'll be spitting feathers.'

I see Dewer emerge from another door, making his way towards me.

'Surely it depends, though, right?' continues the conversation between the officers. 'If the rest of it shows up downriver, it's Northumbria's . . .'

Groans of tired laughter emanate from the doorway. I reel backwards, letting out a sound of my own – a wail.

Dewer arrives. He must have heard the banter too, because he looks panicked. He takes my arm and tries to lead me away.

I pull free. I stumble backwards, into the eyeline of the doorway where the officers are chatting. They see me and go quiet, looking anywhere but at me.

'You think it's fucking funny?' I say to them. '*My* sister?'

Dewer gets between me and the room, glaring at the officers, then pulls the door closed.

Chapter 29

GEMMA

It was the sort of place her sister would like, she thought. Loads of black-and-white photos that cost more than she earned in a month. But she only wanted a card, and chose a bird.

'Can I borrow a pen?' she asked at the counter.

'Of course,' said the man. He watched her curiously as she wrote on the back.

Words had never been her strong point, an E at GCSE English, compared to her sister's top grade. That's why it had been Sarah who gave the eulogy at the funeral, somehow papering over how depressing and crap their mum's life had been with words like 'struggle' and 'health problems' that masked the cold reality of empty vodka bottles, bouncing checks and periodic wet patches on the furniture where she'd passed out.

Gemma wrote honestly and briefly, then realised she

couldn't remember her sister's address besides the name of the building she lived in. Devereux House. That would have to do. She finished writing the card, then paid and thanked the shopkeeper for the pen.

Mark was waiting outside with his rucksack on his back, tapping his foot. 'Happy now?'

'Thank you,' she said. 'I know you don't understand. Right, I just need a stamp.'

He huffed a bit as she went into the post office a couple of doors up. In truth, it could've waited. She very much doubted her sister was expecting an RSVP anyway, but she'd woken with the urge to send it for some reason. Like she needed to get her affairs in order before the day ahead. She bought a couple of sandwiches too, and a chocolate bar.

She felt listless, having slept badly, which was hardly a surprise. Every noise in the corridor, every rattling of the central heating pipes, lifted her from slumber to full consciousness, her senses tingling and alert.

Keeping up the deception, they'd told the woman on reception at the hostel that they were going to drive out and explore further afield. It was true in a sense, but rather than picturesque walking trails, they were hunting a suitable place where the twenty thousand pounds could be left and collected without detection. The total amount wouldn't be much bigger than a house brick, Mark reckoned, depending on the denomination of the notes. They thought about a supermarket, or a public toilet, in one of the nearby towns. Maybe a train or bus station – a bag left under a bench, or on a café chair, or in a rubbish bin. But already Gemma was worried about the possibilities. What if it was found by someone else before they got to it, or their enemies were keeping a close eye from nearby? The risks seemed too great. They needed a spot that couldn't be watched.

They returned to the car park at the hostel, and Mark threw his rucksack in the boot. As he rounded the car, he halted. 'What the fuck? Someone's keyed it!'

Gemma rounded the driver's side. Someone had indeed done a number on the bodywork – several deep-looking scratches stretched from near the top of the wheel arch across the door.

'How long's it been there, do you think?' she said.

Mark shrugged. 'Hard to tell.' Then he smiled. 'It'll take thousands off the value though.'

She didn't laugh, but swept a cautious glance in all directions. 'Hey, you don't think someone's trying to tell us something?'

Mark looked unconvinced. 'They've got our phone number, babe. If they wanted to warn us off, they'd call.'

He had a point. If the people at the house knew where their car was, there was no reason to be subtle about a warning. Nevertheless, the sooner they got this over with, the better.

They drove out of the village, towards a place called Ravenow. With the sun out, and the leaves just starting to turn, the colours of the landscape came alive. It really was a beautiful place. Brighton was great in many respects, but in recent years the allure of the coast had faded. She'd once looked at its great expanse with a sense of expectation and potential, but that had slowly morphed into something quite different. More recently, it felt like a wall, a natural barrier that stopped the people who'd drifted south from going any further.

At the side of the road, Gemma saw something and called on Mark to stop.

'Why?'

'There!' she said.

A yellow grit bin sat at the top of an overgrown farm path with thick tree foliage overhead.

Mark drifted a little further then pulled over. A van drove past.

'What do you think?' she said.

The salting container was situated in a dip, and any vantage point that looked on was easily visible.

A smile grew over Mark's face as he looked around. 'Stay here a sec,' he said.

She remained in her seat as he got out and walked over. A couple more cars drove past, but paid them no attention. When Mark returned, his grin was even wider.

'It's perfect,' he said.

Gemma wouldn't have gone that far, but it was out of the way. And the road had enough traffic that they could pass through without drawing attention. It would be the work of ten or fifteen seconds to stop, get the money and keep going. Driving west, literally into the sunset, considerably richer.

'So what now?' she asked.

'We should go for a walk!' he said.

★   ★   ★

The funny thing was that she really enjoyed it, the walking, for the most part. They steered clear of the house itself, sticking to the other side of the village. They hardly spoke

206

about the plan and what might happen that evening. The subject was there all along, of course, appearing occasionally like a mountain out of the mist. But for the most part, she could turn her attention from it. Maybe there wasn't much more to be said.

As they walked, they passed other hikers, who bid them hello and occasionally stopped a moment to speak about the weather. Gemma could almost, at times, imagine herself living in an alternate universe, in which they really were two lovers of the outdoors, simply enjoying a pretty corner of England. In that world, the boots on her feet fit perfectly, and the map and rucksack didn't feel like a costume donned for a play. The sort of life her sister probably led – wholesome and uncomplicated.

They ate the sandwiches she'd bought from the post office by a thunderous waterfall called Bleak Force. Mark would look at her occasionally and smile. She knew it was meant to be reassuring, and she wanted, desperately, to be reassured. Superficially, it really had gone according to his plan, and Brighton seemed like a distant country. If they pulled this off, it could actually be a fresh start. But each time she tried to imagine it – driving back down south several thousand pounds richer – the dream evaporated as quickly as the waterfall's spray as it crashed into the rocks. She couldn't shake the unpleasant sensation that they were just riding their luck. Whoever it was on the other end of the phone, they couldn't be stupid. And Mark might be right that twenty grand didn't mean much to them, but that wasn't what Gemma was worried about. The faceless man probably cared a lot more about being embarrassed than he did about the money itself. And worried they'd inevitably come back for more. He couldn't know that they really were happy to walk away after one pay-off. He'd be doing everything he could, using every second and every avenue available, to work out who they were. One snatch of the conversation stuck with her, playing on a loop.

Mark: *'We know who you are.'*

'I don't think you do.'

Because he was right. They didn't know who he was. And they didn't know what he might be capable of. It *might* have been an empty threat – a bluff. If it wasn't, they'd only find out when it was too late.

Mark's confidence was unwavering and Gemma wished she shared it. She scoured her mind for holes in the plan – ways the people at the house might work out who had blackmailed them. What if someone at the hostel had overheard their conversations and had connections to the people at the house? Or maybe someone had seen her planting the note on the bike after all. If so, they could just be waiting for the right moment to strike. But why wouldn't they have done so already?

They reached their car again just before five in the evening. Two hours until the people at the house were due to call.

Driving back to Hartsbridge, they went over final details. Mark wanted to pick up the cash on his own. At first, she protested, but he made a good point.

'Think about it, babe. If it goes tits-up, it's better we're not together. You stay at the hostel, just in case.'

Though it made her uncomfortable, she knew he was

right. If – God forbid – he was caught, the only leverage they'd have would be the threat to call the police.

'But it won't go wrong, babe,' Mark insisted, letting go of the wheel to squeeze her hand. 'We've got this far, right?'

Despite all her doubts, they had.

Chapter 30

SARAH

'Open wide, please.'

I do as Constable Dewer asks. He's wearing gloves, and runs the long Q-tip on the inside of my cheek. He then deposits it inside a plastic bag. I can't see the point, but I'm far too tired to object.

'How long will the results take?' I ask.

Dewer writes on the bag, and then slips it inside another envelope. 'This'll go to Carlisle by courier. They can normally do the sequencing in twenty-four hours. I can give you a lift back to Hartsbridge now if you want?'

I thank him, and gather my coat and belongings.

Doug has sent a message saying he's already halfway up the M1, so he should be here in another couple of hours.

Dewer leads me back out into a corridor, where a couple of uniformed officers go silent at my approach. I wonder if they were the same ones joking about Gemma. I'm only a little angry still. I can't really hold it against them – it's not my place to judge how they deal with the shit they must see.

When we're back into reception, Dewer tells me he'll be along shortly, and disappears again, so I wait.

Thirty seconds pass, before there's a commotion at the front doors, which slide open. Raised voices. A man shouting 'Leave him be, for God's sake! You don't have to do that!'

'Just stay back, sir!'

Four police officers barrel through the door. They've got a flailing man aloft between them, each gripping a limb. He's grunting and thrashing. I see he's got blood on his hands, but it's the hair that's a giveaway. Reuben Fletwick.

The other man – the one protesting – accompanies them. He's wearing some sort of protective hairnet on his head. I recognise him from the meat-processing van I saw Reuben being driven away in the other day.

'Have you even called his sister?' he says. 'She needs to know.'

One of the officers nods towards the security door, and the man at the desk presses a button. There's a beeping sound, and they bundle Reuben through. The man tries to follow, but the desk sergeant manoeuvres himself into his path.

'You can't go through there, sir?'

'He's got a disability!' says the man. 'He's bloody terrified.'

Constable Dewer reappears. 'What's going on?'

The man spots him. 'They've nicked Reuben.'

'For what?'

'They're saying it's about a murder.'

Dewer looks at me, and gathers himself. 'Okay, Andy. Has anyone spoken to Carla?'

He shakes his head. 'I followed them straight from work.'

'Give her a ring,' says Dewer. 'Let her know he's here.'

'They carried him in like a bag of spuds!' He takes off the hairnet and wrings it in his hands. He appears genuinely distraught.

'Don't worry – he'll settle. They won't question him until he's got a responsible adult here.'

'Question him for what? Murder? That boy never hurt a fly, and you know it.'

Dewer looks uncomfortable. 'Listen, I'll go and check on him, all right?'

'No need for that,' says Sergeant Nelson. She's appeared from the corridor. 'I'll make sure he's okay. You get Ms Kline back to her car.'

Dewer doesn't argue.

Nelson addresses herself to the man called Andy. 'You know the suspect, do you?'

Andy nods. 'He's my nephew. He's not done nothing.'

'If that's the case, then we'll soon find out,' she says. 'Why don't you take a seat? I can get you a cuppa if you want.'

The man's already reached into his pocket and taken out a hip flask. I've no idea if it's legal to drink in a police station. No one stops him.

* * *

Dewer's quiet as we drive out of Bishop Auckland, stopping briefly so I can buy some paracetamol for my raging headache. I remember to pick up the antihistamines too, to deal with the cat hair. With dusk falling, and Doug on his way, it looks like one more night in the village is inevitable.

213

On the road again, I wonder how Dewer is feeling about Reuben, because I don't know what I think either. I had my suspicions, but what were they based on other than the fact he's a bit different?

'Is there any evidence that man had anything to do with it?' I ask.

'I can't discuss that with you, I'm afraid.'

'Even though it's my sister he's believed to have killed.'

'*Because* of that,' he says sternly.

Silence descends again. We leave the last of the perimeter housing estates behind and climb back into open country. It all looks the same to me, but I think we're going by a different route. There's a mast on a hill in the distance, and it's not in the same place as before. I guess he might be doing it to spare the pain of travelling back past the bridge again. Soon I see signs for Hartsbridge. I'm near the spot where I turned and drove up to see the wreck of Mark's car.

'It must be hard when you know people round here,' I say.

Dewer glances briefly in the rear-view and I catch his troubled, dark eyes.

'It can be, yes. I don't get much cause to be round Hartsbridge, though. The odd bit of oil theft, or missing machinery. We don't have a lot of . . .' He's about to add something, then seems to stop himself. My mind fills in the blank. *Murders.*

'Did you grow up in Hartsbridge?' I ask.

'Ravenow,' he says.

He stops the car, slowly pulling over beside mine.

'Are you okay to drive?' he asks. 'I can follow on.'

I tell him that's not necessary, that my fiancé will be arriving soon. He seems glad to be rid of me.

Back in my own vehicle, I press the ignition, only to get a strange, choking sound. Fucking great! This is all I need. The car's practically brand new. My first thought is the battery – did I somehow leave the electrics running? I don't think so, because the car was locked.

I try again and it starts, thank God. I pull out from the lay-by, and I've only gone five hundred metres towards Hartsbridge when the most horrendous smell comes through the vents. I stop again, opening the windows. Something is *not* right. I keep it running, and slowly make my way back to the pub car park. One of the outdoor tables is occupied and I can see some wrinkled noses. Curious eyes watch me get out.

I've got a breakdown number in my wallet, and I figure it might be worth calling it now – you never know how long it'll take them to get out and there might be parts needed.

Before I do, I pop the bonnet. My knowledge of cars is rudimentary, but if it's just a battery boost I need, there are cables in the boot.

'You good?' calls a voice.

Archie has arrived outside, carrying two hot plates with a tea towel. He deposits them, and picks up several empty glasses.

'I'm not sure,' I say.

'What's up?'

I'm not especially keen to talk to him – has he not heard of the discovery downstream? – so I just say it's my car. He puts the glasses back down again and wanders over.

'Want me to have a gander?'

'Be my guest. I don't know what's wrong with it.'

He slides his fingers under the bonnet, finds the catch and hoists it up.

Smoke and a foetid smell rise from the engine block, and then his face scrunches up. 'Jesus fuck.' He brings a hand to his mouth.

I look in. Tangled in the engine housing, completely limp, is Blackjack. The cat's body is smoking slightly, and there's blood leaking from her slack mouth.

'Oh God,' I say. 'I had no . . . I mean, how did she even . . .'

Archie props the bonnet open on the stand. To my shock, he simply reaches in, scooping up the remains of the poor cat with his bare hands. 'You daft thing,' he says sadly. 'Daft, daft, thing.'

Everyone's watching, and a couple from the table approach more closely. There are cries of shock and disgust. I can't get my head around how the cat managed to sneak in there. I'm no car expert, but I suppose there might be a way in through the underside. If so, it must have been this morning, either before I went to the crash site, or maybe after I'd been back to the pub. But why didn't it make a sound, or scramble out when I started the engine? Did it somehow get electrocuted?

'I'm really sorry,' I say to Archie. 'If I'd known she was in there . . .'

He walks off, in a daze, around the back of the pub. I'm discombobulated, suddenly, by the instinct to feel sorry for him, despite my misgivings.

I close the bonnet again, and another thought occurs, much more horrible. That someone put Blackjack in there.

It must be possible to open the bonnet without the key –
maybe through the grille at the front. There doesn't seem
any way I could know, for sure, but if this is someone's way
of getting rid of me, they needn't have bothered. I'm more
than ready to leave this place and never return.

I get in and try to start the car again. It does so, with no
problem at all.

I'm exhausted, utterly spent, and walk towards the side
door of the pub. I just want Doug to get here, and to feel
normal again, whatever that means.

Chapter 31

GEMMA

'One hour. Leave it and drive away. And don't try anything silly. If I'm not back, the police get called, and it's all over.'

Mark looked at the phone, then slid it in his pocket.

'What did he say?'

'It's on,' said Mark.

They stood in the shadow of a wall at the side of the hostel. The owner had said three more guests were due that evening, so making the call in the room had been too risky.

'So they've got the money?'

'So he says.' He put his arms on Gemma's shoulder and drew her towards him. She could feel his heart beating under his ribcage.

'Be careful, all right?' she said.

'You know I will.'

'If anything doesn't look right, don't take risks. Come right back here and we drive away.'

He nodded. 'I've got to go. Just sit tight.'

The plan was for Mark to drive past the grit bin, go to Ravenow and use the supermarket, then drive back again. On the second pass, he'd fish the money from the bin, but instead of coming straight into Hartsbridge, he'd take one of the turn-offs and drive for a while to make sure no one was following. When he was happy, he'd come back to the village and grab her. Finally, just to be sure, they'd sell the car for scrap in Carlisle. Mark was sure he could find a place to do it off the books.

'If I don't hear from you by ten, I'm calling the police.'

'Didn't we say ten-thirty?'

'Ten-thirty, then. I'm serious, Mark.'

He kissed her, tenderly. 'Me too. Don't fret.' He backed away, until just their hands were touching. 'See you in a bit, babe.' Then he walked down to the car, climbed in and started the engine. She watched him drive down the hill until the red rear lights disappeared from sight.

Back inside the hostel, the manager, Carla, was eating fish and chips on the counter, watching a programme on the computer. Some sort of comedy, Gemma thought, from the canned laughter.

'How are you finding Hartsbridge, then?' she asked. 'The weather's been good for you.'

'Great. Lovely,' said Gemma. Her stomach was in knots and nerves tugged at the corners of her smile. 'It's a beautiful part of the world.'

'I wouldn't argue with that,' said Carla. 'Have you done much hiking elsewhere?'

220

'Loads,' said Gemma. 'Europe mostly.'

She wasn't sure why she said it. Maybe because she'd been fantasising about the campervan again.

'Cool. Any recommendations?'

'Oh, you know. The Alps . . .'

'French or Italian?'

'Listen,' said Gemma. 'We're actually going to check out, I think. Move on.'

Carla put down her wooden fork and wiped her hands. 'That's no problem. You've paid up, so there's nothing outstanding. Just drop the key in the box there when you're ready to leave.'

Gemma thanked her.

'It's probably not a bad call,' said Carla. 'It's due to turn tonight. Tomorrow's going to be a wet one!'

Gemma went back to the room. The other guests hadn't arrived yet.

She sat on the bed, feeling more alone than ever before, her own phone gripped in her hand. Mark had taken his phone and the burner. She wanted to speak to someone. Anyone. But who was there? Absently scrolling through her contacts, she paused on Sarah's number. She hadn't heard her sister's voice for years. She couldn't even imagine how she'd begin to explain Mark's scheme. She could see her sister's face in her mind's eye. It was the same look she'd given her the last time they'd been together on the rainy day they cremated Mum. Worse than disappointment. Worse than anger. It wasn't a million miles from the dispassionate look in the eyes of Tyler's friend in that cold bedroom, watching her undress. Pity. A look that said, *So this is what you've stooped to. This is what you've become.*

She didn't press call. There was nothing to say. Far too late for that. They'd come from the same womb, but their lives were ten thousand miles apart.

Chapter 32

SARAH

Archie has disappeared, but Tara takes the news of Blackjack's fate so much better than I expected. I wonder if she's just putting on a brave face, though, in recognition that my own grief trumps hers. The news of the discovery in the river has clearly reached her, because the first thing she utters is 'I dunno what to say. I really don't.' I shouldn't be surprised she's heard – we're only a couple of miles from the bridge.

I apologise for the third or fourth time about Blackjack, and she tells me it's not my fault.

'He's always sneaking in places,' she says. 'Never much of a mouser anyway.'

A sombre pall hangs over the bar. Three elderly ladies sit together, two drinking tea and one with a sherry. At the bar sits Nige, wearing a football shirt and jeans. He's got a half pint in front of him. I suppose he's pretty much part of the furniture in The Headless Woman.

'You all right, pet?' he says.

'Not really,' I reply.

'Get the lass a drink,' he tells Tara.

She goes behind the bar, grabs two bell-bottom glasses and lifts them to the optics. She sets the measure of brandy in front of me. 'On the house,' she says. 'We could all use one, I think.'

I hate brandy, but it's a kindness she didn't need to extend, and it almost makes me well up. I take a bar stool and pick up the glass. 'Thank you.'

The tiny sip burns my chapped lips, but I take another and swallow with barely a grimace. They're both looking at me, expecting something. I've got nothing to give. The only sound is the rattle of the other customers' teacups.

I down the drink and lay the glass on the bar. 'Would you mind pouring me another of those. I might take it upstairs.'

She does so, and I try to insist on paying, but she won't have it.

Back in my room, I empty my coat pockets on the bureau. The burned fifty-pound note is in there. It still makes no sense. Nelson said they thought Mark and Gemma were in debt, but why were they carrying fifties around? And how could that possibly have led to her arm being severed and dumped in a river?

I open my laptop on the bed, and sip the drink, propped up on the pillows. The Alice article is still on screen. Reuben, beside their teacher, looks back at me. Could he really have done it? I can see why the police might have their suspicions. He must live at the hostel with his sister. He could get access to the rooms. It makes me feel nauseous to think it, but if he works at an abattoir, he's probably no stranger to . . .

The police must have something else too, something they're not telling me. I wonder where the Alice investigation led them, sixteen years ago. Are they dusting off that file too? My eyes rest on Alice. It's all too easy to see a premonition in her wiser-than-her-years features, like she somehow knew or expected the tragedy that would later befall her.

I close up the computer, feeling the familiar itch at the back of my throat. Blackjack might have gone, rest in peace, but his presence lingers. My bag's right there, and I reach for it, to take the tablets. My fingers find the photo too, of me and my sister from the birthday party God knows how many years ago. I knock back the antihistamines and paracetamol with the brandy, raising the glass briefly in memory of the poor cat. Then I lie back on the pillow, forcing myself to look at Gemma. At us. Even though I haven't laid eyes on her for years, it's almost impossible to believe that she's gone.

The tears come slowly at first, but soon I'm quietly sobbing, with the picture clutched to my chest. I could've done so many things differently. I could've called her at any time after the funeral. Maybe that's all it would have taken. A single phone call, to swallow my pride, for her to swallow hers. A concerted effort for perhaps thirty seconds and we could have built bridges. Talked about our lives like other sisters. If all she needed was money – again – sure, I could've helped her. She might never have been up here. She'd have been on my hen night, talking after a few drinks about how she really didn't like the bridesmaid dress I'd picked out for her.

There are footsteps coming up the stairs, pounding, and Tara's voice. 'You can't go up there!'

I scramble off the bed, wiping my eyes, and get to the door just as there's a fist crashing on the other side. I open it, and see Carla there, her red hair in wild spirals. Tara's behind her, still fighting up the stairs.

'What did you say to them?' Carla demands.

'Say to who?'

'The police of course.' She stabs her finger in my direction. 'You told them that Reuben did something to your sister, didn't you?'

I take a step back and she remains where she stands, not crossing the threshold. 'I didn't say anything,' I tell her. 'Only that Gemma was staying at the hostel.'

'Yeah, right! With the *freak*, I suppose?'

'No, of course not! Honestly, I'm not lying.'

'Carla, come back down,' says Tara. 'This is a misunderstanding, I'm sure.'

Carla turns on her. 'We've had a brick through the window already,' she says. 'Was that a misunderstanding too?'

'It'll be kids,' Tara replies. 'You know what they're like.'

Carla takes a deep breath. Her cheeks are flushed, and she puts her hands on her hips. I'm not sure if she's about to launch another volley.

'I promise,' I say quietly. 'The first thing I knew was when I saw your brother at the police station. I'm sure they'll sort it out.'

Her eyes flare again, but there are tears in them too. 'They're keeping him overnight,' she says desperately. 'You don't understand what this'll do to him.'

I reach out, and touch her arm. She doesn't flinch.

'It took years to get him past the Alice thing. It's happening again.'

226

'Come downstairs, pet,' says Tara. 'Let's get you a cuppa.'

Carla shakes her head. 'I need to speak to a solicitor,' she says. 'They're going to question him in the morning.' She looks at me, and smiles sadly. 'I'm so sorry about your sister. I hope they find the person who did it. But it's not Reuben, okay? You've got to believe that.'

I nod back, resisting the polite urge to say I do. Because, really, it would be a lie. She clearly loves her brother dearly, and would do anything to protect him, but I can't let her emotions govern mine. I don't know what Reuben Fletwick is capable of.

I wait a few more minutes, before heading downstairs. I need some food, but I've no intention of eating in the bar, with everyone watching. Doug should be here any minute and I yearn to see him. I need some semblance of normality and a connection to life before the horrors of Hartsbridge. The ladies are still there, gossiping away, as is Nige. Tara's depositing another drink in front of him. Archie's back on the fruit machine.

'I'm sorry about that,' she says. 'She was up them stairs quicker than a ferret down a rabbit hole.'

'I understand,' I reply.

'For what it's worth,' Tara continues, 'I don't think Reuben has owt to do with what happened to your sister.'

Archie turns casually. 'I always thought he was a dirty little perv.'

'No one asked what you thought,' I say.

Archie actually gives a shit-eating grin.

'Is something funny?' I ask

'Nah, darlin',' he replies. 'Course not.'

'I'm not your darling.'

A couple of the old ladies are looking our way.

'No offence meant,' says Archie. He rattles another coin into the machine. 'Course, if it weren't him, there's someone out there still,' he adds, nodding towards the door.

This is some sort of game to him. He's enjoying himself.

It's a struggle to keep a lid on my temper. 'Tell me, you said you never saw my sister. Is that really true?' I know it's the brandy emboldening me, and there's suddenly an edge in the air.

'Told you, didn't I?'

'You didn't seem very sure,' I reply. 'I'm wondering if she might have made her way up to Brocklehurst Hall at some point. You go up there too, right?'

'Just to help out Bill,' he says.

'And were you there when the fire service was called out? You said it was a hoax, Nige?'

Archie's face hardens, and Tara looks on uneasily.

Nige nods. 'We don't know where the call came from.'

'Someone messing around, I expect,' says Archie.

'And if I ask Bill Farrah, he won't have seen my sister either?' I press.

'Steady on,' mumbles Tara.

'You'd have to ask Bill, wouldn't you?' says Archie.

'He was very keen to stop me going up to the house earlier,' I comment. 'I wonder what's up there. In fact, someone vandalised my car too.'

Archie's face breaks into a laugh, and he turns to me fully. 'I don't know what you're on,' he says, 'but it sounds like you're accusing me of something.'

'Yeah, that's not right,' says Tara. 'Maybe we all need to calm down.'

228

'I'll calm down when I know what happened to my sister,' I retort, my focus still very much on her son. 'From the very first time I showed you her picture, you knew something. You watched me. You freaked out when you saw me looking at the CCTV upstairs . . .'

'He's explained that,' says Tara defensively.

I ignore her. He's a big boy, and shouldn't need to hide behind his mother. 'I wonder, what would the police find if they looked too?'

Archie only smiles smugly. 'You're barking up the wrong tree, darlin'.'

That 'darling' is one too many. I walk towards him, slamming both hands into his chest. He's off balance and it knocks him backwards, but he reaches up and grabs my wrist. For a second, we're wrestling.

'That's assault!' he says.

'Go fuck yourself,' I say.

Then his eyes look past me, as the door opens.

'Sarah?' says Doug.

He rushes forwards, and though Archie's released his grip, it's too late to stop the trajectory of Doug's fist. He catches Archie on the side of the jaw, and he falls sideways, sprawled under the bar.

Chapter 33

GEMMA

They knew. Oh fuck. She didn't know how, but that didn't matter. The point was, their cover was blown.

She'd just placed the room key on the counter when she felt the hairs rise at the nape of her neck. It was dark outside, but she could see a solitary figure sitting on the wall outside – the biker from the pub. He was smoking a fag, eyes on the door to the hostel, and though he was twenty or thirty metres away, something in his posture made her stomach drop. Her knees turned to jelly.

They *knew*.

She tried to stay calm as the woman took the key. 'Going on anywhere interesting?' she asked.

'Actually, I think I left my phone charger in the room.'

The manager paused, frowning, then slid the key back over. She didn't appear to have clocked the guy outside, or at least she wasn't worried about him. 'Sure.'

Gemma could hardly breathe, but she resisted looking over her shoulder again, until she was opening the door into the corridor. This time he saw her and straightened up. He started walking towards the building.

Gemma broke into a run. There was a fire exit at the far end of the hallway. Get through it and she would be able to flee back onto the road. She'd no idea where she could go, but she just needed to put some distance between herself and the man. She needed to call Mark.

She reached the door and tried to shove it open, but the bar wouldn't budge. 'No, no, no!' she said. She tried again, with the same result.

A sound behind made her spin around. It was the ginger-haired guy, just emerging from the communal washroom. He looked at her and smiled.

'Help me!' she said, pushing the door ineffectually.

He walked up to her and reached to the top of the door, where a bolt was drawn across. He drove his shoulder into the door, which opened with a bang. She handed him the room key and fled.

At the back of the hostel was a yard that opened onto the road. But the other side met a steep bank that offered the cover of trees. She decided it was a better option, and jogged over. Nettles and brambles snagged at her clothes, but she scrambled through, until she came out on the other side on a narrow track. One way would lead back into the village, and she was torn. There was a chance she'd find safety, but, more likely, he – or someone he knew – would be waiting. She walked the other way, until the lane swung round and seemed to pass behind houses that looked more modern, with garages at the rear. She stopped for a moment, listening hard in case she could hear him following.

There was nothing.

She set off once more, jogging past the houses, and taking out her phone, ready to call Mark, but her fingers weren't working properly.

The *snick* of a twig snapping. Then the crunch of footsteps. Maybe the mute in the hostel had pointed him in her direction.

She turned, and there he was — at the end of the alleyway. 'Oh shit, oh shit . . .'

'There's nowhere to go!' he shouted.

She ran as fast as she could until she reached the back of some sort of deserted scrapyard. She skirted the metal mesh fence around the outside. Then she was back on tarmac, running along a single-track lane between drystone walls. There was nothing ahead — just the shadows of trees lining the roadside. No streetlights. No people. No houses. Somehow she'd ended up on a country lane leading out of Hartsbridge. Her booted feet slapped the road, and her heart was slamming into her ribs. He'd catch her. She knew she couldn't keep it up.

Then, out of the gloom, like a miracle, two headlights appeared. There was barely room to pass, but Gemma lifted her arms in a mad wave, calling out for it to stop.

Thankfully, it did. She ran around to the side of the car and saw an old man through the wound-down window.

'You all right?'

Gemma looked back. The car's headlights picked up the strip of dark tarmac, and a fine mist of dew. Apart from the gently stirring leaves, there was no sign of life. But her pursuer must be down there, somewhere.

'There's someone following me,' she said.

The man squinted through the windscreen. 'Can't see no one.' He looked at her curiously. 'I can give you a lift, if there's somewhere you're going?'

Gemma wasn't sure what to say. Hartsbridge wasn't safe.

'Do you live near here?'

'Other side of town,' he said, 'but I can take you to the pub if you'd like?'

'No, not there,' she replied. 'I just need to think. I don't suppose I could come to your house?'

'I don't see why not,' he said. 'Get on in.'

She went to the other side, and he reached over to undo the lock. The car was older than the one Mark drove, and she thought it might be red or maroon. The leather of the seats was patched and worn, but she didn't care as she sank in. Almost at once, she felt safer.

'Thank you so much,' she said, brushing her wet hair from her face.

'What's your name?' asked the man, as he set off again. He smelled of tobacco, and short grey bristles coated his gaunt features.

'It's . . . Sarah,' she said. 'Nice to meet you . . .?'

'Patrick,' he replied. 'But you can call me Paddy.'

Chapter 34

SARAH

We're back up in the room, with Doug flexing his fingers as I lay with my head on his chest. 'I've never punched anyone before. It really hurts.'

'We're lucky they didn't call the police,' I say.

'He's all right, isn't he? I just saw him grabbing you.'

We left Archie downstairs, with a bag of frozen peas on his cheek. I don't think he'd have brought the police into it anyway, and Tara did her best to defuse the tension by offering everyone another drink on the house. I'm guessing it wasn't the first time her son's been in bother. Secretly, I can't say it didn't please me enormously to see the grin wiped off Archie's face.

For the briefest moment, I can almost pretend everything is good again. Doug's familiar body, his arm over me, his scent – they're making things better.

'You're sure you want to stay here?' asks Doug. 'There'll be other hotels half an hour away.'

I'm too tired to think about it, and certainly too tired to hit the road again.

'No. Let's leave first thing.'

Just going over the events of the last two days has taken twenty minutes. I try to tell it in some sort of order that makes sense, filling him in on each of the characters in this story, but it's almost impossible without frequent tangents.

'But you still don't know *why* Gemma was here?' says Doug.

'Something to do with money, maybe,' I reply. Then I realise he doesn't know about that either. I'm getting frustrated with him for not keeping up, but that's not fair. I've only been in Hartsbridge for a couple of days, but so much has happened. 'They were staying at the hostel, but they didn't want anyone to know. They used . . . false names. Carla said that something might have happened, on the day of the accident.'

'Sorry, who's Carla again?'

'She runs the hostel. With her brother.'

'Oh, right. The one who went to school with Alice Brocklehurst.'

'Yes, but I don't think that's important . . . he's got a disability. The police are still speaking to him. I don't know what to think about any of it.'

He squeezes me. 'Sarah, I think you're in shock.'

'Probably,' I say. Thoughts are tangled in my brain. Pull at one thread, and another comes too, knotted around it.

'Have you eaten anything?' asks Doug.

That's a good point. Not since the cake at Neil's, late morning. 'Barely.'

'I'm going to go downstairs and ask if they'll rustle something up,' says Doug, easing me off his chest.

The clock says it's close to ten p.m. 'I doubt they're still serving. And you just knocked out the chef.'

Doug smiles. 'Let's see, eh? I can be pretty charming at times.'

★ ★ ★

I hear her calling my name and wake up in bed, in the room we shared as children. It's dark, and when I reach for the bedside light, it doesn't switch on. That scares me. In the half-light, I can see my sister's bed is empty, the sheets a tangle. The indent of her head still marks the pillow.

'Gemma?' I whisper.

She doesn't answer, but I'm almost certain I heard her voice calling my name and it was close by.

'Where are you, Gem?'

There's no reply. But then I notice – there's a low opening in the wall that wasn't there before. Just a rectangle of black without a door. At least, I don't recall it.

And I don't know what's on the other side, except with a dawning sense it's bad.

I'm certain, though, that's where Gemma is.

I don't want to get out of bed, because I don't want to go into that hole. I know if I don't, something awful will happen to Gemma. But I'm too frightened to go and help her.

In the hole, something bad might happen to me too.

I lie down again, hoping that if I go to sleep, I'll wake up and she'll be back in her bed. But as soon as my head rests on the pillow, she calls again, and this time there's no doubting what I heard.

'Sarah?' She sounds afraid.

I can't do it. I pull my duvet over my head, trying to block out any sight and sound.

That's when the wind starts – right in my bedroom – a gust lifting the duvet at my feet. I try to pin it down, to close the crack, but the gust builds to a gale until it's ripping at the duvet like a pair of hands, trying to tug it off my body. I'm fighting, trying to hold it down, but in the end it's too much because the wind is pulling me too, and I have to grip the bed itself to stop myself being torn out. The duvet vanishes, my shield gone, and I feel horribly exposed. My fingertips still hold the bed as my body is lifted into the air. I don't want to let go, but I have to. I can't hold on without my sinews cracking.

The moment I release, the wind dies, and I'm left floating in the air, no purchase on anything, like an astronaut in zero gravity. The gentlest of forces tugs me towards the little door, and there's nothing I can do. The darkness is coming, and it will swallow me. I don't want to look, so I curl into a foetal ball. The closer I get, the more my fear grows, until it's in my blood, pumping through every inch of me, and I'm a pure ball of terror.

Then I wake.

Beside me in the dark, Doug is sitting up. 'Are you okay?' he asks sleepily.

I'm sweating, but I tell him to go back to sleep, then climb out of bed to go and splash water on my face.

The dream is slow to let go. I haven't had it for thirty years, but it was like stepping back in time. Strange how the mind works. I suppose it's understandable, given what's happened, that I should hear her calling again now – a voice from the past, the forgotten pathways of my consciousness refiring. A voice from wherever Gemma finds herself now.

★   ★   ★

The next morning, Doug's up before me, wearing a towel, his hair still wet from the shower.

'Morning, sleepyhead,' he says, leaning over and kissing my hair. There's a faint light coming through the curtains.

'What time is it?' I ask.

'Seven,' he answers. 'I could *not* sleep on that mattress.' He's got my suitcase open on the end of the bed, packing it. 'I thought we should get going early. Beat the traffic.'

'I should call the police,' I say, sitting up properly. 'See if there's been any more news.'

'Sure,' says Doug. 'We can do it on the way. Oh, guess what. In the least surprising news ever, Olly and Liz are off.' He's surprisingly upbeat.

I groan. 'Does that mean Liz isn't coming?

'No, but it means we have to change the seating plan.'

My phone rings and Doug grabs it, eyeballing the number. 'Someone's keen. Unknown.'

I hold out my hand and he passes it over.

'Ms Kline. I'm phoning regarding your telecoms enquiry.'

A woman's voice, and it takes a moment to recognise it's Felicity's.

'Oh, hi. Any luck?'

'Yes, can you talk?'

I smile at Doug, who looks vaguely interested. *Who is it?* he mouths.

I wave him to butt out, and turn away.

'Go ahead,' I say.

'I've managed to identify the last time your sister's phone was pinged from the nearest towers. It's in a village called Hartsbridge, in County Durham.'

'Yes, that's where I am now. Can you be more specific?'

'Oh, much more,' she replies. 'I'm going to send you an encrypted link with the approximate location to five square metres. Password is your middle name. Is there any email address you'd prefer me to use? I'm guessing it's not the work one.'

I laugh uncomfortably and give her my personal email and she explains the link functionality will only exist for the next hour.

'I owe you,' I say. 'Wait, how do you know my middle name?'

'Good luck,' she replies, before hanging up.

'That sounded intriguing,' says Doug. 'Care to share?'

I didn't fill him in the night before about the phone trace, simply because it slipped my mind and seemed irrelevant given how the rest of the day panned out. So I tell him that I've asked someone to look into the last location of Gemma's phone.

His eyebrows shoot up. 'Aren't you a bag of tricks? Is that legal?'

'The police wouldn't help,' I tell him.

'That isn't exactly what I asked,' he says.

I tell him to pass my laptop, and he does so, then flops on the bed beside me.

240

I open up my emails, and find the message from Felicity in my junk mail – just a single dodgy-looking hyperlink from an address that reads insightsteam@happiness.com. The sort of thing you'd ignore or delete in a heartbeat. But when I open it up, it prompts me for a password, so I enter Hazel. It was apparently my gran's name on Dad's side, and I never liked it or used it professionally. I've no idea how Felicity knows it either, but I suppose it's hardly a challenge for her to gather such information given the far more juicy things she routinely unearths.

The file is a satellite map, showing most of the north of England, but there's a red cross-hair right in the middle. Beside it, a box reads a grid reference of a dozen or so digits, and also a date – the first of September, at 20.56. My heart misses a beat. That's the night of the fire that consumed Mark's car up on the moorland road.

I use the zoom function, and the resolution shifts from shades of green to individual fields and forests, and then roads too. I make out the boomerang shape of the village, but the cross is off to one side, and centres on an individual building.

I know at once what I'm looking at, because it's right on the river itself, and I can even see the carport off to one side.

It's Paddy Draper's house.

Chapter 35

GEMMA

Patrick Draper didn't live far from the village at all, and Gemma balked as he steered the car underneath a shelter to the side of a house. She had the acute sense of being pulled in two different directions at once. She wanted to leave, to get as far away as possible, but she couldn't until she knew Mark was safe. If they'd tracked her down, did that mean they'd found him too?

'This is going to sound weird,' she said, as he switched off the engine, 'but please don't tell anyone I'm here.'

'You in some sort of trouble, are you?' he replied nervously.

'Not exactly,' she said. She looked across at the house. They were supposed to be not drawing attention, but it probably didn't matter now. All that was important was getting out alive. 'Does anyone else live here?'

'Only me and the dog,' he said. 'Wife died years back.' She worried for a moment he'd withdraw his offer. Then he slid the key from the ignition. 'You want a brew? Summit stronger?'

She thanked him, and followed him to the back door of the house, watching the road the whole time. If the biker had seen her get into the car, there was a good chance he'd know the owner's address. She couldn't stay long.

The wood of the door was cracked and peeling, and around the handle it had been filled untidily with some sort of expanding gel. The window frames were disintegrating and through the single-later pane she could see a kitchen sill lined with overgrown plants spilling from their pots.

He inserted the key and opened the door onto a stone floor. An old sheepdog with one milky eye shambled forward, tail swaying gently from side to side. Patrick stooped to stroke its head. 'We've got a visitor, Chappie.'

The dog sniffed at her knee, tail going faster.

The place wasn't well looked after at all. The air smelled musty, and a little bit damp, and the kitchen was a hotchpotch of free-standing units. A small calendar with a picture of the Eiffel Tower hung on a nail, and still for July. A large, cracked butler sink dominated the window-side.

Patrick filled up a kettle, and placed it on the ancient electric-ring hob.

'Do you work in the village?' asked Gemma.

'Used to look after the school, until it shut down.' He gestured into another room. 'Tek a seat in there if you like.'

A beaded curtain separated the rooms. Gemma took out her phone. 'I need to ring my boyfriend. Do you mind?'

He shrugged. 'Make yourself at home.'

Gemma pushed through into the other room. It was the same story of decay. A threadbare carpet, an old gas fire with a dog bed in front of it, a boxy TV and facing it a single armchair with its back to her. In the corner, a small square dining table. Damp stains bloomed from one corner across peeling wallpaper. On the mantlepiece were several porcelain animals. A dresser completed the room, its shelves lined with a set of plates showing lurid floral patterns. Gemma was no stranger to slummy flats, but this was something else. A time capsule from a decade she'd never experienced. She felt sorry for its owner.

She certainly didn't much want to sit down on the armchair, so she went to the table and took one of the chairs, calling Mark's number. It was almost nine p.m.

He answered after a couple of rings.

'I've got it, babe! It's all—'

'They're onto us,' she interrupted.

'You what?'

'They *know*,' she whispered.

'Hold up, hold up. How d'you know?'

'Because the guy from the pub just came to find me. Mark, listen. You can't come back here.'

'Where are you?'

'Somewhere safe,' she said. 'For now. But I don't know what to do.'

He didn't speak for a second or two. 'Nah. How did they find out? Are you sure?'

She bit back the urge to shout. 'I'm fucking sure, okay? Where are you?'

''Bout three miles away,' he said. 'Pulled over in a truck stop. There's no one following, I'm sure. We're good. Babe, there's twenty grand here.'

She could almost see the childlike gleam in his eyes, as he

looked over whatever holdall the money was contained within. She could almost feel the weight of the wads in her own hands.

'I can come and get you,' said Mark.

'No,' she said.

'I won't stop. Straight to you, then we're on the road.'

'No, Mark! We don't know how many there are. They'll be waiting. You can't come back to the village.'

'Then what? How am I supposed to get you?'

'Hold on a sec.' She pulled open her bag and took out the map of the local area. She found her position and saw, about a hundred metres back up the road, a path ran up towards the moorland surrounding Brocklehurst Hall. It cut more or less a straight line for two miles until it reached a road to the north of the village. It seemed to be very much in the middle of nowhere – the last place they'd look. Looking closer, she saw that it led eventually to the telecoms mast that could be seen from the higher parts of the village.

She told Mark about it. 'We could meet up there,' she said. She trailed the road past the mast with her fingertip. 'If you take the road out of Ravenow past the church . . .' She followed it with her finger. 'Then the third left, you'll be on the same road. You'll be passing north of the house. It looks to be about four miles or so, but you can't miss the mast.'

'Okay, but how are you gonna get there?'

She wondered about asking Patrick for a lift, then thought better of it. The fewer people involved, the better. 'I'll walk,' she said. 'Should only take me an hour, maybe less.'

'It's pitch-black, babe. Just let me come and get you.'

'Mark, listen. Don't you dare, all right? If I take the path, they won't see me. But if they see your car, if they get the plate, they'll be able to find out who we are. We're still safe

246

at the moment. I'll be fine. I've got my phone-torch,' she said. 'Go straight there, to the mast. But if you think they're on to you, just drive, all right? Promise me.'

'All right, promise. Love you, babe.'

'Love you too.'

She hung up. Patrick was standing in the door holding a tray with two mugs and several biscuits on. He'd taken off his boots, and his toes were sticking out from a hole in the end of one sock. Gemma grimaced at the sight of his gnarled yellow toenails.

'Here we are,' he said, laying the tray on the table.

'I'm really sorry,' said Gemma, 'but I've got to go.'

Patrick straightened, and looked at her with sad grey eyes. 'You shouldn't,' he said gruffly. 'It's dark out there. Not safe for a little girlie like you.'

The temperature in the room seemed to dip suddenly, as if a door had been opened somewhere. Gemma felt the goose pimples pucker across her arms. He was standing over her. She sidestepped, picking up her bag.

He reached out with a hand, and for a second she froze, expecting him to grab or hit her. Instead he held his hand in front of her face like a sculptor appraising the contours of his work, not quite touching but far too close for comfort. She flinched back.

'You're marked,' he said.

She had no idea what he meant, and stepped further away, eyes on the bead curtain, wondering if she could escape round the other side of the armchair. There were no weapons, but if she could get one of the plates, maybe she could smash it over his head.

'I want to go,' she said calmly.

'You mustn't,' he replied. 'Not now it's marked you.'

'What's fucking marked me?'

He was clearly insane, and looking round his dwelling, maybe she should have clocked that earlier.

'Just fuck off,' said Gemma. She crossed the room, and pushed through the beads. The dog was at her feet, and whined in pain as she tripped over it, landing on her knees in front of her door. As she half-clambered up, she managed to get her fingers on the door handle. She opened it an inch before a hand slammed it shut once more.

Chapter 36

SARAH

'You need to let the police handle it,' says Doug.

I know he's probably right. I should phone them now – Nelson *or* Dewer. Tell them to meet me at Draper's house. I almost do. They might well still have Reuben Fletwick in custody. If Felicity's info is reliable – and there's no need to doubt it – he has nothing to do with it. But there's another reason I can't.

'I'd have to explain how I got the trace,' I say.

'So what?' says Doug.

'It could lead to Felicity. I'd get into all sort of trouble at work.'

'Does that matter, now? If this guy had anything to do with your sister, no one's going to care.'

'And if he *doesn't*, they *will*,' I reply. 'We could just go there and see. He was at the crash site, I told you. He knows something. We wouldn't even have to mention the phone at all.'

Doug still looks unsure.

'Please,' I say. 'If we see anything suspicious, we'll phone the police. I promise.'

'It's not just that,' he says. 'You don't know what we'll find. If he's involved – if he did something to Gemma . . .'

He doesn't have to say anything else. I remember the arm perfectly well. I know what might be in Patrick Draper's house.

I touch Doug's arm. 'You'll be with me.'

He doesn't put up any more arguments, so I quickly dress without showering and without finishing the packing. Downstairs, the pub is quiet, and we let ourselves out through the back door.

The drive is short – we take Doug's rental car. He seems calm; I'm not. I tell myself that I'll know straight away if Patrick Draper had something to do with Gemma's death. I'll see it in his eyes. I've never been closer than fifty metres from him, but it's no coincidence he was watching over Mark's car. Is this something to do with the cat nonsense he spouts? Does he go around vandalising property? Was Gemma just in the wrong place at the wrong time and somehow pissed him off? Could it really be that banal?

We park up just off the road, in front of the house. The red Volvo is still in the same spot as yesterday. We go to the front door. Before we've even knocked, there's a sound on the other side – a thump and a scrabbling noise, and my heart jumps into my throat.

I hear more scratching, then a high-pitched whine.

'I think it's a dog,' says Doug. He lifts his hand and knocks with the meat of his fist.

No one comes to the door.

'Let's go around the side,' I say.

'Sarah . . .' he warns.

I'm already on my way. I walk around, past the carport. Doug's looking up and down the outer walls. We pass a window with curtains drawn. There's a shed at the back, and a garden on two levels. A flagged path leads between weed-filled raised beds, to where a rusted old lawn roller leans against the trunk of a drooping horse chestnut, the seed pods brown with blunted spikes. Off to the side is a set of ugly concrete steps leading to a track past a greenhouse with several panes missing and then off to the end of the garden where there's some sort of plastic manhole cover in the ground.

The back door is wooden and in need of repair. There's a pane of misted glass and I can see the dog blurred on the other side. It looks like a sheepdog.

I put my hand on the handle, and to my surprise it turns and the door opens. The dog rushes out, tail between its legs, and doesn't stop until it's beside the car door. It drops onto its belly and watches us.

'Mr Draper?' I call into the house.

There's no answer.

'We can't just barge in,' says Doug. Then his nose wrinkles. 'Christ, what's that?'

It reaches me a split second later – a foul stench in the air that makes me gag. I wish I hadn't opened the door, but now I have I can't turn back. I'm past what's right, and ignore Doug, entering a small kitchen area. There are two pieces of burned toast under an old grill, and the sink is full of washing-up in a slick of filthy water. A dog turd curled at the bottom of one of the units explains the smell. A bead

251

curtain hangs partly loose from the door frame, as if it's been torn free.

All the moisture has gone from my mouth, so when I next say Patrick Draper's name it comes out thick, my lips gluing at the corners.

The room beyond is dark, and I find the switch. When I flick it on, a single wall lamp over the fireplace comes to life, but the wattage only gives out a soft golden light. There's no one home. A narrow set of steep stairs leads to my right.

'Let me go first,' says Doug.

He eases past me, onto the steps, which creak under his weight. I follow him, using the rail to steady myself. At the top are two doors, opposite one another, both closed. Doug opens the one on the left.

'Bloody hell,' he says. He looks back at me, a mystified expression.

I join him. The room is devoid of furniture, stripped back to the floorboards. The walls are peeling wallpaper and bare plaster. There are pictures tacked to all of them – what appear to be charcoal on off-white paper. Others are screwed up on the floor, and marked with boot prints, like they've been trampled. They all show the same thing – a large black cat, sometimes in close-up, sometimes a face-on or in profile. They're good, for what they are, conveying movement, ferocity and sheer feral bulk. Others defy logic, showing the creature on its hind legs, or with a human, smiling mouth, or walking on hands and feet.

Doug shakes his head. 'This guy's got a screw loose,' he says.

I'm still in the doorway – there's a movement at my feet. The dog's back, tongue lolling. He looks blind in one eye.

When I crouch down to stroke its head, it cowers away and goes to the other door across the tiny landing. It lifts a paw and lays it on the wood, whining again. I can't hear anything coming from the other side.

Neither Doug nor I move for a few seconds.

'Patrick?' I say. 'Mr Draper, are you in there?'

The dog is going at the door with both paws, and starts to bark too. Whatever's on the other side of that door is driving it mad. If I could wind back time, right then, I would. I'd never have come here. But it's far too late for that. The moment I enlisted Felicity's services, this was always a possibility. The least I can do is open the door and face whatever consequences there are.

Doug gets there first. He goes to the door, hand on the handle, and speaks up close. 'Mr Draper, we're coming in.'

Then he pushes the door open quickly and steps inside. 'Oh Jesus.'

My feet carry me closer, but Doug throws out a hand.

'Don't!' he says. 'Stay back.'

I do as he says, like he's cast a spell. 'Is it Gemma?'

Doug is breathing hard, his eyes still on the room I can't see. He shakes his head. 'I think it's him,' he says quietly.

It's not relief, but it breaks the spell, and I approach nearer. 'Sarah, don't . . .' he says again. 'He's killed himself.'

He doesn't stop me, but he doesn't move aside either, so I have to squeeze past.

On the other side, a bedroom reveals itself. My eyes travel over a chest of drawers, the top covered in lace. A dressing table with a mirror. A rug on a wooden floor, stained with an arc of blood. The metal posts of a bed. Two bare human feet, hairy with filthy, curled-up yellow

253

nails. Then legs in jeans. More blood, thick and sticky, pooled and soaking into a duvet. The top half of the body is drenched over its chest, the face turned away. Several gouts of blood have sprayed across the headboard and onto the wall. A drop of blood drips from the edge of the saturated duvet onto the floor.

I let my gaze settle on the dead man's neck, where it looks like it's been punctured. There's a dark hole about the size of a fifty-pence piece. His eyes are closed. I round the end of the bed and see that in his bloodstained right hand he's holding something. I think it's some sort of bone-handled corkscrew – the sort of thing I buy Doug for his birthday when I can't think of anything else.

'Hello, I need the police.' Doug's on the phone. I hear him give the details of our location and what we've found, then say, 'Yes, I'm sure. He's gone.'

Before I can stop it, the dog hops up onto the bed.

'Down,' I say.

The dog ignores me. It lowers its nose to the man's inert face and begins to lick at the sticky blood. I should be disgusted, but there's something undeniably moving about the gesture.

'They want us to wait outside,' says Doug, gesturing towards the door. 'Come on, fella,' he addresses the dog.

The sheepdog cocks its head, panting, then sinks down onto the bed, curling its body tightly so its muzzle rests over the tip of its tail

Neither Doug nor I have a mind to move it.

Chapter 37

GEMMA

'You're marked, I tell you. Just like her. Like Alice. I saw your car.'

Patrick said the same thing several times, and it made no sense at all. Did he mean the scratches? He stood over her, his body pinning hers to the door, both hands pressing it closed. His eyes were pained and wild. Gemma recognised the look. She'd dealt with rough residents at the care home. Old men with dementia could get aggressive and even violent, sometimes with little warning. Most of the time, it didn't matter. You could talk them round, or get out, or call for help from one of the blokes on shift. But this felt different. No one was coming today.

'I don't know who Alice is,' she said, trying to keep her voice calm. 'Please, I need to go. Someone's waiting for me.'

'*It*'s waiting for you. Out there. You told me yourself – it were after you.'

'Wait? The guy from the pub?'

He looked confused, and closed his eyes, shaking his head like he wanted to dislodge something inside. 'Not him! *It*. The creature. The cat.' He slammed both hands into the door, and spit flecked from his lips. 'Won't you open yer bloody ears, girlie? It'll rip your guts out!' He stared defiantly, daring her to contradict him.

'Okay, okay!' she said. 'I'll stay here. Just give me some space, all right.'

He seemed to relax a little, easing his weight off the door. 'Good,' he said. 'I'm only trying to look after— Ugh!'

He doubled up with a grunt as she thrust her knee into his groin, then toppled to one side. Gemma pulled open the door, which caught on his foot. She yanked the door again, hard, bashing his leg out of the way and making him groan in pain. Then she ran out of the house into the night.

She located the path leading off the road, over a stone stile built into the wall. It wasn't quite pitch-black, and she found the track was fairly easy to follow. Periodically, she looked back and checked there was no one following, and when she guessed she was four hundred metres or so from the house, she paused to catch her breath and call Mark.

Only she didn't have her phone. She patted all her pockets, then fished desperately in the rucksack as the truth slowly stole over her. She'd left it in his house. It must have fallen out when she tripped over the dog. Either that, or somehow she'd dropped it on the path, but she was pretty sure she'd have heard it hit the rocky ground.

'Fuck,' she breathed.

She weighed up the risks, and decided she couldn't go back. He'd be madder than ever. She'd told Mark an hour, and he'd be expecting her by the mast tower. And now she couldn't call him, it was more urgent than ever. The phone would lock itself. Even if, by some miracle, it fell into the hands of their enemies, there was no way it could lead to her.

She took out the map and walked on, watching the shadows of grey clouds scudding overhead. The only light came from the moon, and she realised if the clouds thickened much more, she'd be in complete darkness. It wouldn't matter how good the path was then – she wouldn't be able to see a thing.

It was tough going over the uneven ground, and though she was treading carefully, it took her by surprise at times, jarring her knees or sucking her feet into muddy patches. She could see fifteen metres ahead, twenty at most, but beyond that loomed nothing except a dark wall – a darkness she'd never even thought possible. Gemma had the unnerving sense that she could just keep going, forever, into that black oblivion, walking until she stepped off the edge of the world.

She checked the map, holding it right under her nose to reflect any meagre light there was. There were no landmarks on the route, no walls, or fences, or even the remains of buildings. On either side of the path were squiggles that meant marshland, and that thought made her shudder. Lose the path, and she could quickly find herself in trouble, up to the waist or maybe deeper in swampy bog. There'd be no guarantee of getting out again.

She pressed on. She tried to find hope to cling onto. If Mark was right – and she had to trust him – they hadn't followed the car, and it was only she who was compromised. And maybe they didn't really know at all. The guy from the pub might just have been working on a hunch — a hunch she'd proven correct. There was no way to tell.

It happened slowly, and at first she didn't want to accept it. The clouds were thickening, a thin mist descending and stealing over the hillside. The fifteen metres of path ahead became ten, then less. She felt her eyes straining with the effort of trying to pick out much to either side. The moon was no longer guiding her, completely obscured. So, with her eyes on the ground, she pushed on, as fast as her legs could carry her without actually breaking into a run.

With no way to judge distance other than by time, she checked her watch frequently, mentally substituting a minute for a hundred metres. Doing so only made the minutes seem to drag more slowly than ever, further disorientating her to the point she felt herself separated completely from the normal rules of space and time. Here she was, moving somewhere between land and sky into the unknown.

Her right foot turned over a loose rock. She actually heard a creak of the ligaments along her arch, and she almost fell, letting out a gasp of agony. Bile rose in waves in her throat, as she stopped, all her weight on her left leg, waiting for the throbbing pain to subside. Terror rose up in its wake. The foot hung, hot and heavy and loose from the ankle. She didn't know if she'd be able to walk.

Taking a few deep breaths, she gritted her teeth and placed the foot gently on the ground. It hurt like mad, but it held her weight. Proceeding with greater care, eyes on the path, she hobbled along. She'd made it this far. If she had to crawl, she would. Her hair had become damp with the heavy moisture in the air. Each step sent shock waves from her foot right up into the back of her skull, but in a few dozen steps, the intensity softened. The darkness was close to absolute now – the path only visible for five or six metres in front of her.

A shrieking noise broke the silence, making her slow. It came from the left and the shrill bird cry died in a long echo, followed by a rapid snapping of wings. Just a bird. A pheasant, maybe, that she couldn't see, disturbed from the heather. In its wake came another sound. One that glued her to the spot. This was more deliberate, a soft compression. Then another.

Footsteps, prowling.

Chapter 38

SARAH

Yet another car drives past, slows, faces peering out in curiosity at Mill Cottage, no doubt intrigued by the police car parked outside. I catch the face of a woman and smile. I suppose I'm part of the show now.

No one on the scene knows what to do with the half-blind dog. His name, we've learned from his collar, is Chappie. He wanders about, into and out of the house, throwing curious glances at the comings and goings of the half a dozen police officers. He seems happy enough, his tail wagging. Whenever he comes over to me, I lay a hand on his warm fur. It's comforting to touch something alive and uncomplicated, when my sister's fate is still a mystery.

The facts all point in a simple direction though, and there's no point denying it to myself. Gemma was here, and what possible explanation could there be for that other than being brought here against her will? Her phone either ran out of batteries here or was switched off in Patrick Draper's house. And now he has killed himself, in his bedroom, maybe the very day he was watching me searching for Gemma. He wasn't right in the head, that much is clear from what I learned at the pub and the drawings upstairs. But there are still questions. Why my sister? Was she just in the wrong place at the wrong time? And how does Mark's fate tie into this?

The police officers on the scene so far are all in uniform. Since the paramedics went in to confirm the death, they've donned booties and gloves so they don't disturb the scene too much.

Doug and I are waiting at the side of the house, sitting on a low wall, and feeling like spare parts. His arm is over my shoulders. It must have been ninety minutes since we found him, and an hour since the first officers arrived on the scene. They took the barest details from us and have spent most of the rest of the time on the phone. Every light in the house is on, and there are flashing blue lights from the two cars parked on the road. They catch Doug's features. He looks annoyed. He's asked a couple of times when we can leave, but the officers just ask us to hold tight for now. We've already spoken about what we'll say – that we found the door open, and followed the dog upstairs. Half true, and it hardly matters anyway.

They haven't brought the body down yet. I suppose it'll go in the ambulance at some point, maybe after they've taken photos. From there, to the same morgue as my sister's remains. That seems somehow wrong if he was the one who took her life in the first place.

Yet another car pulls up. A grey BMW. Sergeant Nelson

gets out of the driver's side, and Constable Dewer the opposite door. They speak briefly to the officer on the front path, who notes down their details. Nelson spies us, but makes a beeline for the front door. Dewer hesitates, and comes over. He gives a friendly nod to Doug.

'Ms Kline.'

'Constable Dewer. This is my partner, Doug.'

They shake hands.

'You both all right?' he asks. 'Must've been a shock.'

He hasn't seen what's upstairs yet. 'Shock' doesn't quite do it for me.

But I say 'yes'.

'Has anyone taken a statement from you yet?'

We shake our heads, and Dewer calls over to someone called Barry. A stout, balding man in his late forties comes across. 'Constable Smith will take your statement, Mr . . .' He looks to Doug.

'Thomas,' says Doug. 'Doug Thomas.'

Dewer turns to me. 'Ms Kline, if you'll follow me.'

Panic rises from my chest. 'Wait, we're doing it separately?'

'Protocol,' says Dewer. 'Nothing to worry about.'

I throw a glance at Doug as I follow Dewer. I know I shouldn't be worried. We agreed not to mention the phone. And there's no suspicion in Dewer's face. Like he said, it's just procedure.

Dewer opens the back door of the police car so I can take a seat, then sits in the front himself. He turns on the heaters.

'Why were you even here, Ms Kline?'

I trot out the half-truth: that I saw Draper watching me the day before and wanted to talk to him.

263

Dewer stares at me like he knows, or at least suspects, I'm lying. Maybe he has a sense for falsehoods, or maybe this is the same tactic he used before, letting me fill the silence.

I hold his gaze, and add, 'I thought he might know something, that's all.'

'A bit risky, no?'

'I had Doug with me.'

He doesn't write anything down and maintains eye contact.

'And what led to you entering the house?'

I take him through it. The dog, the open door, then climbing the stairs and the discoveries in the two rooms: the pictures in one and the body in the other. I keep it basic, partly because I don't want to relive the horror, partly because I don't want to contradict anything, however small, that Doug might be saying to the other officer.

'I heard he was obsessed with the idea of a big cat, but those drawings were *weird*. The same thing, over and over again.'

'Paddy always was a strange one,' says Dewer. 'He was a decent sort though.'

'I think he killed my sister,' I say quietly.

Dewer looks at me. 'Why?'

I could tell him about the phone right now. That's the missing piece of the puzzle he can't even see. 'Look what he did to himself,' I say. 'Who does that unless they've got a guilty conscience?'

'People kill themselves all the time. Especially lonely old men.'

'But he was watching me, yesterday. And someone in the pub said he had a connection with the school, with Alice . . .'

'We have someone in custody already,' says Dewer.

He means Reuben, of course. I realise then that I can't keep quiet.

There's a knock on the window, and I see Nelson leaning down. Dewer winds it down. 'Need you inside, Constable.'

'Have you found something?' I ask.

'Sit tight, Ms Kline,' she replies.

I obey, not through any sense of deference to authority, but because the warmth of the car is comforting and I don't know where else to go or what else to do. I watch them both walk back towards the house and wonder if Nelson will buy the excuse for my presence too. There's a chance, I realise, that they might get a warrant to look at my communications devices. The link from Felicity is pretty well disguised, but a thorough search has a decent chance of uncovering it.

No. I'm thinking too far ahead. I'm not a suspect here. The story I told Dewer stands up. For now. If they don't let Reuben go sharpish, I'll need to rethink though. I can't leave Hartsbridge if he's still the prime suspect.

Looking back out of the window, I see the paramedics are entering the house again, this time carrying a stretcher between them.

Doug comes to the car, so I get out.

'Something's going on,' he says.

Together, we walk back to the house. Sergeant Nelson, Dewer and two other officers are standing to one side of the front door, inspecting a small polythene bag. When Nelson sees me watching, she says something to Dewer, who lowers it out of sight. It couldn't be more obvious they're trying to hide something.

'What's that?' I call, walking over.

Nelson moves to intercept me, but I rush past her. 'Ms Kline . . .'

'It's Gemma's phone, isn't it?' I say.

Dewer turns to face me. The arms are behind his back, holding the bag. 'It's evidence,' he says.

'If it's something to do with Gemma, I deserve to be told.'

'It's not related to your sister's disappearance,' he says.

'You're lying.' I try to get past to look, and Dewer throws a frustrated glance at Nelson. 'Just show me!' I say.

'Fine,' says Nelson. 'It can't hurt.'

Dewer takes out the bag. There's a tag on it, with writing, but I can't read it. The inside of the bag is coated with specks of blood. I recognise the yellow colour of the object, but it's not a corkscrew. There's no metal. It's a single scythe-shaped piece of bone, maybe three inches long, with a wicked sharp point.

'Is that a claw?'

'Something like that,' says Dewer. 'We've no idea if it's genuine.' He lowers it again.

It certainly looks real. It's discoloured at one end. It's like nothing I've ever seen outside a wildlife documentary, buried in the hindquarters of a struggling impala. It sets off some deep-seated flight response in the recesses of my brain, but seems to have no place here, in this setting.

'Why would he have your sister's phone?' asks Nelson. She's looking at me hawkishly.

I look at Doug. He gives the smallest of nods. He wanted to tell them before, and maybe it's not such an issue now. These people aren't my enemies.

'Gemma was here,' I say. 'I tracked her phone.'

Dewer looks dumbfounded and Nelson takes a deep breath. '*You* tracked her phone. How?'

'Does it matter?' I say, meeting her challenge. 'The point is, it was here, a day after her boyfriend died.'

None of them speak for a moment.

'I didn't have a choice,' I add. 'I needed to find her.'

Nelson nods slowly. 'Okay, Smith – we're going to need a forensic team out here, right away.'

'On it, boss,' says the officer.

Nelson looks at me. 'Ms Kline, I appreciate this is hard for you, but it would be good if you could stay in the vicinity for the rest of the day.'

'Do we have to?' asks Doug, a little petulantly. 'She's been through enough.'

'At some point, I'm going to need to see this trace.'

'I'm afraid you can't,' I say. 'The person I got it from only made it available for a limited time.'

'How convenient,' replies Nelson. 'So I only have your word for the whereabouts of your sister's phone.'

I'm not sure why, but something in her attitude seems to have changed. She's not quite the kind and compassionate officer who dealt with me at the station. Maybe it's because I've embarrassed her, getting one step ahead in the case. Maybe she really thought Reuben Fletwick was her man. I assume he'll be released quickly in light of all this.

'Why would I lie?' I say.

'We could check ourselves now, boss,' suggests Dewer. 'Probable cause should be enough for a warrant.'

Nelson glares at him.

I back off, towards Doug again. 'Can we get out of here, please?'

Doug nods and wraps a protective arm around me.

'You should get some rest,' says Constable Dewer, more gently.

I can't imagine what he means. It's eleven-thirty in the morning. I'm hardly going to take a nap. 'We'll be at the pub,' I say to them. 'If you find anything, I need to know.'

'Don't worry,' says Dewer. He looks across at the house, a little balefully. 'We'll be here all day.'

Chappie wanders in between us, like an actor stumbling onto the wrong stage. His tail is wagging. 'What'll happen to him?' I ask.

Dewer looks at the dog. 'We'll call the warden. He'll go to one of the shelters.'

Chappie looks up at me, hopefully. One of his front paws is still flecked with his owner's blood.

Chapter 39

GEMMA

'Mark?' she called.

Of course it wasn't him. It was coming from off to the side of the path. In the wetlands. There was no reason for Mark to be there.

Patrick Draper then. He must have followed her.

Rain had started to fall, invisibly. Through its patter, she though she heard another step, perhaps ten metres away. Maybe closer. She could physically feel her ear canals, primed for any sound. And there was something else. A low breathing. A rumble from deep in a heaving chest.

She crouched down to the path and picked up a rock slightly bigger than her fist. 'Leave me alone!' she shouted. 'I'll fuck you up!'

She lifted the stone in her hand as she continued up the path, eyes fighting the darkness. She heard no more noises, but she fancied she could feel the presence keeping pace, beyond the limits of her vision. If it was Draper, she reckoned she could probably overpower him. And if she got a lucky strike with the rock, even better.

Then, quite suddenly, she saw a tall metal fence right in front of her, the tips of the posts split into spikes. Just on the other side, rising high above her, the skeletal shape of the mast. Her heart leapt, and she laid her hand on cool metal, grateful just to touch some sign of civilisation. A bright point of light appeared to one side, blinding her. All she saw was the shape of a figure rushing in. She yelped and lifted the stone.

'Gem! It's me!'

The light dropped and Mark's pale face appeared. She buried her head in his shoulder and felt his arms wrap her up.

'I've been calling and calling,' he said. 'Fuck, babe, I thought . . .'

'I lost my phone,' she told him. She turned around. 'I think there's someone out here.'

Mark shined his camera torch back along the path, and swung it to either side. It hardly penetrated the grey mist, but she couldn't see anyone.

'Let's go,' he said, and started leading her along the fence, and then there was hard ground under her feet again. They arrived at the car, all its lights off. Reaching for the door, she paused, her eyes snagging on the scratches.

'What's up?' said Mark. 'Get in.'

'He said it was marked.'

'Hey?'

'I think he was the one who scratched the car,' she said. '*Who*?'

'Patrick,' she said. 'The man from the village.'

Mark shrugged. 'Don't matter now. We'll get some new wheels soon.'

They climbed in. On the back seat was a blue bag of thick polythene, full.

'Is that it?' she said.

'It's all there,' Mark nodded, then rounded the other side of the car.

He jumped in and slammed his door, turning the key. Gemma panicked as the engine turned over several times with a wheezing sound, before growling into life. Then Mark leant over and kissed her hard on the lips. For a second, she forgot everything. Being chased from the hostel, the weird old man, the noises in the dark. They'd done it. They'd won. There was more money than she'd ever seen on the back seat. They could go home.

Chapter 40

SARAH

We drive back towards The Headless Woman, but pull over once the house, and the police, are out of sight. Doug says we should pack up and go. It's still before noon, so we could easily get back to London before nightfall. He says the police can't keep us here. 'You're the lawyer, aren't you?'

He doesn't seem to understand, or maybe he's choosing not to. 'I don't want to go. Not yet.'

'There's nothing we can do here,' he says. 'You've got to let the police get on with things.'

'I need to *know*,' I reply.

'We do know though, don't we?' he says. 'Sarah. She's gone. You said it yourself. She was at his house. Don't torture yourself by sticking around this place. None of this is your fault, or your responsibility.'

It'll be torture anywhere I go, trying to work out what exactly happened to Gemma.

'Just a few more hours,' I say. 'While they carry out a search of his house.'

'And if they don't find anything? Do you want to move up here permanently?'

'Doug, she's my—'

'Sister, I know,' he says. 'But you're my fiancée, and I hate seeing you do this to yourself.'

'Another night at most,' I say. 'Then whatever happens, we go home.'

'What about work?'

'They'll understand.'

I'm certain the police *will* find something. They have to. Patrick Draper didn't look like the sort of man who would have been able to hide evidence from experienced investigators. Even if it's just a hair, or a bloodstain, or something belonging to Gemma.

We go back into the pub and straight to the room up the back stairs. My half-packed suitcase is still on the bed. 'I'm going for a soak,' I say. I need to get the stink of Draper's house off me.

I go into the bathroom, splash warm water on my face, and start to fill the bath. The pipes clank ominously. Doug comes in after a couple of minutes, carrying his phone.

'Check this out,' he says, extending it towards me. He's googled images of big cat claws. Sure enough, they look almost identical to the object in the evidence bag. 'I wonder where he got it.'

He's trying to release the tension and I'm grateful. 'You can probably buy them on eBay,' I say. Not that Patrick Draper seemed like the e-commerce sort.

'I need a drink,' says Doug. 'And if we're not going anywhere . . .'

'I think they're closed today,' I reply, recalling what Tara told me before.

'Place like this never *really* closes,' Doug says with a smile. 'Anyway, Tara and I are good friends again.' He did indeed manage to coax two bowls of soup the night before, so he must've somehow convinced her to forgive the violence he visited on her son. Whether Archie feels the same way is another matter.

'Maybe say we'll be here another night.'

'You're sure you wouldn't rather—'

'*Please*, Doug.'

He holds up both hands in defeat, backs out of the bathroom, and tosses his phone on the bed. I sit on the edge of the bath, testing the temperature as it fills.

Maybe Doug's right that it's pointless being here, but there are still too many unanswered questions. Things I'm missing. Did Mark and Gemma have a connection with this place I know nothing about? Or did they simply find themselves in the wrong place at the wrong time? I want to understand why, because I know if I go back to London without some grasp of why my sister died, this will eat away at me. I couldn't help her, just like I couldn't help Mum.

Once the bath is luxuriously full, the bathroom filled with steam, I undress and slide in. When I close my eyes, all I can see is the claw. I can't help imagining the force and determination Patrick Draper used to puncture his throat. The question is why. Just because the police were closing in? Because of me? Maybe it's futile to dissect his psychology. The drawings in his house speak for themselves. He wasn't in his right mind. The horrible truth is that my sister found herself, somehow or other, in his presence. And that was her undoing. Did she see something she shouldn't, prompting a violent reaction? Did she just say the wrong thing? If he was really serious about the cat business, maybe she took the piss.

Annoyingly, I've nothing to wash with – my toiletries are all in the shower. Doug's travel bag is on the shelf by the sink though. I reach over, trying not to drip on the floor too much, and hook a finger through the handle. Inside, there's some shampoo and shower gel, so I fish them out. Something else, something small, plops into the bath. I reach under the bubbles, feeling with my fingers, and find it. It feels like a cufflink, but as the suds fall off, I realise it's not.

It's an earring, silver with a blue teardrop pendant.

The water seems to drop a couple of degrees, as I'm taken back to a few days earlier, when my colleague Katriona almost bumped into me in the hallway and I resisted the urge to ask where she got them.

Fuck, *no* . . .

My mind throws up the briefest of defences. Just a fleeting, token stab at making excuses as to why Kat's earring might have found its way into Doug's things. Why? I'm not sure, because on the surface it's not a little ironic. I've sat in enough rooms and heard enough tales of disintegrating relationships to be thoroughly disabused of any notions of fidelity. To think that somehow I might be different, or special . . . Well, that's sheer arrogance, isn't it?

It stings, though, like a hand's grabbed my heart and yanked it from its moorings. I'm reeling too much to let it sink in properly. Or maybe it's my own psychological defences that are keeping me numb and somehow indifferent to the enormity of that glittering sapphire. It will hurt, later. I know it will.

I stand up, my mind turning to immediate practicalities and arrangements. Things I can control and must get a grip on. The wedding, the guests. Susanna's flying in, for Christ's sake! The fucking honeymoon . . .

I climb out of the bath and wrap a towel around myself. Katriona? *Really?* Until a minute ago, I only remember a single time she and Doug met, about two months ago when we happened to be out in the same area of the city as Doug and his mates on a Friday night after work. I'd left early when Doug had mentioned karaoke, my idea of hell. Katriona didn't. In fact, looking back, hadn't she said on Monday morning that he was a great singer? That's impressively two-faced.

No wonder she's not coming to the reception.

God, am I *that* blind?

Take me through this, as a cocky barrister might say. How many times since have they met, behind my back? There hasn't been a single night Doug and I spent apart, but I can't say I know what he gets up to in the day, other than his work, which he claims is stultifyingly dull. He would say that, wouldn't he? Kat works hard, like me. Long hours. She's had some issues to sort with her tenants – her parents' old house just outside the M25 . . .

I really am a fool, aren't I?

Her tenancy issue has been going on for several weeks. A run of bad luck. The washing machine flooding the kitchen. A fence blowing down. What was it a couple of weeks ago?

That's right – a key breaking in the lock. We laughed at it, together, as she asked to knock off a couple of hours early.

It seems she was laughing at me.

I feel angry and sick. It's four days since I saw her in those earrings. Had they had something in the diary – some crappy hotel room equidistant from our offices? Doug didn't want me to come here at all – he tried his damnedest to stop me – but as soon as I was out of the flat he must have called her. A window of opportunity. A chance to get back at me, even.

In the bedroom, still dripping, I lock the door with the bolt. His phone is on the bed. I know the code, just as he knows mine. What did we ever have to hide?

I open his messages. There's nothing there. Pete from work. His stag do group from a couple of weeks ago. His brother Hamish. His mum. I sink to the bed, thinking about Marion. His poor mother, just out the other side of chemo. She worships the ground her eldest boy walks on. I don't want to think what this will do to her. The hat she was planning can go back in the bloody box.

There's nothing that looks like it's from Katriona, and I guess he wouldn't be that stupid. Maybe he's got another phone he uses for hook-ups. I might not be the only one with my 'bag of tricks'.

I see his running app, top left of the home screen. He records everything there – distances, times, elevation, heart rate. How many times his cheating feet touch the tarmac every minute. He often went in the middle of a workday, showering afterwards in the office basement. Occasionally, he's off and out before I'm even up though. The app brings up the latest outing he's logged – a fifteen-mile circuit

278

from the flat, Regents Park, looping back along the canal to North London.

It was Saturday, two days ago. I know straight away that's not right. His schedule is six days at a week at the moment, religiously. He had Thursday off. Ran Saturday, but not Sunday. He *always* runs Sunday – says it's his favourite time, through the empty City, out towards Canary Wharf.

Not yesterday morning, though, when I tried to call several times and he didn't answer.

My heart jumps as the door opens and catches on the security lock. 'You all right?' Doug says through the narrow gap.

I close the app and toss the phone back on the bed, feeling oddly calm.

'Just getting dry,' I say, then unfasten the lock.

He comes in, holding a plate with a couple of bags of crisps and a bottle of wine in a cooler.

'Not a huge choice, I'm afraid.'

'Never mind.'

'You've had a bath already?'

'Uh-huh.'

I can hardly look at him. Everything I used to love about his face has soured. Like I'm in the presence of a different person entirely. Why couldn't I see it, because it's so obvious now – it's just a mask. I feel like I've walked onto a stage, with no script and expected to improvise the most dramatic scene of my life so far. I almost don't have the strength myself, but if I don't do this now, I'll never forgive myself. I have the strange sense of Gemma actually looking on. I see him like I know she did.

'Where'd you want this?' he asks, looking around.

I clear the side table, then pick up my clothes and head into the bathroom. Even being naked in front of him disgusts me.

He follows me in, folding his arms around my waist and leaning in to kiss my neck.

I pull away. 'Don't.'

He looks offended. 'I just thought you might need, y'know . . . to relax.'

'Not like that,' I say.

'Fair enough.'

He disappears into the other room. I get dry properly, and dressed, and tie back my hair. Then with the earring tucked in my hand, I follow him. He's eating a packet of crisps, standing at the window with his back to me.

'Good run yesterday?' I ask.

Keeping up the act admirably, he turns to face me, but I see the tiny jerk of his eyes towards the phone on the bed, making a split-second calculation, as if he knows that it's evidence which could damn him.

'Not really,' he says. 'I only got a few hundred metres. My stomach was playing up.'

Quick thinking. It would be almost funny if it weren't so obvious.

'How come you didn't mention it earlier?'

He looks at me while he unscrews the wine bottle. 'Odd question, sweetheart. It didn't seem important.' He begins to pour, frowning. 'You okay?'

'Not really.'

He offers me a glass, and I fight the urge to swipe it out of his hand. That would involve getting close, and that thought makes my skin crawl.

He stands there, arm extended, then pulls back. 'Do you mind if I do?'

'Go ahead.'

He takes a large swig. 'You know, the barmaid was talking downstairs about this big cat business. I don't know how you've coped up here on your own. These people are bonkers.'

I can't do it any more. It's actually pitiful watching him squirm. 'I want you to go, Doug.'

'Pardon?' he says.

'You heard. Pack your stuff, get in the car, and go.'

'Hey, I know you're upset about Gemma, but I've just got—'

'Don't,' I say. 'Don't fucking try. I know, all right.' He's holding my stare. 'I *know*.'

He pauses. 'I really don't have the foggiest what you're talking about.'

There was no doubt in my mind anyway, but his laughable acting confirms everything. The condescension is maddening.

I toss the earring, and it lands on the bed between us.

'It would have been better if she was a stranger,' I say, 'but *Kat*? I have to work two offices over.' I laugh, bitterly. 'Do you think she'll have the decency to quit?'

Doug puts down the glass, lowers his eyes. Will he make one more stab at denial?

'I know this won't mean much at the moment, but it's over.'

'What's over?'

'Me and her. I told her yesterday morning – that's why I went to meet her. It was a stupid mistake.'

He must be living in some sort of parallel universe. 'You're right,' I say. 'It doesn't mean *anything*.' I take a deep breath. 'Please, go.'

There's a knock at the door, and we both turn towards it. Talk about timing.

'Just a minute,' says Doug. He gets up and opens the door, clearly grateful for the reprieve.

'Sorry to bother you,' says Tara. 'The police are here. They need to speak with you.'

We share a glance, the argument forgotten for a moment.

Chapter 41

GEMMA

Mark drove slowly as Gemma rolled him a cigarette, using the map on her knees. She lit it and passed it over. It had started to rain harder, so he kept the windows closed. She tried to tell him about the man at the hostel, but he simply blew a jet of smoke.

'They must have been guessing,' he said. 'I mean, how could they have known?'

'Maybe they saw me drop the note.'

'Nah. Think about it. If they really knew it was us, why dump the money at all? They could have come for us both, any time they wanted.'

Gemma supposed it made sense. She felt stupid. Now she'd run, they'd know for sure. She said as much to Mark.

'No way they can find us though, is there?' he said. 'Fake names. No ID. We live at the other end of the bloody country.'

'What about the number plate on the car?' she asked.

'It's registered to Carlton Place,' he replied. It had been their address three years ago. 'Babe, stop fretting.'

The car's headlamps picked up the road ahead and they caught the silver rods of rain.

Gemma couldn't share Mark's bravado. Their faces were well known. What if the people at the old country house worked through it logically, putting out feelers via all the people they supplied? Was it really beyond the realms of possibility that word might get back to Brighton and Kash, and someone might give their names?

Panic made her scalp tingle. If there'd been an option to give the money back, then and there, she'd have been tempted. Winding back the clock wasn't possible. Burned bridges couldn't be rebuilt. They'd make it back to Brighton and settle their immediate debts with Des. But that might not be the end of it. She couldn't help thinking that what they'd done here would come to bite them, one way or another. Mark might be able to brush it off, but he was like that with everything. For her it was different, and she already anticipated the sleepless nights as it gnawed away at her consciousness.

That was *if* they stuck around. The money they'd have left over would be enough for a fresh start somewhere else. A few months anyway. And there were care homes everywhere, always begging for experienced staff. She sat back, breathing a little more easily. Maybe there was light at the end of the tunnel. She'd wait until they were back to bring it up.

Something hit the windscreen with a splintering crash. Mark fought the wheel, the rubber screeching on the road, and came to a halt.

'What the fuck was that? A bird?'

The glass had held, and whatever had hit them left a starburst of cracks. Gemma was sure it hadn't been a bird, but something much heavier.

Two headlights appeared ahead, springing from the darkness, like the eyes of an animal fixed on its prey.

Chapter 42

SARAH

Tara leads me from the bedroom, and Doug tries to follow.

'Stay out of it,' I say under my breath.

He gets the message, pausing at the top of the stairs. 'Sarah, I want to—'

'I don't care,' I say. 'This is nothing to do with you.'

I head downstairs. Constable Dewer is waiting discreetly at the side door. He's ashen. It's only a couple of hours since I saw him at Draper's house.

'You've found something?' I say.

'Is there somewhere private we could talk?'

I look towards the bar – there are several people in there, but Tara points along the corridor. 'Use the lounge,' she says. 'There's no one about.'

We follow the corridor, through a door marked private, and find ourselves in another vestibule. There's a small kitchen and, to one side, a living room with sofas and a

TV. Dewer invites me to take a seat. I tell him I prefer to stand.

'We need to let you know that we've carried out a preliminary search of Patrick Draper's house.' He sounds formal, like he's reading from a script. 'In the course of that search, we looked into an old well shaft at the rear of his property and discovered human remains. They're yet to be formally identified, but our initial impressions are that they belong to a woman in her early thirties.'

'Gemma.'

'We believe so, yes.'

Now I do sit, letting gravity fold my body onto one of the sofas. It feels unreal, but I know it shouldn't. All the evidence so far has been pointing this way.

'Where is she, now?'

Dewer swallows. 'The remains are on their way to the hospital morgue in Bishop Auckland,' he says. 'They'll be examined over the next few hours, in order to confirm the identity and determine an exact cause of death.'

'I have a picture of her, if that helps,' I say.

Dewer grimaces. 'That will be of limited use, I think.'

'What does that mean?'

He looks at the floor. 'There's some decay, because of the immersion in the stagnant water. And I'm sorry to say the body is disarticulated. We haven't yet been able . . . We haven't actually found all of it.'

I have nothing to say to that. *Disarticulated*. Cut up. It shouldn't be shocking, given what was discovered in the river. But there's only one bit they need to find, really, in order to identify her.

'You can't find her head.'

Dewer's only gesture is another glance at the floor. 'It may be that it's somewhere else on the property,' he continues. 'As soon as we have anything concrete, we'll let you know. Ms Kline, you have my deepest condolences.'

'You can call me Sarah,' I say.

'I'm sorry, Sarah. I really am.'

I suppose that's it, then. He looks ready to go, and I don't blame him. But something doesn't entirely make sense.

'I don't understand – if you found the body in the well, how did one arm get into the river?'

'We don't know,' says Dewer. 'We're working on the assumption it was deliberately placed there.'

'He wanted someone to find it?'

The constable shrugs. 'Paddy Draper was clearly not of sound mind – it might be a mistake to read logic into his actions. We're just following the evidence trail at this stage.'

'Thank you,' I say, shakily. 'I know this can't be easy for you or your colleagues either.'

He smiles, with sympathy. 'Don't worry about us, please. If there is anything else I can do for you, let me know.'

Find the rest of her, I think. *Find her head.*

'Are we free to go?' I ask.

'Of course. We have your contact details. We'll have to release a statement to the press. It will just say the body of a woman has been discovered at a property in Hartsbridge. Your name, and Gemma's identity, won't be mentioned. I need to warn you though, I can vouch for the discretion of my immediate team, but it's possible more details will leak. If you receive calls from numbers you don't recognise, it might be best to ignore them.'

'I understand. One more thing. My partner and I are

having . . . difficulties. Please don't contact him if there's any more news.'

'Of course.' He wishes me goodbye without enquiring anything more, and I'm grateful. I watch him leave the room, and remain seated for a few more minutes, considering my next move. I feel more alone than ever, and there's a pathetic sliver of me that wants Doug, even now. Anyone to share this with. And I know full well he'd do it. He'd take care of everything.

I can't go there, though. It wouldn't be real. Any words or gestures of comfort would be a facsimile of affection and make it harder to extricate myself from him. This is my cross to bear, and I know I can do it. I owe it to myself, and to Gemma.

I pick myself up and leave the room. The noise of the bar seems like another world I'll never be able to enter again. I don't want to go back to the room yet, in case Doug's still there, so I walk outside instead. Then I see Doug is already there, by the open boot of the rental car. He spots me too, closes it, and walks over to me.

'There's nothing to say,' I tell him, when he's still a few metres away.

'Don't be like that,' he replies. 'What did they want?'

I keep my arms folded. 'It's none of your business, Doug.'

He stays at a distance. 'I know you need space,' he says. 'I know that.'

'You've no idea what I need,' I say.

He sighs. 'I just spoke to Kat. She wants to call you later.'

'Ha! Don't worry – I'll see her in the office kitchen in a couple of days. That'll be a hoot.'

'We can be adults about this,' he replies. 'Let's meet, back in London. I'll go to Olly's.'

'Go wherever you want.'

'Okay.' He holds up a hand, bowing his head. 'We can sort this out, though. I know we can. It was a stupid mistake.'

'You said that already.'

'And I'll keep saying it,' says Doug. 'I'm not giving up on us.'

I can't believe I'm hearing this. Does he really think . . .? Surely, he can't.

'There is no "us",' I clarify. 'There was no *us* from the moment you stuck your dick in another woman.'

He flinches. 'It wasn't like that.'

'Oh, so you were playing Scrabble?'

'Work was bad,' he begins. 'You were so busy—'

'Don't even go there.'

'You know I love you, more than anything. Kat meant nothing.'

'Fucking stop, Doug! She meant nothing to *you*. This is all about *you*.'

He lets out a deeper sigh, and there are tears in his eyes. 'We're supposed to be getting married on Saturday,' he says, pleading.

If that's supposed to be some sort of guilt-inducing ultimatum, he's so far off the mark, I almost laugh out loud.

'Doug, even if I could forgive you – and believe me, I *never* will – I just found out my sister has been chopped into fucking pieces and dumped in a hole in the ground. Do you honestly think I'd go anywhere near a wedding dress in five days' time?'

'I . . . I . . .' He's run out of bargaining chips.

'Get out of my life. Stay out of my life. I never want to see your face again.'

I walk past him, back through the front doors of the pub. The sign of The Headless Woman swings gently in the wind. It's like a sick joke in search of a laugh.

Chapter 43

GEMMA

The headlights were brighter than their own and completely blinding. The car didn't move. It stayed there, the invisible occupants watching.

'Oh fuck,' said Mark.

'Who is it?' asked Gemma. Though she already had a good idea. It was a Land Rover.

One of the doors of the other car opened, and an older man stepped out. Though Gemma couldn't be sure, she thought he was the other man they'd seen on their second day in Hartsbridge, meeting the motorbike rider at the country house. He was large, and heavyset, with a scarred cheek.

'Turn around!' Gemma urged. 'Go the other way.' The road, she knew, led back past the mast tower the way Mark had driven in.

Mark put the car into reverse, but stalled. 'Come on, come

on!' he said, starting the ignition again. The man climbed back into the other vehicle, revved its engine and crawled towards them. Mark succeeded in sending the car shooting backwards. The rear end slipped off the road, throwing Gemma's head back. He crunched the gears into first. They lurched forwards and drove off, quickly gaining speed. Gemma looked back to see the other car following. It came after them, keeping pace, even when Mark accelerated to sixty miles per hour. The road was fairly straight, winding slowly downhill. It was barely ten feet wide. Two miles and they'd be on the main road. Get there, and they'd have a better chance.

'He's going to hit us,' said Mark, with surprising calmness.

A thump went through Gemma's spine as they jerked forwards. Mark gripped the wheel and kept them on the road. He pushed harder on the accelerator, and the lights behind shrank back. They were losing height, coming down through sheets of rain that made it hard to see much at all.

Another light appeared, a dull red, just off to one side of the tarmac. A motorbike, parked up, the rider on the back. He was holding something in his hands, pointing downwards towards the bottom of their car. Too late she realised what it was and threw up her hands.

'Mark, he's got a—'

The barrel discharged a gout of fire and a bang.

The car jerked right, losing the road and skidding through heather. Mark yanked the wheel and brought them back. Gemma saw the road curving ahead, dipping away between two shallow slopes. The Land Rover was still behind them, and catching now.

'Keep going! Keep going!' shouted Gemma.

'It won't go any faster,' said Mark. He was peering over the wheel, and the wipers were on full speed.

Gemma kept her eyes on the road behind, searching for the lights of their pursuer. The Land Rover had dropped out of sight beyond the curve, but she saw its beams lighting up the heather on the other side of the slope.

'Fuck – hold on!'

Mark hit the brakes as they came to a sharp bend, marked with arrows, but the wheels locked.

'Look out!' cried Gemma.

Her hands reached automatically for purchase on the dashboard as she was flung sideways in the seat. They were heading straight for the sign. The car's rear end flew out, and they spun right around in the road. Then a horrible crunch, and she couldn't see anything and the window at her side burst inwards, tarmac and sparks shooting past her face. For a split second, everything was silent, before an enormous thud threw her violently into Mark. Another yank ripped her back again. The car seemed to be coming apart on every side, with glass and metal smashing together. She tried to put her arms over her head, but every part of her body felt powerless, compelled by forces beyond her control. Mark cried out, a terrified howl.

The car was rolling, over and over, and she thought it would never stop.

Chapter 44

SARAH

Doug had the decency to take the earring with him, a token effort to clean his personal crime scene.

I get back into the bath, having run more water. I keep the hot tap going, until it's pouring wastefully down the overflow and the water is almost scaldingly hot. The pain is good. It's fitting. It tells me I'm alive.

Sliding underneath, into a peaceful oblivion, I can hear my own heartbeat, surprisingly slow and steady, a reminder that despite everything the day has thrown my way – I'm going to survive. I stay under the water, with my nose breaching the surface for air. My sister is gone, and my relationship's in tatters. God knows how things will work out at the office.

I know it's wrong to focus on regrets. We're always telling clients that – it's about the future now, and what we make of it. Doug was right about one thing. This *isn't* my fault. I might not have been the best sister, but

Gemma was an adult too, and she carried her own fair share of prejudice and problems. She wasn't my responsibility. Not any more. Why can't I accept that?

Gone are the days I used to wash her hair in a bath just like this, when Mum was too pissed to get up the stairs, telling her to close her eyes and tip back her head. I was the one who made sure she brushed her teeth properly and had the right clothes clean for school. Made her eat her fruit and vegetables, even when she swore – correctly, it proved – that cucumber made her vomit. I taught her to cross the road. I held her hand, at least until she wouldn't let me.

And when she left home at fifteen, when she pushed me away, I let her.

I get out when the water is going cold and dry myself in front of the steamed-up mirror. In the other room, the cold air entwines my ankles and shoulders. There's no sign that Doug was ever here, other than the tray with the wine and the uneaten crisps. The dent left by his head on the pillow. There are three missed calls on my phone though – all from him. What's he thinking now, I wonder, on the long lonely drive back to London? Does he still harbour some vain hope of a reconciliation? Again, my mind travels to the inevitable unravelling of the carefully made wedding plans. I fight off the onslaught of anxiety. Not today. There'll be time to spread the bad news.

I pour a glass of wine and take one sip. It is warm and unpleasantly sweet, like my taste buds are off. There's a bit of noise from outside – a peal of laughter. At the window, I see a minibus in the carpark, with teenagers climbing out in walking gear. Some sort of school trip, maybe. Somehow the world is carrying on, oblivious to the dead bodies and my personal misery. Gemma doesn't mean anything to them, and why should she? It's not even three, and there's really no reason to stick around now. If I leave in the next hour, I can probably get back to London before dark. I think about ringing Bea, or Laura, or one of the other girls, arranging a drink. I could probably crash at one of their places. I don't fancy going back to an empty flat. The thought of having to *explain* rises up like an impossible wall.

Getting dressed, I head downstairs.

To my surprise, Nige is sitting at the bar. His cheeks are flushed and pink, and I see he's on the shorts. Can't blame him, really. Carla's there too, with another young woman I've not seen before. From the way they're sitting, heads close, legs slightly intertwined, I guess they're a couple. Tara is pulling a pint.

'All right, pet?' she says. 'Your fella not with you?'

With everything that's happened since, she seems to hold no grudge about the punch.

'No,' I say. 'He left.'

Tara is good enough to take the hint and not ask questions. She probably doesn't want to get involved, because I can't believe she didn't hear anything *at all* of the argument. No one else seems to bat an eyelid either.

'How's Archie?' I ask.

'Nice little shiner,' she says ruefully. 'He's had worse.'

'That's . . . good, I suppose.' I look around – the fire's not burning. There are chairs on several tables. 'I thought you were closed on a Monday.'

'We are, really,' says Tara, nodding at the door. Sure enough, the bolt is drawn across.

'This is the VIP day,' adds Carla, with a wink. 'Locals only.'

'Oh, I can . . .' I point to the stairs.

'Don't be daft,' says Tara. 'What can I get you?'

'Actually, I'm going to leave,' I say. 'I just wanted to thank you all, for your help.' I turn to Carla. 'How's your brother doing?'

She gives a tight smile. 'They released him,' she says. 'No evidence. He's at his uncle's for the night.'

'They're still tearing Paddy's place to bits,' adds Nige morosely.

'I just can't believe Paddy was capable of it,' says Tara. She looks up at me. 'No offence, pet.'

'None taken,' I reply.

'Honestly – I always liked him,' says Carla. 'He helped restart our emergency generator one year.'

'Just shows, you never really know someone,' remarks Tara. She looks at me. 'Did you see those pictures, at Paddy's?'

I nod. I'm at a loss how the information can have reached them, but I suppose, in a place as tight-knit as this, word spreads. 'They were *strange*.'

'He was obsessed with the cat,' says Nige.

I half-turn to go. It's not that they're making me feel unwelcome – far from it – but there's no doubt my presence here in Hartsbridge, and Gemma's, has disturbed the peace somewhat. I need to leave them to get on with their lives and pick up the pieces. Yet there's another part of me that keeps my feet rooted to the worn carpet. I *was* a stranger, but I'm not anymore. I'm part of this his place now. And Hartsbridge, in just a couple of days, has become part of my story too.

'Neil from the schoolhouse told me he and Bill Farrah once came to blows about it,' I say.

'Aye,' Nige nods. 'Paddy wouldn't stop with the nonsense. We thought it was a wind-up, and for a while Bill saw the funny side too.'

'So what changed?'

Nige sinks his drink. 'In the end, he managed to persuade someone to come and take a look, like a journalist. Lord knows where he found this fella. He actually went up to the big house – this was maybe three years back. Bill got the hump and told him to clear off. Anyhow, I don't think this journalist was a credit to his profession. He published something in a magazine, talking about Alice and all that.'

'I think I may have seen it,' I say, recalling the 'Beauty and the Beast' article.

'Well, Bill found out, didn't he?' continued Nige. 'He came looking for Paddy. Stand-up row it were, right out front. Farrah laid him out.'

'Paddy never set foot in here after that,' adds Tara.

'Seems an overreaction,' I comment.

'Bill always had a soft spot for Alice,' explains Nige.

I recall the first night when I was here, and Farrah stormed out. 'D'you think it might have been more than that?'

I feel I know these people now, so I'm not shy about asking. It seems so obvious to me.

Tara and Nige share a glance with each other, and I know I'm not the first person ever to say it.

Then the phone behind the bar rings, making us all jump, and Tara goes to answer it. 'Oh, hi,' she says. Then her eyes switch to me. 'Yeah, hang on.' She offers the phone across.

'Hello, Sarah. It's Constable Dewer. I tried calling your phone.'

'It's upstairs.'

'There've been some developments,' he says.

I steady myself. 'You've found . . . the rest of her?'

'It's complicated,' he replies. 'Would you be able to come to the hospital in Bishop Auckland?'

'Now?'

'If that's suitable,' he says. 'The matter is sensitive, and we'd like to talk face to face.'

Chapter 45

GEMMA

When she came to, the first thing she heard was water. There was pressure in her head and pain across her chest. She realised she was upside down.

'Mark . . .' she mumbled. Panic surged through every vein, heightening her senses.

Some sort of fan or motor was running, rattling weakly. There were rocks in front of her, water babbling over the top. The windscreen had completely gone, and one of the car's headlights lit up a few metres of grass and a stream ahead.

'Mark?' He wasn't in his seat any more. Instead, his body was all wrong, somehow forced beneath the dashboard, crumpled underneath the wheel in the footwell. Blood matted his hair and face. His eyes were wide open, staring at nothing. 'Babe? No . . .' She reached for her seat belt and found it. As soon as she pressed the button, she dropped, landing on her shoulder on the car roof. Water soaked into her clothes, and she managed to turn her body. 'Mark?'

He didn't answer. She climbed towards him, extending an arm to put her fingers under his throat, trying to feel for a pulse. She couldn't get anything.

'Mark!' she shouted, as if that might somehow snap him out of it.

She could smell smoke, and heard the crackle of flames. Behind the seats, grey plumes were starting to rise from the back of the car. There was money everywhere. She couldn't see what was on fire, but the smoke was thickening. She had to get out.

The door to her side had buckled and only opened a fraction before jamming. She scrambled out instead through the windscreen under the car's angled bonnet, hands sinking into freezing water and finding the slippery stones beneath.

'Get her!' shouted a voice.

She looked up and saw the Land Rover parked on the road above. She couldn't see the bike, but the rider was on the roadside, still holding the shotgun. 'No!' she screamed. 'He needs an ambulance! Please!'

The door of the Land Rover opened, and the driver stepped out. He walked across to the man from the pub with the gun, and put his hand on the barrel, pushing it down. Then he looked up and down the road and said something to his companion. Behind Gemma, the fire was taking hold, licking out from one of the windows.

'All right, love,' called the older man. 'You get up here now.'

Gemma didn't budge. 'My boyfriend's in there,' she said. 'I think . . . I think he's really badly hurt.'

Neither man on the road said anything. Gemma went around to the other side of the car, but the wind had changed, blowing black smoke right into her face. With that and the heat, she couldn't get close. Mark wasn't moving at all.

The young man with the shotgun began to climb down the steep bank, gun held aloft on one hand with the other grabbing the heather.

Gemma started to walk the other way, downstream.

'Oi! Stop!' he shouted.

The gun went off with a crack. The heather shuddered near her feet, and her leg went out from underneath her, struck hard. Then came pain – a dull ache. She reached down automatically to the spot above her knee. Her jeans were torn, and the flesh below was pulpy. It took a moment to process that she'd been shot. She heard footsteps splashing towards her.

'You made me do it, you stupid bitch,' the man said, a little fear in his voice. 'I wouldn't have hurt you.'

Gemma was on her hands and knees, trying still to process what was happening. Mark was dead. In another few seconds, she would be too, whatever this kid was saying. What other outcome could there be? They couldn't let her live.

She felt a hand grip the top of her arm and tried to scramble away.

'Don't be daft,' he said.

As he hauled her up, her fingers closed on a rock. She spun around, swinging, and smashed it across the side of his head. He groaned, the gun dropping as his knees folded. She couldn't see the Land Rover or the road or the older man. Behind the guy she'd struck, the car was blazing, sending plumes of foul-smelling smoke into the sky. No human sounds came from within, and through her stabbing grief, Gemma was grateful. She turned and ran, dragging her injured leg. She felt the bleeding with every pulse, leaking out of her. She had to get away, even if she had no idea where she might be going.

The rain soaked her to the skin, and she shivered uncontrollably. She knew she couldn't go much further before collapsing, and it was only fear that kept her upright. Each step sent shock waves of pain and brought tears to her eyes. She left the river, climbing blindly to higher ground and away from the road. In her mind, all she could imagine was the vast expanse of open land on the map. Eventually, if she kept in the same direction, she might find another road, but she had no idea how far it might be, or if she would make it. Looking back, she could see the faintest orange glow from the flames.

She could hardly believe Mark was gone, but she had to accept it. There'd been no life in his wide, unfocused eyes. If the fire took him, he wouldn't suffer.

She walked on, following no path, until she knew there was no way they could find her. Then, with nothing left, she fell headlong to the ground, bringing another wave of agony. This time, when she tried to stand, she couldn't. She wanted to sleep, but if she slept, she knew with complete certainty that she wouldn't wake up again. So she crawled, hands and knees sinking into mud. She made it a few more metres before she felt rocks under her fingers and stabbing into her knees. She couldn't see much at all, other than the ground dipping ahead.

And then she was sliding, rocks shifting under her weight. She tried to flail for purchase, but she couldn't stop and turtled up, rolling over and over until she slammed into the bottom of the slope on her back. Her head hit ground so hard, she was sure her skull would crack. Blinking at the rain that spattered her face, she tasted blood in her mouth. She couldn't move. Her arms and legs were like dead weights. Her eyes wanted to close. And so she let them, just for a moment.

Chapter 46

SARAH

It takes a while to find a space in the hospital car park, and I'm practically running when I enter reception. There's no sign of Constable Dewer or Sergeant Nelson, and a queue at the desk. I call the sergeant's number, but get a disconnected tone. I join the line of people.

After a few minutes, it's my turn, and I try to explain that the police have asked me to come here. The man behind the reception screen takes the details with painfully slow taps on his keyboard and asks me to take a seat.

'They said it was urgent,' I say.

He gives me a well-practised passive-aggressive smile that makes any sense of entitlement shrivel, and asks me to take a seat again. I do as I'm told, fingers itching to dial Nelson once more. I manage about four minutes before doing so. The result is the same.

There's a flash of annoyance. They summoned me here, and now I'm left in the lurch.

The digital clock on the wall counts down the time at half-speed, and I watch the other visitors gradually peel off along separate corridors. Staff come and go. Half an hour passes. Then an hour. I don't call Nelson's number again, but I occasionally catch the eye of the receptionist. Did he even call anyone to say I was here? Or maybe I misheard Dewer? Was it a different hospital? Maybe there's more than one in Bishop Auckland. Or did he say to come to the police station, after all?

I scroll through the phone on my lap, looking for the general number of the station. I've just found it when I see a pair of sensible black shoes arrive, and my eyes travel upwards. It's Sergeant Nelson.

'I'm sorry to keep you waiting,' she says.

'Oh, that's fine. I did try to call, but it wouldn't connect.'

'No. There's no signal downstairs. Would you like to follow me?'

'This is very cloak-and-dagger,' I say, gathering myself. I've got pins and needles in one foot and flex my toes.

She doesn't look in the mood for jokes. 'Ms Kline—'

'Call me Sarah.'

'Sarah. This way, please.'

I walk by her side, until we reach a branching corridor and a bank of elevators. She presses the down button.

'Aren't you going to tell me what this is about?' I ask.

'We're not entirely sure at the moment,' she says.

We get into an empty lift, and she presses -2, which is labelled 'Mortuary'. I realise then that we're going to see her.

310

Gemma. I fight the urge to hit the alarm button and stop us in our tracks.

When the doors open again, it's onto a grubby corridor. There are a couple of orderlies wheeling an empty trolley, which they push into the vacant elevator as we exit.

'Is she here?' I say.

'Don't worry,' replies Nelson. 'We won't ask you to do anything you feel uncomfortable with.'

That's good to know, but I'm still completely in the dark as to why I'm here.

Nelson leads me into a small room. There's a table and chairs, and calming pictures of seascapes on the walls. She closes the door behind us and lays her satchel on the table. 'Have a seat.'

I do so, partly because I feel there's something substantial coming.

'I don't want to get your hopes up,' says Sergeant Nelson, 'but the arm we found in the river . . . It's not a DNA match with the sample you provided.'

Her words leave me reeling, because they don't make any sense. 'What does that mean? It's not my sister?'

She places a level hand on the satchel, as if it contains the relevant information she's talking about. 'Not exactly. Ms Kline, Sarah – forgive me if this comes across as insensitive – but how sure are you that Gemma *was* your biological sister?'

I laugh. 'You're kidding me?'

Her face is still deadly serious.

It's not something I've ever had cause to think about. 'I remember when Mum was pregnant. When she was born.'

She's looking at me meaningfully, and I slowly grasp what she's implying.

'You think my mother might not have been *my* mum.'

'Is that a possibility?' she asks.

'It's . . . I mean, no. I have a birth certificate. She's my sister. People always said we look alike. But what about the DNA of the rest of the remains?'

'That's yet to be processed,' says Nelson.

I remember something. 'Wait, you asked before if she had a tattoo?'

Nelson nods briskly. 'And you said no.'

'Well, yes – not on her arm.' I point inside my hip, where I remember the flower. 'Right here. A rose, about an inch across, maybe slightly more.' Nelson gives little away, so I add, 'Constable Dewer said earlier the remains weren't in good condition.'

'There's some . . . putrefaction,' says Nelson, 'as would be expected after several days. Would you mind waiting here for a moment? I'm going to see if the pathologist is free.'

I say that's fine and sit still while she leaves.

Alone, I feel a surge of heat under my breastbone, spreading outwards. I don't want to believe it yet. It feels like folly even to acknowledge the hope lurking at the threshold of my rational mind. But I can't keep it at bay. If it isn't her, it isn't Gemma, she could still be . . .

No. Mistakes get made in labs all the time. The arm – it might not be from the same body. And how does the ring fit into this? If it's not my sister's body, why was her ring on its finger?

After less than a minute, Nelson enters again, with a fresh-faced, handsome young man of East Asian heritage in a doctor's coat. He carries a brown envelope in one hand. He smiles. 'Good afternoon, Ms Kline. I'm Dr Kim.' I greet him in return. 'This is a sensitive issue, I understand. I have here some photographs of the remains we've examined. They've been cleaned, and the genitalia are covered in the images. I can also obscure any of the obvious trauma. Would you be able to identify the exact location of this tattoo for us?'

'I think so, yes,' I tell him. 'It was on the left side.'

Dr Kim shares a glance with Nelson, smiles again, then opens the envelope. With his back to me, he arranges the contents on the table.

'If you'd like to come and look?'

I stand up, not really sure what to expect. And it's not bad at all. The image, which is partially covered at the bottom by the brown envelope, shows a section of a woman's body from the top of the thighs to the waist. The skin appears to have a slight indigo tone, and I don't know if that's from the lighting or the effect of decay. The woman is not slim, but ascertaining the age of the partial body is next to impossible. The genitals are covered by a square of green cloth, but there's a discernible clear strip of fair hair leading towards the navel. There's clearly no tattoo, nor any mark suggestive of removal. The lack of that particular feature should be enough on its own, but even without such evidence, I'd be sure this wasn't my sister. The hips look too wide, and though my sister might have put weight on since I last saw her, this feels like a very different person.

'It's not her,' I say.

'You're quite sure?' asks Nelson.

And now I think back, I don't know why I didn't see it before, with the arm, at the police station. That hand was too plump, the fingers too short. Mum always said we had our father's hands, pianist's fingers. He'd played beautifully, she said. It was just about the only nice thing she ever said about him.

'Ninety-nine per cent,' I say.

'Very good,' says Dr Kim. 'Oh, there was one other thing, sergeant. The X-rays you asked for have come back. Our victim has a compound fracture of the lower tibia and fibula – likely occurring in childhood.' He looks at me. 'I suppose that doesn't match your sister either?'

I shake my head. It doesn't. But now there's little doubt in my mind whose body lies in the hospital mortuary. Because I saw the cast on her foot, in a photograph from almost two decades ago.

'It's Alice Brocklehurst,' I say.

Chapter 47

GEMMA

Gemma thought she heard a voice but woke to complete darkness, groggy and in pain. Her lips were cracked. She was lying on a soft surface, arms and legs outstretched. It was cold, and she realised she was wearing only her knickers and T-shirt. She was inside though. Her first thought was a hospital.

The voice had said a name, and it lingered at the edge of her memory. *Alice.*

When she tried to move, she couldn't. Pain shot through her leg. There was something holding her ankles and wrists. Thick straps, maybe leather. She tried to lift her head, but her brain throbbed.

'Hello?' she said.

Her voice sounded oddly muffled, like she was in a small space.

Oh God. They'd found her.

She tried not to panic, and turned her head, waiting for her eyes to adjust to the gloom. She couldn't see any windows. The ceiling was painted in a strange wavy pattern.

She made out the frame of a bed. A small desk, with a child's teddy bear sitting on top. There was a rocking chair. Someone sitting in it. Her heart lurched.

'Hello?'

The figure in the chair didn't move, and the longer she stared, the more certain she was that it was a mannequin of some sort. It sat bolt upright. Still, she didn't want to take her eyes off it. It seemed to be wrapped in something, from head to toe.

Gritting her teeth against the pain, she tried to move her body, flexing her back, and pulling on her wrists again. The straps dug into her skin. Her leg throbbed – it felt like a fire under her muscle.

'Hello?' she shouted again. 'Is anyone there?'

No one answered. The figure in the chair was motionless.

She screamed as loud as she could, and it burned her dry throat. The room seemed to swallow the sound.

Chapter 48

SARAH

'It can't be,' says Nelson. 'Alice Brocklehurst went missing sixteen years ago. Dr Kim, how old do you estimate the victim is?'

'I'd say late twenties at least,' he says. 'I'm sorry, who is Alice Brocklehurst?'

Nelson ignores him. 'What makes you so sure it's her?'

I explain about the school photo, and the cast. I wonder if she did it riding – wasn't that her thing? 'Can't you check her medical records?'

Nelson looks completely at sea. It's only just sinking in for me, too. If it's her – and it seems hard to imagine it's not – she was alive for years after she disappeared. She was hidden somewhere. Did Patrick Draper have her all that time?

'I need to make some calls,' says Nelson. 'Dr Kim, I'll need you too.' She turns to me. 'Ms Kline, I'd appreciate if you stay here.'

She doesn't give me a chance to answer, before rushing from the room.

For a few minutes, I feel curiously elated, like I've just solved the mystery of Alice's disappearance myself, but the sensation soon fades to a more doubt-filled hollow. What does it matter that this is Alice Brocklehurst? There was no chance she could be alive, and the fact of her death, coupled with my sister's ring, hardly makes it more likely Gemma might still be breathing. It just means Patrick Draper is a serial killer.

At the same time, I work through the logic. Maybe not. Why would he take the ring and put it on Alice Brocklehurst's finger? Who was he trying to deceive? What was he trying to hide? And then it hits me, with a chilling certainty. If he kidnapped Alice Brocklehurst, isn't it likely he's done the same to Gemma? Taken her – not to kill, but to keep. What if he put her somewhere only he knows?

Knew. Past tense. Any secrets that sick bastard had died with him.

I get up on my own with just my circling thoughts for about forty minutes before the door opens again and in walks Nelson. She's followed by Constable Dewer.

'Ms Kline, I want to thank you for your assistance,' says Nelson. Her tone is businesslike. 'Constable Dewer here will take you back upstairs.'

I feel disembodied, thrust out of the drama. I've gone from being a character on stage, in the spotlight, to an extra watching from the wings.

'Oh, right? And then what?'

Nelson gives me a beady stare. 'We're in the middle of a complex investigation,' she says.

'I know. It's my sister who's missing, remember? I think he kidnapped her. She could be out there now, somewhere?'

'As soon as we have any further information, you'll be the first to know.'

'You're still looking for Gemma, right? Think about it – Draper kept Alice alive until recently. Maybe he hasn't killed Gemma at all.'

Her face betrays little emotion. I look to Dewer, but he seems like a fish out of water.

'What's wrong with you people?' I say. 'You think it's okay to drag me here, make me wait for bloody ages, then send me packing the moment you've got what you want?'

'We found nothing at Patrick Draper's house relating to your sister,' says Nelson.

'Then he must have put her somewhere else, mustn't he? Do your fucking job!'

'There's no need for language like that, Ms Kline. I know you're upset. My suggestion would be to get some rest back in Hartsbridge.'

'How can I do that? My sister might be alive.'

'And if she is, we'll find her,' says Nelson. 'I promise you that.' Her phone rings and she looks at it. 'I've got to take this. Constable Dewer, if you could see Ms Kline to her car.'

★ ★ ★

I remonstrate with Dewer all through the elevator ride, out through reception and into the car park, where dusk has fallen. He bats my concerns back with calm forbearance. He seems jaded, a little distant, and I remember that he knew Alice too, when they were kids. This must be a shock for

319

him too. We reach my car, and I ask him if Draper had other properties – places the police might search.

'You saw his house,' says Dewer. 'He could barely keep that standing.'

I remember then that Tara said something about tunnels. 'Aren't there places on the moors – underground? Old mines, or something?'

'Probably,' replies Dewer. 'But they're closed off.'

'*All* of them? Shouldn't you get a search party out?'

Dewer sighs, at the end of his patience. 'Sarah, I don't know what to say. I wish we could help, but there's not enough concrete evidence to put something like that into motion.'

'You searched for Alice Brocklehurst!' I snap. 'The whole village turned out.'

He nods, and his eyes are hurt. 'We did,' he says quietly. 'Trust me, we searched and searched. Two days and nights. Some for longer. And we didn't find a thing.'

'I won't give up,' I say. 'I can't.'

'Nor will we,' says Dewer. 'You have to give us space. The gaffer's under a tonne of pressure already. She won't take kindly to you forcing her hand.'

I know he's trying to placate me, but I see kindness in his eyes too. He's not my enemy.

'Just let me know if you find *anything*,' I say.

He nods, then walks back towards the hospital.

★ ★ ★

It's dark as I drive back to Hartsbridge once more, taking the lonely country road with the deserted moors spread out on either side under, cast on an almost silvery glow. Slowing to a fifteen-mile-an-hour crawl, I'm acutely aware that I'm just a dot in this landscape. It might be pretty come the summer, but nothing about this place recommends itself for human habitation, and the people who'd made their homes and livelihoods here have done so despite Mother Nature rather than with her assistance. You'd only have to go back a hundred years, and this road would have been a cart-track at most.

From what I know of Patrick Draper, he wandered these rolling hills for years. He knew it like the back of his hand, the paths and gullies, the places no one would ever look. Who's to say there's not a shaft entrance, off the beaten track, which only he knew about? He could drive his car out here at night, take one of the many tracks, lights off, and he'd be invisible.

There might be a frost tonight. It's cold enough. I want to pull over, and scream my sister's name, on the flimsiest chance she's here somewhere and might hear. But that would be madness. As mad as believing there's a wild cat out here, ready to pounce on unsuspecting hikers.

And now I think I understand why the Brocklehursts moved away. Because the worst part of it is the not knowing. As the days turned to weeks and months, they must have looked out every day over the bleak and empty landscape, not knowing if she was out there, being slowly digested by the acidic peat, her body carrion for buzzards and crows indifferent to the feelings of her family. Once the police had given up, once the search parties had stopped, it would have been easier just to leave the nightmare of uncertainty behind.

Chapter 49

GEMMA

Somehow, Gemma had slept. When she woke again, a door that she hadn't seen before was open in the opposite wall, throwing a dull red glow into the room that made her surroundings clearer. The figure had gone. She scanned the room quickly, just in case it had moved to another position, but she comforted herself that she was alone.

In the dim light, she saw the room was maybe twenty feet across, pretty much square. The walls were covered in the same material as the ceiling – like the inside of a giant eggbox. Even the door was coated with it. Hundreds of little cups. She'd seen something similar before, and it took a second to realise where. A sound studio. Soundproofing.

Whatever happened in here wasn't meant to be heard.

She fought the urge to scream again. 'Please,' she called. 'I won't tell anyone. It was all a mistake.'

She heard footsteps, and in the doorway a small shape

appeared. It was a woman, wearing a skirt and cardigan. She turned on another switch and strip lights on the ceiling flickered into life, bright enough to make Gemma squint.

The woman pushed in a trolley loaded with a bowl, and other items Gemma couldn't see. She looked at least eighty, with sparse white hair. Her lips and chin folded in around toothless gums.

'Welcome, welcome,' she said. 'How are you feeling, flower?

'Where am I?' asked Gemma. 'I need to go to hospital.'

'Nonsense,' replied the woman. 'We can get you fixed up here just fine.'

She pushed the trolley closer, and Gemma writhed to get away.

'You've been up to mischief, Alice,' said the woman. 'You're home now.'

'I'm not Alice,' she said. 'My name's Gemma.'

'You look like Alice. Come on now, have a sip of water.'

She held a cup, and Gemma lifted her head to drink. It spilled a little, but tasted incredible. She tried to gulp it down.

'Not too much,' said the woman, taking the cup away.

'Where am I?' repeated Gemma.

'You're home,' said the woman. 'No need to worry.'

'Please,' she said. 'I don't know what you want, but I can't stay here. I have a job. In Brighton. My friends will be looking for me.'

The old woman pulled on a pair of blue surgical gloves and stood over Gemma.

'Hold still, and this will hurt less.'

Gemma froze as the woman reached down and snipped the dressing off her thigh, nodding approvingly.

324

'Lucky he found you when he did,' she said. 'Horrible night to be out on your own.'

'Please. Listen to me. I don't want this. I don't want to be here. My . . . my sister's getting married next week. She's invited me. I'm . . . I'm a bridesmaid.'

'Oh, that's lovely,' said the woman. 'But I don't think you'll be able to go.'

She dipped a cloth into the steaming bowl, wrung it carefully, then applied it to Gemma's thigh. It stung, and she hissed through her teeth.

'There's still shot in there,' said the woman, picking up a pair of callipers. 'Oh, Alice, what have you been up to?'

'Wait!' Gemma protested. 'No! Stop! I'm not fucking Alice, all right.'

The old woman looked cross. 'You're going to have to stop making a racket,' she muttered, pointing upwards with the callipers. 'He's got a short temper these days.'

'Listen,' said Gemma, quietly but urgently. You've made a mistake. I don't know who Alice is. I'm Gemma. Gemma Kline.'

'We all make mistakes,' said the old woman, leaning closer to her leg. She reached across and offered Gemma a piece of wood, about six inches long. 'You're Alice now. He chose you specially. Here, bite down on this.'

Chapter 50

SARAH

Back in Hartsbridge, pulling into the car park at the pub, I feel exhausted by it all. The wondering, the uncertainty. I'm caught between two completely distinct emotions, both directed at hypothetical Gemmas. Grief for the one who's dead, killed by Patrick Draper, the one to whom I never said goodbye. But angry at the one who's alive, the blithe spirit who passed through this place and continues her existence elsewhere, oblivious to the chaos in her wake. It's easier to be angry, because at least there's hope in that version of events.

But what am I supposed to do now? Stay, on the off chance more information comes to light? That could be a long wait, going by the attitude of the police. No, I have to return to London and try to rebuild the pieces. I can't put my life on hold.

Climbing from the car, I wonder absently how much the

scratches on my door will cost to sort out. It's a minor irritation, in the scheme of things. Did Patrick Draper use the same claw on his neck that he'd vandalised my car with? It seems a fairly pathetic attempt to warn me off, more likely to arouse suspicion than quell it. But he clearly wasn't of sound mind, so it's probably a mistake to look for logic in his actions. I suppose at the very least it suggests he did know something about Gemma.

It was hard to think about at the time, with the gore still fresh in my mind, but it's a strange way to kill oneself. Oddly theatrical for a man who seemed to live a such a pared-down life. And where did he get the claw from in the first place? Can you really buy such things online? I don't know exactly why it's troubling me, but I feel like I'm missing something.

I come in through the back doors of the pub. Peering into the bar area, both Nigel and Carla have gone. It's just Tara leaning over her magazine.

'Hiya, pet,' she says. 'We were wondering where you'd got to.'

I didn't explain the nature of Dewer's call to the pub before, and it feels wrong to do so now. I'm sure, even with the astonishing speed of gossip in Hartsbridge, that the latest revelations won't yet have reached the village from the hospital. Alice means something to these people, and I'm sure it's not my place to share what I know, despite my personal connection to the case.

'It's not really important,' I tell her. 'Actually, I think I'm still going to check out.'

'Now?' she says. 'It's getting late.'

'I can pay for the room,' I say hurriedly. 'I just think I want to get on the road.'

'Don't be daft,' she says. 'Normally I ask folk if they've had a good stay, but—'

A door opens, and Nige comes through from the gents, a little unsteady on his feet. 'Come to keep an old fella company?' he asks.

'I'm afraid not,' I tell him.

'The young lass is leaving us,' says Tara. 'Besides, it might be time to call it a night, don't you reckon?'

'Can't say I blame her,' replies Nige. 'I'll bid you a safe trip home then.'

He asks to settle up, and tells Tara to have one on him.

'You're a gent,' she says. She tells him what he owes, and Nige opens his billfold wallet and offers over a card. It's as he does so that I spot the familiar red colouration of a fifty-pound note peeping out from the top of one of the slots inside. Actually, there are several. He sees me looking and snaps it closed quickly, but the blush rising up his cheeks tells me I've seen something I shouldn't.

'Well, be seeing you all,' he says with a nod to me, but no eye contact.

I wait a second, wondering what I've just witnessed, then it slips into place and I follow him out of the back door into the car park. He's walking faster than seems natural for a man of his stature, and coupled with the drink it's a slightly comic, silent-movie shamble. I call after him, and he comes to a stop. We're both standing in the street.

'Nige, I have to ask,' I say.

He turns slowly. 'What's that, dearie?'

'You know what,' I say. 'I went up to the place where the car came off the road. I found a fifty-pound note – burned. You were up there too, weren't you? The night of the crash.'

329

'What of it?' he says.

'I'm guessing that's where you got those?' I nod to his pocket.

He shakes his head and his jowls wobble too. 'Don't know what you're talking about.'

'You're a terrible liar,' I say. 'Please, be honest. How much was there?'

He walks back towards me, slowly. I don't feel scared. Not of Nige. He looks sheepish.

'I didn't want to take any,' he mutters, 'but all the boys did. It was floating in the bloody air.'

'From the car?'

'Aye, most of it was burning. There was all sorts. I know it was wrong.' He takes out his wallet. 'Here, you have it.'

'I don't want it,' I say. 'And I won't tell anyone. Don't worry.'

He gives a shuffling nod. 'Thanks for that. I'd lose my job. We all would.'

'Take care, Nige.'

'Same to you.'

I watch him head off down the road, trying to engage my scrambled brain to take in this new information. So it wasn't just a single note – there was lots of it. And if Gemma and Mark had money, who did they owe it to? It's just another question I'll probably never answer. It seems unlikely that it's connected with Patrick Draper though.

Back in the pub, Tara's switching off the lights in the main room.

In the remaining illumination, cast from lamps behind the bar, the rhino's horn throws a long shadow. I'm certain it's illegal to import things like that now, but I suppose in the days of Thomas Brocklehurst, such objects all had a price.

I realise then what bothers me about the claw found in Patrick Draper's hand.

'Penny for your thoughts?' says Tara.

I turn to her, where she's wiping a table in the far corner. 'You knew Paddy, didn't you?'

'As well as anyone in the village,' she replies.

'And when he talked about the cat, did you believe him?'

'Course not.'

'But he believed it himself?'

'In his own way, I think he did, aye.'

'But he never showed you anything? No photos? No fur . . . No claw?'

She shakes her head. 'If he had, mebbe people wouldn't a tekken the piss,' she says. 'Don't tell us you're a believer too now?'

'Ha. No. Listen, thanks for everything. I'm going to get out of your hair now.'

'Take your time, pet.'

Upstairs, I'm going to pack my things, but the same thoughts are worming away. I open my laptop, and find the article about Alice again. *Beauty and the Beast*. The name of the writer is on the byline – a Fred Castle. When I google him, I get several hits, but I narrow it down to journalistic results, and soon find him. He goes by 'Frederick' these days, and if it's the same man, he's moved up in the world. He works for a Scottish broadsheet, writing reviews. It doesn't take long to find an email address, but I need to speak to him now. I could use Felicity, but that seems like overkill, so instead I keep trawling. I'm not holding great hopes for

331

LinkedIn, but there he is. And there's a mobile number. I call it.

'Hello?' A northern accent, but not strong. Maybe with a hint of Geordie.

'Is that Mr Castle?'

'Speaking.'

'My name is Sarah Kline. I'm sorry to bother you, but I was wondering if I could ask about a feature you wrote some years ago. It was about a village called Hartsbridge, and the disappearance of a young girl called Alice Brocklehurst.'

He chuckles. 'I won't say it was my finest work. Sorry, though. What's this about?'

'I'm doing some follow-up work,' I tell him.

'I shouldn't bother. It's a load of claptrap. You've read my article, yes?'

'I did indeed. I wanted to ask you particularly about an unnamed source you interviewed. Was it, by any chance, Patrick Draper?'

'That's the chap. A real loon, but he took me in for a while. Had me traipsing all over those fells, showing me this and that. Mostly freezing my bollocks off. This is a real blast from the past.'

'But you never saw a big cat?'

'Trust me, you'd have read about it. In the end, that wasn't the story, which is why I focused on the missing girl and her family. Even went up to the house, but got shown the door pretty sharpish. It was a bit cheap, but my editor was breathing down my neck for something. You know how it is. I'm not proud.'

'Did Draper ever show you a claw?' I ask. 'A big cat's claw.'

'Did he buggery. All he showed me were some pictures he'd drawn. I told him we didn't print pictures. To be honest, they gave me the creeps.'

'Thank you,' I tell him. 'You've been very helpful.'

'Listen, if you do a piece of your own, do us a favour and leave me out of it? I'll never live it down if my colleagues read it.'

'You have my word.'

Off the phone, my blood is tingling. If Patrick Draper had this claw in his possession, if he was so keen to convince others that the cat existed, why did he never show anyone when he had the chance? I almost call Nelson, but I know she'll give me short shrift for interfering. Yet my own theory is no less believable than theirs. Someone killed my sister and Mark because of money – I don't know how they got mixed up, but that's why Gemma was here. The same person who kidnapped Alice Brocklehurst. A person who had access to a huge estate, and who was very keen to stop me, or anyone else, going anywhere near. Farrah. It's so obvious now. He used Patrick Draper, his old enemy, as a fall guy, dumping Alice's body, when she died, in his old well, killing him with an implement that seems to fit perfectly with his weird persona.

I head out of the room. Archie's at the other end of the hallway, in the office. I feel a prickle of fear. Did he hear some of my conversation to the journalist? I've no idea how he's involved, but he is. He works closely with Farrah. He's been lying from the start.

I gather myself and walk past him. He doesn't speak, but his eyes follow me, the angry bruise across his cheek under his left eye.

I load my suitcase in the boot and pull out of the car park, into the unlit streets of Hartsbridge.

I know exactly where I can find the answers I need.

Chapter 51

GEMMA

Gemma must have passed out, but when she woke again, the first thing she realised was that her wrists and ankles were no longer shackled. She sat up, fighting a wave of dizziness, and swung her legs off the bed. Her thigh was heavily bandaged. She tried, gingerly, to put weight on it, but felt at once it wouldn't hold her up.

She needed to pee, very badly. There was no toilet, but there was a bucket in one corner. She hopped across towards it, every step sending stabbing aches up her pelvis and lower back. Desperate, she hitched down her knickers, crouched and did her business.

She hopped back to the bed, and sat down. Just the exertion of crossing the room left her head beaded with sweat. Her stomach growled. She guessed she must be at the manor house, in some forgotten cellar. She'd no idea who the woman was, but she didn't look like a drug dealer, that much was certain.

Gemma felt a wobble of her lip as she thought of Mark, dead in the car, but she didn't let herself cry. There wasn't time for that now. They'd kept her alive, for some reason. Only one thing mattered. She had to work out a way to escape.

The moment it crossed her mind, a small hatch in the door opened – not at head height, but about one metre off the ground. It let in a dim red shaft of light.

'Hello?' she said.

There was no answer. A dark shape appeared on the other side of the hatch, obscuring the light.

She looked around the room for a weapon, knowing full well there wasn't one.

Apart from the bucket. She picked it up, backing away from the door.

'Whatever you think I've done, I'm sorry,' she said.

The lock opened with a clunk, and the door opened a fraction and stopped. She could sense the presence on the other side, daring her to come closer. She remained where she stood, trembling.

The dark shape filled the crack in the door. She heard sounds. Sniffing.

For the first time, she realised it wasn't human. Perhaps some sort of guard dog. They were trying to scare her.

The door closed again. She heard the bolt draw across.

Chapter 52

SARAH

I park up in the driveway of the old schoolhouse and there are lights on inside, so I guess it's not too late to call. As I approach the front door, a security beam above the gable end of the house picks me out and casts a shadow fifty feet long.

I knock at the door, and see a twitch of a curtain. I give a little wave, and the most apologetic face I can muster.

When he opens the door, Neil's wearing a dressing gown and looks perplexed.

'Gosh, are you all right?' he asks. 'I heard you were at Patrick's house. Is it true he took his own life?'

'That's why I'm here,' I say. 'Can I ask you something?'

He looks at his watch. 'Now?' He's right. This must seem odd. It's nearly nine p.m.

At that moment, a particularly fierce gust picks up petals from the roses and flings them into his porch.

'You'd better come in,' he says. 'I'll boil the kettle. No cake though, I'm afraid.'

'That's all right,' I say. I'm grateful to be indoors, out of the wind.

We go back into his kitchen, and he carries the kettle to the sink.

'The police retrieved what looks like a claw from Patrick's house,' I explain. 'It appears he used it to cut his own throat.'

Neil crosses himself, and looks a bit sick. 'And still no luck finding your sister?'

I shake my head. 'I know she was at his house, but I'm still hopeful. People can't just disappear.'

He smiles, and I'm sure he's thinking of Alice Brocklehurst too. 'Then I'm hopeful too. She seemed a nice young lady, for the brief moment I met her.'

I want to change the subject. 'I wonder where Patrick got it,' I say. 'You said your father euthanised the cats at the house – have you any idea what happened to the bodies?'

Neil frowns. 'Now that's a question,' he replies. 'It would have been fifty years ago. One suspects they'd have been incinerated.'

'Up at the manor?'

He shrugs. 'I couldn't tell you. My mother might know something, but she's in bed now. What is your thinking? That someone kept one of the claws, all this time?'

I think of the scratches down the side of my car.

'I don't see how Patrick got hold of it,' I say. 'But someone at Brocklehurst Hall, on the other hand . . .'

'There's only one person up there,' says Neil.

'Who hated Patrick Draper.'

The kettle starts to whistle.

'Hate's a strong word,' says Neil. 'They didn't see eye to eye.'

There's a noise from inside the house, and a voice calls, 'Neil?'

He sighs. 'Coming, Mum,' he calls back. 'Sorry about this.'

'No, I'm sorry,' I say. 'I'll make the tea.'

He walks back out of the kitchen, and I take a couple of mugs down from the pegs, then fish teabags from a tin on a shelf. I can hear them muttering to each other in another room. She sounds annoyed and I'm sure I hear the words 'What does she *want*?' and I feel bad for waking her up. There's a plate by the sink, covered in crumbs, with four pieces of cucumber on the side. I stare at it for a few seconds, then smile uneasily to myself.

Neil returns as I'm pouring the mugs.

'Everything all right?' I ask.

'She gets confused, that's all, bless her. Sometimes she still thinks Dad's around. She doted on him. Not that the old bugger deserved it. Cared more about a cow and her calf than he did his own wife and child.'

He says it wryly, but there's definitely sadness there too.

'So what actually happens up at the manor now?' I ask.

'From what I've heard, he grows some vegetables – sells them at farmer's markets and the like. But mainly he's there to stop trespassers. Don't know why the family don't sell it, to be honest.' He opens the fridge and takes out milk. 'I'd keep away if I were you. I reckon you're barking up the wrong tree.'

'You really think so?'

As he stirs the tea, I notice there's a small smear of blood along the side of his hand. I try to look away, but he's

339

seen me looking and turns it over. 'Look at that,' he says. 'Bloody roses, eh?' After he's binned the teabags, he points to the chairs on the other side of the room. 'Have a seat,' he says.

We walk round opposite sides of the kitchen unit. There's a large rug in front of a wood-burning stove, a chesterfield on one side and an armchair opposite. I sit on the latter, and Neil places the mug down on a coaster on the low table. It's solid wood, an irregular lateral slice through what must once have been a huge tree. The whorls and rings have been polished to a high shine, apart from at the far end, where a smudge of fingerprints ruins the pristine effect.

'You were talking about Paddy Draper,' he says, 'and this claw?'

'Yes, I can't work out where it came from, except possibly from the house. You know, some sort of relic, like the rhino's head in the pub!'

Neil frowns. 'Seems unlikely to me. I know a lot of the goods from the house were sold off – I can't imagine taxidermy is much in fashion any more. Especially the more exotic stuff – a little in bad taste, don't you think?'

I hadn't thought of that. If Draper simply purchased the claw from someone at the house, maybe it never crossed his mind to claim it was evidence of a cat on the fells. My Farrah theory is falling apart a bit.

'Did your father mention any of the big cats being stuffed?' I ask. 'You said before you thought they were destroyed.'

'He didn't,' says Neil, sipping his tea. 'But it might be that they were separate animals – already preserved, if you get what I mean. Thomas Brocklehurst had a thing for hunting

340

as much as preserving. A complicated chap, you might say. You're sure this claw was even genuine?'

I only saw it for a moment. 'I think so.'

I take a sip of the tea, which is still scalding. A clock on the mantelpiece tells me it's almost quarter past nine and I'm aware I'm probably outstaying my welcome.

Neil must have caught my glance. 'You don't have to rush,' he says. 'It's good to have some company. Mum's not always stimulating conversation.'

'I'm sorry,' I say. 'I can see how much you care for her.'

He shrugs. 'Somebody has to. To be honest with you, I've been looking after her most of my life.'

I can tell, from the way he lets it hang, that he wants me to ask more. 'Because of your father's work?'

'Because of who he was,' he says. 'He used work as an excuse. He found animals less complicated than human beings, I think.' He looks down into the fire, distantly. 'I had a sister, you know. She was born on our kitchen floor – delivered by my own father.'

'Gosh,' I reply, because I can't think what to say, or where the story is going.

'It's one of my first memories. I was three or four at the time. I remember all the shouting and screaming, but my father told me not to come into the room under any circumstances. Fancy telling a toddler that, eh?'

I nod dutifully.

'Anyhow, she was stillborn. Dad buried her in the back garden. Hard to believe, but this was the early sixties, and you could get away with it. The next day, Mum tells me, he went back to work.'

'That's . . . awful. I'm really so sorry.'

'Not your fault,' he replies. 'Like I said, he wasn't senti-mental. I'm not sure Mum really got over it, though.'

The clock chimes once for the quarter-hour, and it seems to break him from his spell.

'So what will you do now?' he asks.

'Head home to London, I suppose.'

'Of course,' he says. 'The big day!'

I don't have the energy to tell him about *that*, so I nod and sip my tea. But as I do, I wonder how exactly he knows about the wedding at all.

I smile, to cover my inkling of dread. 'Did I tell you I was getting married?'

He pauses with his own mug, and frowns. 'I suppose you must have. When you came to the shop perhaps?'

I try to think back to that conversation. Only a few days before, but I can't see why I would've said anything – it's an odd detail to share.

Silence swells to fill the room, broken only by the ticking of the clock. I've a queasy sensation in the pit of my stomach, like I've eaten something bad. I'm acutely aware, all of a sudden, of where the door is. I'm closer to it than him, but not by much.

'Of course,' I say breezily. 'It must have been. I bore myself sometimes!'

He stands up, slowly, and I hear the creak of his knees. He walks across to the wood burner. He opens the doors, and drops in another piece of wood from a basket.

I stand up too. 'I'll be on my way,' I say. My voice cracks on the last word, giving me away. He reaches towards a stand that holds a poker. In a single move, faster than I would've thought possible, he swings it at my head.

I leap back and the poker misses by a whisker. But I trip

on the table, sending tea spilling off the side, spattering onto the parquet tiles.

'You shouldn't have come here,' he says. His face has changed, the soft edges gone.

'Then let me go,' I say.

He cocks his head and smiles. 'I don't think that would work out.'

He advances on me in heavy strides and I turn and run, only to see his mother standing in the doorway in a nightdress. I run to the other side of the kitchen counter, with Neil at my back. I can't see a knife, but the kettle's still there beside the Aga. I grab it and pull off the lid, flinging the contents blindly back at him.

There isn't much in there, but it catches him across the face and the effect is instantaneous. He drops the poker and both hands go to his eyes. The most awful howl of pain fills the air and he drops to his knees before folding up onto the floor, screaming like an animal. I feel a hand on my hair, yanking, but I grab it and pull free. The old woman comes with me, slamming into the kitchen cabinets with a moan and collapsing beside her son. The poker's by my feet and I pick it up, brandishing it over both of them.

'Where's my sister?'

Neil is trying to stand, reaching for me, and before I know it, I've hit him on the back of the head and he drops again, this time landing flat on his face and not moving. I don't know if he's dead, and I don't care. His mother is cradling her arm, sitting against the fridge.

'Tell me where she is!' I say.

She looks at Neil, then me, her eyes blazing with contempt. 'You broke my arm!' she says.

I advance on her, poker held high. 'I'll break the other

one if you don't tell me where Gemma is.' I know I'm not actually going to hit her with it, but I'm happy to scare her to death. 'Where is she?'

She gurns for a moment, then sends a gobbet of sputum at my feet.

I turn around and shout my sister's name. Then I walk through the house, into a bedroom that I guess, from the bed bars, belongs to the old woman. There's a wet room kitted out with bars and other aids too.

'Gemma?' I shout.

The next room is Neil's. Spotless, a perfectly made double bed. Men's toiletries on a dresser and a telescope at the window. No sign of Gemma.

But she's here, I know she is. And she's alive. Why put cucumber in a sandwich only to take it out? He made it for *her*, I realise. He didn't know . . .

I reach into my pocket for my phone, before remembering I've left it in the car.

Shit.

Back in the kitchen, Neil hasn't moved. Surely I didn't hit him hard enough to kill him, but who knows? The old woman is crouched over him, talking in his ear. I walk across the room again, shouting at the top of my lungs. And then I see the spilt tea. It's run away from the mug, between the floor tiles and is soaking into the rug. There must be a slight slope in the floor.

Checking Neil's still prone, I grip the legs of the table, and pull it off the rug. Then I pull that aside too. Underneath, set into the floor, is a hatch about three feet wide, hinged near the wood burner. There's a metal ring at one end, but it's not locked. I hook my finger in and pull it upwards. At the same time, a set of steps unfolds downwards in an almost graceful, well–oiled concertina.

'Gemma?' I shout again.

The old woman has stood up. 'Don't you go down there!'

I point the poker at her. 'Fuck. You.'

It's dark, but I can see a concrete floor below. I pause. If I just go down, there's nothing to stop the old hag closing the hatch. So I take the poker dropped by Neil and jam the end, two handed, into the hinge. With some firm stabs, and some wriggling, I smash and prise it from its screwed moorings. I'm sweating by the time I'm done. Neil remains motionless, and it strikes me that he might actually be dead. I feel oddly dispassionate at the prospect of being his killer, turning my attention back to the steps. I clamber down carefully, using a rail to balance. There's a cord hanging from the ceiling and I pull it. A blood-red glow lights up workbenches and pieces of paper hanging from pegs on a string. A darkroom. There's another door, off to one side. On the other side, muffled, like a sound of someone drowning, comes a voice I'd recognise anywhere. I walk across and turn the handle.

A woman is tied to a bed, half-naked, a gag across her mouth. It's so gloomy, it's not until I'm right beside her that I can truly feel relief. It's followed quickly by horror. I can't fathom in that moment what's happened to her, what she's been through, so I just tell her I'm here and I'm going to get her out. She bucks on the bed, making it shake, and her eyes are wide enough that I can see the whites all around. I pull the gag gently off her mouth, and she starts to sob my name.

'Keep still,' I say. 'I've got you.'

The thick leather straps come away and she throws her arms around my neck. Through the aroma of sweat and unwashed hair, the smell of her skin takes me back twenty-five years to the nights she had nightmares and still needed me close to get back to sleep.

I pull away to unfasten the ankle straps, and she's hyperventilating with tears as she asks how I found her.

'Later,' I say. Her leg is bandaged around the thigh. 'Can you walk?' I ask.

'Yeah, I think so. Mark's dead, Sarah.'

I help her off the bed and her legs buckle, but I steady her. 'I know. Easy does it.'

She doesn't want to walk towards the door.

'Come on,' I urge.

'Is he out there?' she asks.

'I've dealt with him,' I say grimly.

She looks at me with astonishment, like I'm some kind of superwoman, rather than her big sister.

We climb the stairs again, me sending her up first in case she falls. She blinks into the light above as I emerge at her side. Now I can see her body in more detail, I gasp. Both her eyes are black, and there's a cut across her cheek. Her lips are scabby. Barely any of her lower half isn't purple, yellow or green with bruising.

But I don't have time to take in more details, because a shape rushes at us with a banshee wail – Neil's mother, and she's got a long kitchen knife in her hand. She moves almost comically slowly, but the knife's edge still looks deadly enough. I shove Gemma out of the way. Momentum pushes me the other way. Without so much as a cry, the old woman vanishes into the hatch. Her body crunches into the steps and lands in a heap at the bottom. The knife's out of sight, but she starts to convulse. A puddle of dark liquid slowly spreads out from under her head, and quickly she's still. Gemma looks horrified.

346

'It doesn't matter,' I say.

As I lead Gemma to the door, a large hand appears on the kitchen counter, and Neil slowly rises. Gemma screams and backs away. But Neil can barely stand. There's blood trailing down his neck and soaking the collar of his dressing gown. His eyes are bloodshot, cheeks scalded. He stumbles towards us, only to falter again and fall, sprawling out on the kitchen floor.

Gemma doesn't want to move. Her gaze is fixed on Neil.

'Come on,' I say. 'My car's outside. We're going to a hospital.'

We stumble out into the drive, and I open the passenger side for my sister. Then I climb in too and start the engine, throwing glances at the door in case Neil emerges again. But he doesn't. I reverse straight out into the road, but straight away there's something wrong with the car. It shudders and clanks.

'What's happening?' asks Gemma.

I keep going, but the steering's unresponsive, so I cut the engine and get out. As I feared, the front tyre is flat.

'Someone's slashed it,' I say.

Did his mother do it, with the knife? Or maybe it was him, as he left the kitchen to see her before?

Gemma climbs out too. I look back into the car for my bag and grab my phone. No signal. I think about going back into the house and finding a landline, but there's no way I'm risking it. Not with *him* in there.

'We can walk,' I say. 'It's only half a mile back to Hartsbridge.'

Just being back on the side of the road makes me feel better. We've done it. We're free. The surge across my chest makes me feel light-headed. Gemma is struggling, and I take more of her weight across my shoulder.

'How are you even here?' she asks.

'A long story,' I say. 'You're safe now.'

Lights appear on the road ahead, coming from Hartsbridge. Supporting Gemma, I wave wildly with the other arm, calling out for them to stop. It looks for a moment as if the driver will pass us, but then it comes to a sharp halt. My heart surges again. It's Carla, driving a small car. She looks gobsmacked, and jumps out. 'Holy shit? Are you okay?'

'We need to get to a hospital.'

'Okay, sure – get in.'

She opens the back door and we ease Gemma on to the back seat. Then I get in the passenger side.

Carla slams her door. She looks over her shoulder. 'What on earth happ— You're the sister! I remember you . . . you stayed at the hostel.'

'She was at Neil Packer's house,' I say. I check my phone again. Still no signal. 'I need to call the police.'

Carla's eyes are on the phone too. 'You won't get a signal for another mile. Once we're out of the valley head.' She drives on. 'I don't understand,' she says, glancing in the rear-view. 'Why were you at Neil's place? The police have been looking for you.'

'He was holding me prisoner,' says Gemma. 'He's a psychopath.'

Confusion swims across Carla's face. She's clearly struggling to take it all in, and that's not a surprise.

After another minute or so, I get a bar. I dial 999 before changing my mind and quickly scroll through to find Sergeant Nelson's number.

'Hang on a mo,' says Carla, pulling over quite sharply. 'I need to text Andy. I'm supposed to be picking up Rubes.'

While she sends her message, I call Nelson.

'Hello?'

'It's Sarah Kline. I've got my sister.'

A long pause, then she speaks far more calmly than I expected. 'Is she all right?'

I look back at Gemma, who's sitting up gingerly.

'Yes, pretty much. We're going to the hospital in Bishop Auckland. Can you meet us there?'

Another pause, like there's some sort of delay on the line. I should've waited until the signal was better. 'Yes, of course,' she answers. 'Where are you, now? I can meet you on the way if you want.'

'At the hospital is fine,' I say. 'We're getting a lift with Carla from the hostel in Hartsbridge.'

'Understood. I'll see you shortly.'

'You need to send a police car to Neil Packer's house,' I say. 'He had Gemma all along.'

'I'm sorry, *what*?'

'I think he killed Alice too. Just send someone, quickly. He's hurt, but he'll try to run.'

She's taking a while to compute, just like Carla. 'We will. Are you sure I can't escort you, if you're in danger? I can be with you in—'

'We're fine,' I say. 'Honestly.'

We end the call.

'All good?' says Carla.

I tell her the plan, and she sets off again. She's driving more slowly than I'd like, but it's a twisty road, and she's probably keen not to throw Gemma around too much in the back. Her phone chimes and I forgive her for checking the message while driving. She puts it down and returns her attention to the road ahead.

'Who *is* Alice?' asks Gemma.

'A missing girl,' I tell her. 'She's dead.'

A quarter of a mile later, Carla indicates and takes a side road, running slightly uphill.

'Does this go to Bishop Auckland?' I ask. I don't recall it from the previous journey.

'The main road is closed for maintenance from midnight,' she says. 'It's a bugger, but this way's only a couple of minutes longer.'

She puts on her full beams, lighting up the black tarmac ahead. There's a light drizzle falling, almost as delicate as snow.

Gemma leans forward from the back. 'I don't think this is the way,' she says. 'Mark and I came this way. It leads to the middle of nowhere.'

I look at Carla, who shakes her head. 'You're wrong. There's a cut-through.'

But her voice has taken on a scared edge.

'What's going on?' I ask her.

She sighs. 'Look, I'm sorry, okay.' She looks back at the rear-view. 'You shouldn't have tried to blackmail them.'

Blackmail? So that's what this is about. 'Who are you talking about?' I look at Gemma. 'Who did you blackmail.'

'Please . . .' says Gemma, leaning forward and reaching for the back of Carla's seat.

Carla speeds up, hands tight on the wheel. 'It's your own fault,' she says, shaking her head.

'Turn around!' I say.

She slows and turns onto another track. Thirty metres up, she stops. 'I'm sorry,' she says again. 'I can't help you now.'

I grab the door handle, but it won't open.

Then I open my phone. At the same time, a bright glare illuminates the rear window, then moves around the side of the car. I shield my eyes, and as the light passes, I see it's Archie, with a torch in his hand. In the other, he has a sawn-off shotgun. He points it through the windscreen.

Chapter 53

I sit straight, hands up.

'Don't fucking move!' Archie shouts. It's the second time in as many days that I've had a gun pointed at me, but this time seems worse than when Farrah did so on the forest road. Archie looks agitated, and unpredictable, like he could twitch at any moment and pull the trigger.

I've still got the phone in my hand, and he can't see it from his angle, but Carla reaches across and eases it from my grasp. 'Don't,' she says. She flicks off the central locking and someone opens the back door. It's Bill Farrah. He has no weapon, but he tells Gemma to get out.

She remains where she is and he reaches in and grabs her by the hair, hauling her from the seat.

'Leave her alone!' I yell.

'Out!' shouts Archie, jutting the gun at me.

'Do it,' says Carla. 'He's not messing around.'

I can't believe she's involved. Reuben's sister. She helped me, at the start. My brain wants to search for clues that I missed, but the reality of the gun barrel takes precedence. I get out slowly. It's freezing. There are tall hedges either side of the track. The sky is black. I can't get my bearings. How are they here?

'What do you want?' I ask.

'Very fucking funny,' says Archie. He moves towards me, gun pointed at my chest. I automatically back away to where Farrah is holding Gemma's arm. We're ushered back to the road, where a Land Rover waits. Are these the people she's somehow blackmailed?

'Their car's at Neil Packer's,' says Carla. 'They're saying he's hurt.'

Farrah nods to her. 'Meet Sam down there. Move it somewhere out of sight.'

I've no idea who Sam is. 'Whatever she's done, we can sort it out,' I say.

'What about the police?' Carla asks, ignoring me.

'We've got time.'

Carla walks quickly back to her car. She reverses out of the track and takes off back down the hill.

'Where've you been hiding then?' asks Archie, bringing the gun to bear on Gemma.

'I don't know what's happening,' says Gemma. 'Please, you've got to believe me. I've been locked in that *freak's* cellar.'

Archie's shakes his head. 'Don't. It's pathetic.'

'We've done nothing wrong,' I say. 'It was all Neil.'

'Enough talking,' says Archie. 'In the car.'

I think about running, but it's not possible. I wouldn't get ten metres, and Gemma's in no fit state to run anyway. So we both climb into the back of the Land Rover, onto battered leather seats. Archie slams the door after us. Farrah eases himself into the driver's seat, then Archie takes the seat beside him with the shotgun trained loosely on us.

Farrah kills the lights, and we continue up the same track where Carla parked, which becomes rutted and bouncy. When we reach a gate, Farrah leaves the engine running as he goes to open it, then we proceed through at less than ten miles an hour. He must know the way very well indeed, because there's almost no visibility beyond five or ten metres. Light from the dashboard is all that catches Farrah's grim features. I have the horrible sense we're going to be shot at the side of the road, our bodies left to rot. I clutch my sister's hand. It can't have come to this, after everything we've both been through. I can see she's eyeing the gun. Whether it's fear or a mad plan, I don't know.

The track enters woodland and becomes smoother, on a gentle uphill gradient. Soon enough, as the trees peter out, he switches the lights on again. The dark shape of a huge country house comes into view. I can't see details, but there are crenellations lining the roof and dozens of windows. It's all completely dark.

We veer sharply past one side, into an open space between what look like stables or outbuildings. Farrah stops and Archie orders me out. I do as he says. Gemma gets out on the other side.

Farrah hops down and walks to the door of a small barn with double metal doors. He pulls a key from an extendable ring on his belt and unfastens a padlock, then swings them open. 'You can scream all you want now,' he says. 'Won't do you any bloody good.'

He takes out his phone, and makes a call.

'We've got them,' he says. 'Yeah, both.' Whoever's at the other end speaks for a while. 'And you might want to see what's happening at the old school. Carla's there.'

There's nowhere to run. Another jab from the shotgun sets us moving into the building. There's farm machinery and I see a rat scurrying out of sight behind an old bathtub. Cans of paint line a shelf. An ancient two-wheeled horse wagon, something from the middle of the last century, sits on a tarp like it's being renovated. Farrah picks up the yoke, lays it across his shoulder, and uses his weight to wheel it aside. Then he pulls the tarp aside too. There's a wooden hatch beneath, locked with another padlock. He leans over and unfastens that too, then pulls open the two sides to reveal bright golden light. A blast of warmth rises up. There are metal stairs beneath, and a distinct aroma of marijuana.

'I'm not going down there,' says Gemma.

Farrah looks at her coldly, then steps back. 'Shoot her,' he says.

Archie cocks the gun and I throw myself in the way. 'No!'

Archie pauses.

'Gem, please,' I say. 'Whatever's going on, we can get through it.'

My sister looks at me with desperation in her eyes. 'I'm so sorry. I never wanted you to come here.'

'Down,' says Farrah.

I go first. Beneath the ground, the space is massive. The bit I can see is maybe thirty metres long, ten wide, lined with row after row of raised beds, filled with luscious green cannabis plants. The air is hot, but dry, and there are fans humming out of sight. The light that makes all our faces a pale orange is coming from lamps overhead. Large sheets of polythene hang at intervals, like draping sails. Rubber piping and cables of various colours and thickness run along the floor, branching off around the beds.

So this is why Bill Farrah doesn't like people at the house. I wonder how Gemma's managed to get herself mixed up in it though. Was Mark into all this? Was he some sort of drug dealer? The big sister in me feels a flicker of annoyance, which is quickly subdued when Farrah tells us to get on our knees.

I obey, but Gemma stays standing. 'You don't have to do this,' she says. 'We'll never say a word, I promise.'

'I know you won't,' replies Farrah. 'On your knees.'

Gemma drops too. 'My sister had nothing to do with it,' she adds.

'Not our problem,' says Farrah.

I watch his face, wondering if he's going to give some sort of signal to Archie. My only hope is the police. Nelson must have realised we never made it to the hospital. She must be calling my phone which Carla now has. Will she be able to track it, like Felicity tracked Gemma's? I'm grasping at straws and I know it.

Even if she does, she'll have no idea where we are now.

'So what now?' asks Archie.

Farrah looks at us all, then pulls a pack of papers from his top pocket. 'Watch 'em,' he says.

He walks past us, back towards the stairs.

Archie takes a seat on the edge of one of the planters. I know next to nothing about drugs, but this is some operation. I wonder what this place was before they turned it into a weed farm.

'What are you going to do to us?' I ask.

Archie laughs. 'What do *you* think?' he says, jerking his head at Gemma. My sister's legs are shaking and she has to shuffle so she's on her backside instead. Archie doesn't say anything.

'I don't know,' she says glumly.

'You owe us twenty grand,' says Archie.

'You killed Mark,' she snaps back.

'Is that his name?' says Archie. 'We called him matchstick. Can you guess why?'

Gemma doesn't say anything, but she looks furious.

'Got what was coming, he did — trying to fuck us. You look like shit by the way. Neil Packer do that?'

'You've no idea what he is,' says Gemma, her eyes distant, like she's suddenly back there. 'He found me up there in the hills. Somehow got me back to his. He dresses up, in these skins, like . . .'

'A cat?' I say.

Gemma looks at me with ferocity and fear, her eyes searching for something in mine. 'How do you know?'

The pictures in Patrick Draper's house spring to mind. The strange creature — neither feline nor human. Maybe he *had* seen something up there on the moors.

'He called me Alice,' says Gemma. 'His *new* Alice.'

Archie is looking at my sister, bemused. 'Sounds fucking mental.'

'I hurt him,' I say.

'I hope he's dead,' adds Gemma, definitively. 'And that old bitch.'

We both look up at the distant rumbling sound of an engine, then the softest squeal of brakes. A car door slams. I pray it's the police, but from Archie's nonchalance I guess it's not. This is someone he knows. Is it this Sam, who Farrah mentioned to Carla?

There are footsteps on the stairs, and Farrah comes down first. He's followed close behind by a figure wearing jeans and a dark sweater. My heart leaps when I realise it's Sergeant Nelson, but she doesn't look remotely worried. Still, the same stubborn, hopeful part of me refuses to understand what my logical brain is telling me. She's not here to help us.

She stares at both of us. 'Well, this *is* a shitshow, isn't it?'

Chapter 54

'Who are you?' asks Gemma.

Nelson looks at her as if she's stood in a dog turd. 'Carla's got the car into the woods,' she says to Archie and Farrah. 'We can deal with it later.'

'I trusted you,' I say.

'Oh, shut the fuck up,' snaps Nelson. 'You think I wanted this? I told you to leave it alone, but you couldn't help yourself.'

'So you're a drug dealer too?'

Nelson looks playfully hurt, then waves a dismissive hand at the plants. 'Disgusting stuff, if you ask me. I just make sure no one interferes. And I can trace a burner if any idiots think about trying to fuck us. Isn't that right, Gemma? I must say, of the two of you, you really did get the raw deal with the brain cells.'

My sister lowers her head. I can only guess – whatever exactly their plan entailed - that it was Mark's idea.

The rest of it is falling into place in my head. Something

went wrong and they killed Mark. But somehow my sister ended up in Neil Packer's hands. I can't see how Patrick Draper fits in though and I'm almost resigned to never knowing. I don't see how we will ever get out of this now that our only possible saviour is one of them.

There's a radio crackle and Nelson groans at the caller ID. She addresses Farrah. 'That'll be Dewer – I've got to take this.' With that, she climbs the stairs again.

Constable Dewer. Is he in on it too? Surely not. That's why she's left to make the call. I wonder about screaming, just in case he hears over the line.

'This is such a fucking mess,' says Archie.

'Does your mum know you're here?' I ask.

He barks a laugh. 'What do you reckon?'

'She'd be disappointed.'

'Shut your mouth.'

Nelson returns, looking deadly serious. 'Dewer's at the old schoolhouse now. These two young ladies left quite a scene. Killed the old lady by the looks of it.'

'She killed herself,' says Gemma. 'She was keeping me a prisoner, they both were.'

'And Neil?' I ask.

Nelson sniffs. She doesn't even glance at me, and there's something chilling about the sudden change in her demeanour. Something bad is coming. 'No sign of him at the moment.' She looks at Farrah. 'We haven't got long. I've told Dewer I'm at home but I'll come straight out. You'll have to do something with the car before morning. The hard-working constable's not beyond calling in a helicopter if he takes a fancy.'

'That won't be a problem,' he says.

'Go on then,' she says.

Farrah nods, and leaves again, walking quickly up the steps.

'And these two?' asks Archie.

Nelson points to the back of the bunker. 'Kill them. Quickly. Then wrap them up.'

I've known it was coming, but it's still a bolt to hear her say it so bluntly.

'No!' I say. 'Wait! I've got money. Way more than twenty grand.'

'Get up,' says Archie.

'I can transfer it over,' I add. 'I'm a lawyer. We can make it untraceable. I've got this woman, the same one who traced Gem's phone . . .'

'Stop,' says Nelson wearily. 'There's no point now.'

But I don't stop. I can't. I keep talking. I say everything and anything I can think of. I swear in God's name, and my dead mother's, that we can keep their secrets if they just let us go.

Gemma's silent and subdued as we're pushed and cajoled at gunpoint towards the sheeting at the back of the bunker. I envy her calm demeanour, even as it chills me. Archie looks robotic and bored, like this means nothing. Nelson's face is stone.

I can see there's no getting through, so I change tack, telling them they can keep me here, and let Gemma go. 'You won't talk, will you, Gem? Not if they've got me. Tell them. Tell them.'

'Maybe I was wrong about the brain cells,' says Nelson. 'Do it, Archie.' He raises the shotgun. 'That way, for fuck's sake. I don't want blood on my—'

A strange, strangled sound makes Archie turn. Nelson too.

We're all staring at the entrance, where Farrah half falls, half stumbles down the steps. He's holding one hand across his middle and trying to talk.

'Bill?' says Nelson.

He reaches the bottom of the steps, mouth working like he's got something caught in his throat. Then he coughs, and bright red blood gurgles over his lips. He takes a couple more shuffling steps, before leaning wearily back against the wall. Something drops from his arms, splatting on the ground. Bile climbs my throat and Archie says, 'Sweet Jesus.'

Another length of Farrah's intestines unspools wetly at his feet. His face is deathly pale as he sinks down the wall, settling gently into the midst of his own viscera.

Chapter 55

'Bill?' whispers Archie.

Farrah isn't paying attention.

'What the fuck?' says Nelson. She points to us. 'Stay here.' Then nods to Archie. 'Give me that.'

He shakes his head, clutching the shotgun.

She reaches across to him, and takes it from his hands by force, which looks oddly amusing, given she's a foot shorter and at least twice his age. 'Shells?' she says.

He reaches into his pocket and offers her a handful. She takes them and puts them in her jacket. Then she stalks towards the stairs, pausing by Farrah. He's still alive, but only just.

'Who is it, Bill?' she demands.

He doesn't answer. His breathing shortens to quick, irregular gasps.

Nelson puts a foot on the bottom step. 'Whoever's out there, you'd better fucking run.'

Gemma's hand sneaks into mine and squeezes. 'It's him,' she says. 'It's Neil.'

She speaks with complete certainty, almost reverence, but I don't see how it could be.

'It's not,' I reply. We must be two miles, maybe more, from the old schoolhouse and we left him bleeding from his head.

'If that's you, Packer,' shouts Nelson, 'give yourself up.'

There's no sound from above.

Nelson takes another step, then another. 'I *will* shoot you, you bastard,' she says.

She disappears up the steps, leaving us alone with Archie. He can't take his eyes off the older man. 'We'll get you fixed up, Bill,' he says.

Farrah's talking days are clearly over. He's completely still.

I move towards the steps too, but Archie whips round and shoves me back. 'You're not going anywhere,' he says.

A gunshot goes off with a crack, making us all jump. As soon as Archie turns to the stairs again, Gemma leaps forward and lands on his back. I'm slower to move, not having the first clue what to do as she claws at his eyes with her hands. He spins around, flailing and trying to throw her off, then thuds backwards into the wall. She clamps her teeth over one of his ears and he screams, staggering past me, and into one of the polythene sheets. It rips loose, and tangles at his feet. He falls, taking Gemma with him. She cries out and rolls off, blood covering her chin, and spits something on the ground. Archie's hand is clutching the side of his head as he tries to stand, but before he's up, I grab the corner of the sheet and fold it over him. Gemma snatches up another side and does the same, giving him a kick as well. His limbs are jerking wildly, but the more he moves, the worse it gets. I back into a planter which wobbles. It gives me an idea and I turn and grip the edge. 'Help me!' I say.

My sister grabs a hold too, and together we manage to tip it over, leaping clear as it crashes down onto Archie's body. Soil and plants spill out until we can't see him at all.

'Fuck him,' she says, and I really couldn't agree more.

We both go to the bottom of the stairs and look up. Farrah's blood coats several of the steps. If we don't go now, we might never get the chance. Halfway up another shot rings out. This one sounds further away.

We climb the stairs slowly, side by side, peering out at the top. There's no one in the barn, but there's a spent shell on the ground in the main doorway.

Nelson's in a half crouch, behind the front wing of the grey BMW I saw earlier when she arrived at Draper's house. She's reloading the shotgun and snaps it closed, then rests it over the bonnet, pointing towards the house, sweeping back and forth.

'Come out, you fucker!' she shouts.

Something moves, but it's over to her left and she doesn't see it – a dark shape flitting slowly alongside the outer wall of the stable block, before slipping inside the door. I'm not sure it was a person at all. I pull Gemma the other way.

Nelson hears us and spins around. 'Get back inside!' she orders.

The creature rushes in a shambling gait from the stable block, and it's on her in a flash, knocking her to the ground. The muzzle discharges, and for a split second there's a clear silhouette of black fur and erect ears, and the glint of shining teeth. The shot buries in a wooden door. I can't see a human face at all as it straddles her, hands thumping down repeatedly in white flashes. She's making these noises I've never heard a human make before – squeals and grunts of panic,

367

like a terrified piglet. He doesn't stop as the blood spatters up the side of the car and over his shoulders.

Gemma and I creep around behind the scene of carnage. He's still going, tearing at her body, and the noises she's making are more like involuntary exhalations of air than screams, coupled with meaty thuds as he strikes her. The Land Rover is twenty metres away, and Gemma points to it. 'He left the key in the ignition,' she whispers.

'Are you sure?'

She's already running towards it, and I follow. At the same moment, he stands up from Nelson's corpse and faces us. He starts to run too. We get to the car first and both pile in through the same driver's door. I slam it, and push down the door lock. Gemma scrambles to the passenger side and does the same.

Looking out, he's gone.

'Where is—' says Gemma.

I catch movement in the wing mirror and we both scream as his feet thunder across the roof, denting it inwards. Then he jumps off in a black flash and rounds the front. Retreating a short distance away, he stands there, facing us. As I turn the key and the engine chugs into life, the front lights flash on. I can't quite fathom what I'm looking at. He moves on all fours, more like an ape than a man, but his head is almost entirely concealed inside the skin from the head of a black cat, pulled roughly over his features, so only his eyes and nose are showing. His jaw is that of the cat too, with incisors as long as my index finger, but I can't see how the whole thing is held in place. The rest of his clothes are a pelt moulded to his limbs. I can even make out rough stitching. From his right hand, which is balled into a fist, a single claw extends between his fingers. It's definitely Neil Packer, but the way he moves is completely alien. It would be comical if it weren't for the utter strangeness of the transformation. There's nothing funny about the sheer animal conviction with which he stalks us. I know there's no arguing with this thing. It's not a person at all.

I grab the gearstick and crank it into first. My foot presses the accelerator and we lurch forwards, right for him, only to stall. 'Fuck, fuck, fuck.'

I turn the key again.

'Oh shit,' says Gemma. 'He's coming.'

Neil charges towards the car in long loping strides, then leaps, clambering with agility I can hardly believe, onto the bonnet of the Land Rover. The vehicle shakes, then he draws back a fist and punches at the windscreen. Spider cracks spread from the impact.

I find the biting point this time and we surge forward, throwing him off balance. I speed blindly on, but the front end clips something and the wheel jerks in my hand. Neil vanishes like he's been whipped away and I see the wall of the barn too late to slam on the brakes. We hit the wall with a metal crunch. My arms brace, but my head still hits the wheel before I'm thrown back in my seat, reeling.

I try to ram the gear into reverse, but it won't budge. We're stuck.

I glance across at Gemma. Her eyes widen, looking past me. Then he's at my window. It shatters inwards, showering me with glass, as he reaches in. I press myself against Gemma as the claw rips at the seat leather with long tearing swipes. All I can do is kick out, aiming for his face, but I've got no room to manoeuvre, and panic makes me miss.

369

But it's enough that he suddenly withdraws his arm. I think he's preparing for another assault, but he's staring at something else. He starts to run.

Archie's standing at the entrance to the barn. He wails in terror, and tries to pull the doors closed, then thinks better of it and flees back inside. Neil pursues him, disappearing too. I don't fancy Archie's chances. We don't have long.

'We need to find somewhere to hide,' I tell my sister.

She's looking at the barn. 'Where?'

I point to the house. There's a window missing on the ground floor.

'We'll be sitting ducks,' says Gemma.

'There must be forty rooms inside. He won't find us.'

I don't wait for her agreement and get out of the car. She can't move as fast as me, so I tug her along with me. My head is spinning a little from the crash. Part way, Gemma stops and breaks off, making a beeline for Nelson's car. I call her back, but she disappears for a moment. I realise what she's doing a second before she rises again holding the shotgun in her hand. She staggers back to join me. I wonder if she's ever fired a gun before. There can only be one shell left.

The window is waist high, and she goes first, wincing as she swings her bad leg over. I go next, but I know from the heat across my shoulders that I'm being watched. Sure enough, Neil's coming out of the barn.

He's breathing hard, tired. But he walks towards us.

'Go!' I say.

I follow my sister into the dark house. The room we're in is completely gutted as far as I can see, with empty shelves looping three walls and a huge fireplace and a sculpted ceiling rose. The walls are bare, the paper peeling in large strips. We leave through an open door and find ourselves in an internal hallway, with several other closed doors. There's graffiti scribbled on one of the walls. The whole place smells of mould and it's freezing. I start to think this was a bad choice, after all.

We reach a triple-storey entrance hall with a floor of cracked tiles. A monstrous chandelier still dominates the ceiling, giving off the faintest twinkle amid the palls of grey and crowded shadows. A wide central staircase climbs from the front door, branching left on a right angle, before turning again to the second floor.

Somewhere behind us a door bangs. He's inside.

Gemma starts to climb the stairs. It seems as good a choice as any.

It must be the adrenaline dump, but by the time I'm at the top, I'm exhausted, my legs like jelly. They almost give out completely as I try to keep up with Gemma. More doors line the long gallery, with tall windows at each end. There's a runner carpet along the length of the gallery, parquet flooring at either side. We head left. Gemma checks each room, but I can tell from her frustrated groans that there's nothing to help us. I open the opposite doors. Apart from rubbish strewn about and the occasional piece of abandoned furniture, there's nothing that looks like a hiding place.

As I open the door at the end, it's not a room at all, but a narrow staircase.

And Neil's standing halfway up the steps.

'Gem!' I slam the door again and turn, but he's out a split second later and running after me down the hall. Then I feel a ripping pain straight down my back and fall headlong to the carpet. Rolling onto my back, he's right there. He slashes at me, and I throw up an arm. Pain rakes across my skin. I can feel hot blood already pouring over my hand.

I manage to catch his jaw with a kick and wriggle out, but he grabs my ankle and pulls me back under him. I'm going to die just like Nelson, torn to pieces. He lifts the claw again.

Bang!

Smoke obscures my vision. When it clears, Neil's still there, but behind the cat's bared teeth, I can see the man's mouth moving in strange, involuntary gasps, his tongue thrusting and receding. His arm, the one with the claw, has gone. He turns his cat head towards the missing limb, reaching with his remaining hand, his movements slow and uncertain. In the gloom, black blood starts to spatter on the runner from the stump in frankly astonishing gouts. I scramble out, and watch as Gemma comes around to his side. She's got the shotgun at hip height, and the barrel is still releasing a wisp of pale smoke. She points it at his head, then pulls the trigger again.

It only clicks.

She tries once more, but nothing happens. I guess she doesn't know much about guns after all. One of my arms seems not to function, but I use the wall to get to one knee, backing further away from him. The blood flow from Neil's arm has slowed to lazy spurts, a couple of seconds apart, from torn flesh. He manages to stand up, tottering backwards for a moment. He seems in his own world as he staggers past us both, heading for the stairs, leaving a thick trail of blood. He makes it all the way to the balustrade, before losing his balance and falling forward. With a splintering crack, the top rail breaks and he upends, disappearing over the edge. There's a split second of silence, then an answering thud thirty feet below.

Gemma places the shotgun on the floor carefully. 'You're hurt,' she says.

She's looking at my arm, which drips blood onto the carpet. And when I try to move, there's a feeling of fire across my back, like I've been lashed.

'I'll be okay,' I tell her.

She helps me stand and we walk, leaning on each other, to the edge of the stairs, and slowly descend. Neil's lying at the bottom, head twisted sideways on a patch of cracked tiles, one arm folded underneath him while the remains of the other point towards the ceiling, still leaking blood. The mask has been torn off his head almost completely, giving him the appearance of a two-headed creature, each facing the other, slain midway through a metamorphosis.

We try the main doors, but we can't get them open, so we go back towards the room by which we entered. I can hear distant police sirens as we struggle back out through the window, and by the time we're at the side of the house, three police cars are gliding across the gravel towards us. Dewer gets out of the first before it's even stopped moving, and runs towards us.

'What the hell happened? Where's Nelson?'

I point over to the car where she lies. 'She's dead. I think they all are.'

'Get them out of here,' he says to the officers at his back, then he moves past us, talking into his radio. I hear terms I don't understand, and those I can take a stab at. Cleaning up this mess – all of it – will take a long, long time, and just the thought of trying to piece it together makes my head swim. More officers approach, and blankets are thrown over our shoulders. We're led back to the waiting cars.

Chapter 56

For the next few hours, through the night and into morning, I only see Gemma intermittently. We're taken in separate vehicles to the hospital in Bishop Auckland, triaged in separate rooms. I ask how she is incessantly, despite the reassurances that she's being looked after. In the back of my mind, I fear she might somehow disappear again.

There are police with me at all times – not Dewer, but two silent strangers who talk under their breaths into their radios in codes I don't understand. I hear Nelson's name more than once though and wonder what they found beside her car. From their sombre tone, from all the blood, I assume she's surely dead.

I only see my face for the first time when I hobble to the toilet. I've two black eyes, and an angry cut across the bridge of my nose. Another graze on my cheekbone, and a swollen lip. Photographs are taken with my permission, and I realise I look very much like a battered spouse. We had a client three or four years ago who wouldn't press charges against her husband, despite our encouragement. He wouldn't let her leave the house for days, but she used to message us the evidence via Snapchat. I've got pretty good over the years at noticing little things as I walk around town, and constructing the stories of what goes on behind their closed doors – the small injuries, hidden under sunglasses or carefully draped hair. Is that what people will think about me now? *Poor woman . . . why doesn't she just leave him?* The real story would blow their minds.

It feels good to be looked after, wheeled around through the hospital's labyrinthine corridors, up and down lifts. My wounds are dressed, I go for X-rays (a single broken rib), blood is taken (I'm not sure why). My chart, tucked into a slot at the foot of the bed, is updated by several doctors and nurses.

In the early hours, two plain-clothes police officers are shown into my private room. A man and a woman – he broad-shouldered, crooked nose, looking like a rugby player. She tall and elegant, athletic. They introduce themselves and I forget their names immediately. The woman asks if I'm okay to answer some questions, and sets a Dictaphone down before I've had chance to answer.

They want to know everything – what happened at Neil Packer's house, how I came to be at Brocklehurst Hall. I tell it as it occurred, and it's easier than I expect. I find I can detach myself and my emotion from the narrative, giving the sequence of events in almost mundane detail. They don't interrupt once, or ask any questions at all, but when I've finished, they say they may have more questions for me in the morning, then stand up to leave.

'Wait,' I say, when they're halfway through the door. They both turn. 'Can I see Gemma now?'

'Soon,' the female officer says. 'We still need to ask your sister some questions.'

I nod obediently. I can hardly blame them for caution, given the scene of death and mayhem we left outside Hartsbridge.

* * *

After a stream of doctors and nurses, all carrying out their checks and asking the same questions, I must have slept. I wake when the door opens and Constable Dewer comes in. He's wearing civvies – jeans and some sort of sports cagoule. A baseball cap on his head, which he removes.

I push myself up on my elbows, and pain throbs through the muscles of my throat – it feels like there's some weight strapped to my neck, pulling me back down. It's whiplash, I think, from the crash.

'I've given my statement,' I tell him.

'Oh, I know,' he says. 'How are you feeling?'

'Confused. Glad it's over.' There's no clock in the room, and whatever cocktail of drugs they've given me has scrambled my circadian rhythms. 'What time is it?'

'About four,' he says. 'They're looking after you?'

I nod. Even that hurts. 'You look like you're wearing a disguise,' I say.

'I shouldn't really be here,' he replies with a thin smile. 'Not in a personal capacity.'

'So why are you?'

He sits down, slowly, on the single bedside chair.

'To find answers, I suppose.'

'I'm not sure I've got any.'

He rubs his eyes with profound weariness. His facial hair has gone from five o'clock shadow to designer stubble in the space of a day.

'We picked up Carla Fletwick. She's not talking.'

I remember her wrought emotions, when her brother was arrested. Whatever else she's done, I'm sure that wasn't fake. 'And Reuben?'

'With his uncle.' He sighs and shakes his head. 'What a bloody mess. Tara was at the station, screaming blue murder. We had to call the doctor.'

'You don't think she knew?'

'I honestly have no idea.' He stands up and walks to the window, pushing one of the blinds across. The daylight seems wrong. I can't imagine what he's looking at.

'We've had more details about Alice's cause of death,' he says, with his back to me.

'You don't have to tell me,' I say.

He turns back and shakes his head, as if to say, *Who else can I tell?* 'It's all preliminary, but there's a . . . a chance she died of natural causes. Despite the decomposition, they found signs of a significant, multi-organ infection. There's no evidence he did . . .' He breathes out. A long, shaky breath. 'Neil didn't . . . there's no evidence he, y'know, did anything sexual to her. At least, as far as they can tell. I suppose that's something.'

I suppose it is. A small mercy anyway. I've some knowledge of how doctors ascertain such things when the victim is alive, and I hope to God it's true in this case. Selfishly, in that moment, I'm thinking more about my sister. Gemma hasn't told me anything about what happened under Neil's house, and I don't know how I'd ever even broach it.

It leads to more questions though. 'So do you think he took Gemma *because* Alice died?' I ask.

'I doubt we'll ever know,' says Dewer. From his distant expression, I don't think he's very interested in finding out.

'What about Sergeant Nelson?' I ask quietly.

'What about her?' says Dewer.

'You know she was working with them. Bill Farrah and Archie.' He stands up straighter, like he's affronted in some way, or isn't quite ready to accept it. 'I'm not saying she deserved what happened,' I add.

He nods. 'There'll be an investigation.'

I can sense he's closing down, like he did the first time we met and spoke outside The Headless Woman. Despite my own weariness, it angers me. He's come here – when by his own admission he shouldn't have. He said he wants answers, but he's not giving me anything in return. 'Did you really have no idea?'

He fiddles with the baseball cap in his hand, then does look up and meet my gaze. 'Not about her directly, but a while back, one of the inmates at Haverigg mentioned a Durham copper on the payroll. Most of the time, this sort of thing is just talk. Some lags will say anything for attention.'

He sounds like he's trying to convince himself and failing.

'Haverigg isn't where Archie's father is incarcerated, by any chance?'

Dewer meets my eyes, looking slightly surprised, and nods. 'He'll be questioned, I'm sure. We'll get to the bottom of it one way or another.'

I wonder how it was Nelson became embroiled in the first place, but it appears she might have been a middleman of some sort, keeping the eyes of law enforcement off the house. With so many players dead, will any investigation get to the bottom of it or will it end up swept under the carpet? I'm not sure I have the headspace to care.

But I'm still left with a sense of unfinished business – a lingering question about what exactly Dewer expected I could give him. He looks younger than ever, despite the facial hair – a lost little boy.

And that's when I understand. He must be – what? – thirty-ish. A local boy.

'You knew her, didn't you?'

He looks up at me, eyes tormented, then away. 'Knew who?'

'Alice Brocklehurst.'

He remains quiet, staring at a point on the floor at the end of the bed.

'You said you grew up in Ravenow,' I continue.

'I went to school in Hartsbridge,' he says. 'Walked there every morning and afternoon – three miles there and back, whatever the weather. No, I tell a lie. A neighbour took me in a tractor when the snow was bad.' He smiles, glancing at me briefly and shyly. I try to imagine what he looked like sixteen years ago. Was he in that school photo too, with Reuben and Alice? Did I miss a young Constable Dewer? 'Her parents sent her off to boarding school when she was thirteen. I went to the comp in town. We emailed. Met up in the holidays.'

And from the way he says it, I know he doesn't mean they were just friends.

'Oh my God. I . . . I'm so sorry.'

His jaw clenches and unclenches several times like he's trying to hold something back.

'What was she like?' I ask quietly.

'Wonderful,' he says, voice dangerously close to cracking. 'Down to earth. Normal. Considering.'

'Considering how wealthy she was?'

'Considering the life she had.'

I remember the pictures. The wild animals had all gone way before Alice was born – the seventies, they told me at the pub.

'I heard her parents were strict.'

'Her dad mainly. Didn't want her mixing with the village kids. She thought he used to monitor her emails, so we had to delete them straight after.' He breathes out another long, shuddering breath. 'The day she went missing . . . she was due to meet me. The last time before they packed her off to that fucking school. She never made it. Afterwards, when all the searching started, I was too scared to say anything. I thought they'd blame me.' He raises a fist to his mouth, and speaks behind it. 'I thought she'd show up.'

I don't know what to say.

'I looked for her,' he goes on. 'I searched and searched, long after everyone else gave up.'

Part of me wants to reach out and touch him, to take his hand and squeeze it. But he's too far away, and I know it would hurt to move closer. 'And you found her,' I say instead. 'In the end.'

Chapter 57

I don't believe in parallel universes, but if I'm wrong, maybe there's one where, at this very moment, Gemma's postcard never reached me, or where I ignored it. I'm walking down the aisle, Doug's little niece casting petals ahead. I'm smiling bashfully at the joyous faces of our guests. Susannah's crying in the second row, still a little dishevelled from the mad dash from the airport, and Olly's there too, muttering something funny into the ear of the nervous groom. But Doug only has eyes for me, standing at the front near the registrar's table (complete with floral centrepiece). He's actually welling up and it sets me off too. I feel beautiful in my wedding dress, and from the shining eyes to the left and right, I'm not ashamed to say everyone concurs. The picture's will be glorious, and I know then that it's true what the romantics say – this really is the happiest day of my life.

In this speculative present, I never went to Hartsbridge. I spent the last week working typical days with Katriona in the London office, dealing with last-minute wedding arrangements and never even guessing she was sleeping with my fiancé.

And in this other branching of cause and effect, my sister is still tied to a bed under an old schoolhouse in a village I've never heard of. At the house in the hills beyond, two small-time drug manufacturers are going about their business undisturbed, under the watchful eye of a corrupt police officer. Patrick Draper is still walking the hills, desperate to spot an animal he's sure is roaming there, to prove to himself and anyone who'll listen that he isn't mad.

Maybe it doesn't matter what I believe in. Those realities could all exist, and I wouldn't know. But they don't belong to me.

In the here and now, Gemma and I set off from the half-full car park, following a well-trodden path over chalk farmland. Chappie's good on the lead, tail wagging. The warden couldn't tell me how old he was but guessed over twelve from his teeth. I've always wanted a dog, and though it'll make things trickier in the short term, I couldn't bear the thought of leaving him in a shelter for the rest of his days. I unclip the lead and he shoots off, faster than his years should allow. I'll get a walker back in London, but I'm already planning to work from home a bit more.

Gemma's limping from her leg wound, and I'm fairly sure the doctor wouldn't approve of me taking on a walk of any length with my rib still healing and one arm in a sling. But we both needed space and fresh air, and Devil's Dyke, in the Sussex Downs, seemed doable. The sun is just about at its highest point for an early afternoon in the middle of September, and the sky is cloudless, a pristine blue.

The perfect day for a hike.

I've stitches in my arm and back – forty-one in all. They're a bit itchy, but it's remarkable how quickly a body heals. Some of it will take longer, of course – not least the memories. I've been over it so many times in my mind, reliving it all in lurid detail. There's no escaping the things I've seen, especially when I'm on my own. I know Gemma feels the same, because she's barely left my side for the last five days. When the hospital released us, we stayed on another night in Bishop Auckland in a twin room, sleeping six feet apart like we were teenagers again. I know from her troubled slumber that she has nightmares too. Probably worse than mine.

She doesn't look quite so ghoulish now – her bruises have almost gone, bar a thin purple line beneath one eye. She's wearing my make-up, just like she did when we were kids, only this time it was given willingly. How long she'll stay with me in London, I don't know, and it feels far too early to broach it. From what she's said, she still has friends in Brighton, but enemies too. I know she grieves for Mark, because I find her crying from time to time. She sometimes drops him absently into conversation, and I think I probably misjudged him in the brief time we met. He wasn't my cup of tea, but who am I to judge, based on my own romantic errors?

We pass a middle-aged couple, out with their gambolling red setter, its furry legs covered in mud. Chappie dances around it, comes back to our side, then sets off again, leading the way. Maybe it's our lingering bruises that make us stand out, because the woman does a double take, and once we've passed, I can't resist a look back. They're both staring and glance away hurriedly. Even though we put out a request for privacy through a solicitor, our faces were in the newspapers anyway – mine from the company website, and Gemma's a crop from something far less formal. We haven't personally spoken to any journalists. The police are still investigating exactly what happened in Hartsbridge, releasing little information, but the locals have understandably been talking to anyone who'll listen. Nige was pictured, posing outside The Headless Woman, under the headline 'Mystery of the Hartsbridge Hunter'. He's wearing what looks like his Sunday best. I don't blame him. I wonder what's happened to Tara and how she's come to terms with Archie. I don't think she knew anything about her son's misdeeds, or at least she turned a blind eye if she did. I don't blame her either. She was always kind to me.

Neil Packer has been the subject of much speculation. 'Clinical lycanthropy', they call it. That's one theory anyway, and it's been entertained in the broadsheets. A rare psychological disorder, in which the sufferer believes themselves to be an animal, impersonating its behaviours to a greater or lesser degree. Not confined to wolves, as the name suggests, but mostly focused on canine fantasies. Whether it's involuntary or not seems to be a subject of debate, but it seems to me that Neil did a good job of presenting himself as an upstanding member of the community for most of his life. Apart from his victims, Patrick Draper, as far as I know, is the only person to ever see him in the act. Poor Paddy, ridiculed and ostracised.

I can't see that we'll ever know exactly what drove Neil to act out his part, when it began or how often he did it, but something he said lodges in my head whenever I think of him. The little baby girl, born breathless on the kitchen floor, and buried nameless in the garden. Could it have been some strange, twisted way to compensate? To find a sister and become something his father cared for – an animal himself. That might explain why he tried to *replace* Alice after she died.

But I'll leave the armchair psychology to others. Neil Packer can't tell us anything from the grave, and I expect there's no name that really matches the delusions under which he suffered.

Gemma and I reach the dyke itself, a deep wedge-like valley that follows a gentle sweep through the landscape, the result – so the noticeboard at the car park told us – of glacial flow at the end of the last Ice Age. Walkers trail along the path below like ants in procession. There's a stiff breeze on the lip, but it dies as soon as we drop into the cut. We find a seat on the grass, and Gemma takes out a thermos and two tin mugs. Chappie comes and lies down between us, so I feed him a chew stick.

'We really do look the part,' I say, laughing.

As she pours out the hot chocolate, she asks if there's been any more word from Doug.

I shake my head. After a slew of pitiful excuses, he'd moved on fairly quickly to anger. I can't believe how little I knew him. At least he had the decency to move out before we got back to London. I answered his calls the first few times, but my tone and brevity left no doubt about my feelings. Then it was texts I could tell he'd slaved over, but it was more of the same – veering between denial and anger, protestations of love, and self-pity. Eventually, because of the press enquiries also, I changed my number. In a way, the old one belonged, like my previous life, to a different woman entirely. 'I need to give his mum a call really. I just can't face it at the moment. She'll be devastated.'

Gemma hands me a cup.

For the same reason as the number change, I'll move out too as soon as I'm healed. That flat was *ours*, and I need something on the ground floor, with a garden, for Chappie.

Luckily, we had the website for the wedding. Wasn't *that* good foresight on my part? So it was easy to spread the bad news with a simple message that, due to unforeseen circumstances, we were sorry to call it off. The insurance we took out was in case one of us fell ill, but astonishingly it covers this eventuality too. Not that I care about losing some money if it means closing this particular chapter of my life. I was sad to let so many people down, but felt no terrible guilt. After what happened up there in the Pennines, I find it hard to get upset about much at all. Emotionally, it's like everything is dialled right down, almost muted.

'Never thought we'd be doing this,' says Gemma, sipping hot chocolate from her mug.

I wonder what she means. There must have been times in that basement she thought she'd never see the light of day again, let alone me. Or perhaps she's speaking more generally – two estranged sisters, together again.

'Me neither.'

'You want to go down?' I point to the path at the base of the slope. It looks to be quite steep, and muddy in parts, so I'm glad when she says 'Nah'.

She finishes her hot chocolate with a slurp, and I remember she used to do the same thing with milkshakes and how much it annoyed me.

'What are you smiling at?' she asks.

'Nothing.'

We return on the same path to the track to the car park, and she wordlessly crosses to my far side, to hook her arm with my good one. The touch feels odd – even when we used to walk to school together, I was always a fraction ahead. The tragedy of it hits me like a punch – that the time we needed each other most, we pushed one another away. I promise myself it won't happen again.

Gemma is perhaps reminiscing too, because she says, 'I'd like to visit Mum's grave, but I don't know where it is.'

'I can show you. You want to have a drink at her local too?'

'Ha! Why not?'

The path is busy as we near the end of our walk and the car park is full by the time we reach it again, with a couple of dozen day-trippers disgorging from a coach. We go to my car, which still bears the scars of Hartsbridge, and load our coats and bags into the back. Chappie hops dutifully onto the towel in the boot, and I clean off the worst of the mud, give his chin a tickle, then close it.

'I'm sorry,' Gemma says quietly from my side. 'For everything.'

I'm about to ask what she means, when her eyes widen and she tugs me towards her, shouting 'Hey!'

I see a car, reversing, which jolts to a halt right where I'd been standing. The driver looks back through the rear windscreen, raising an arm in apology.

'Thanks!' I say to Gemma.

'Needs his eyes testing,' she says.

'No harm done.'

We both get in. I recall her apology, a few seconds before,

but the moment seems to have passed, so I don't bring it up again. Taking care, I drive out of the car park, and pull slowly onto the road north, to London. There should be time to stop at the cemetery before dusk falls.

And there'll be plenty of time to talk.

Acknowledgements

Writing a novel is rather like a hike to a destination dimly imagined. For this one, there were false summits, several boggy patches, and less than optimal map-reading. At least once I found myself back at the point of origin. That the end was reached at all is down to my editor Molly Walker-Sharp, who re-tied my laces, gave me a compass, and showed a great deal of patience when I didn't arrive anytime close to the deadline. I also want to thank my unflappable agent Julia Churchill for her guidance and encouragement on what otherwise would have been a lonely journey.

If you enjoyed *The Hiker*, we think you'll love the DS Josie Masters series . . .

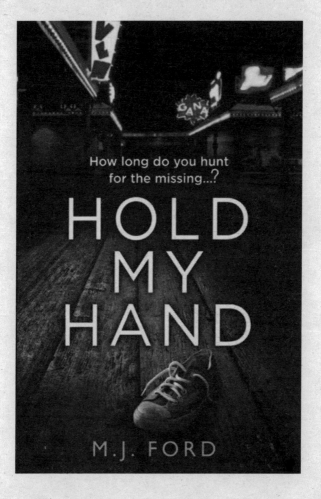